Praise for the Midnight Breed series by LARA ADRIAN

CRAVE THE NIGHT

"Adrian's steamy and intense twelfth Midnight Breed vampire romance adds new dimensions and new conflicts to her near-future world.... This installment is sure to delight established fans and will also be accessible to new readers."

—*Publishers Weekly*

"Nothing beats good writing and that is what ultimately makes Lara Adrian stand out amongst her peers.... Crave the Night is stunning in its flawless execution. Lara Adrian has the rare ability to lure readers right into her books, taking them on a ride they will never forget."

—*Under the Covers*

EDGE OF DAWN

"The eleventh installment in Adrian's strikingly original Midnight Breed series delivers an abundance of nail-biting suspenseful chills, red-hot sexy thrills, an intricately built world, and realistically complicated and conflicted protagonists, whose happily-ever-after ending proves to be all the sweeter after what they endure to get there."

—*Booklist (starred review)*

"Adrian once again engulfs her readers in a world or Breed loyalty, fierce passion and emotional overload.... I guarantee you will be begging for more."

—*Guilty Pleasures Book Reviews*

"A well-written, action-packed series that is just getting better with age."

—*Fiction Vixen*

DARKER AFTER MIDNIGHT

"Fantastic! We recommend this book to anyone who loves action packed, intense reads with gripping characters and spectacular storylines woven into a phenomenally crafted world. If you haven't started the Midnight Breed series yet, we highly suggest that you bump it up to the top of your list and get started today. "

—*Literal Addiction*

"A riveting novel that will keep readers mesmerized... If you like romance combined with heart-stopping paranormal suspense, you're going to love this book."

—*Bookpage*

DEEPER THAN MIDNIGHT

"The Midnight Breed series is one of the consistently best paranormal series out there.... Adrian writes compelling individual stories (with wonderful happily ever afters) within a larger story arc that is unfolding with a refreshing lack of predictability.... Deeper Than Midnight rocks!"

—*Romance Novel News*

Praise for Lara Adrian

"With an Adrian novel, readers are assured of plenty of dangerous thrills and passionate chills."

—*RT Book Reviews*

"Ms. Adrian has a gift for drawing her readers deeper and deeper into the amazing world she creates."

—*Fresh Fiction*

Look for these titles in the *New York Times* and #1 international bestselling

Midnight Breed series

. . . and more to come!

Other books by Lara Adrian

Historical Romances

Dragon Chalice Series
Heart of the Hunter
Heart of the Flame
Heart of the Dove

Warrior Trilogy
White Lion's Lady
Black Lion's Bride
Lady of Valor

Lord of Vengeance

Romantic Suspense and Paranormal Romance

Phoenix Code Series
(with Tina Folsom)
Cut and Run
Hide and Seek

Masters of Seduction Series
Merciless: House of Gravori (novella)
Priceless: House of Ebarron (novella)

BOUND TO DARKNESS

DARKNESS

A Midnight Breed Novel

C

NEW YORK TIMES BESTSELLING AUTHOR

LARA ADRIAN

ISBN: 1939193052
ISBN-13: 978-1939193056

www.LaraAdrian.com

Available in ebook and trade paperback. Unabridged audiobook edition forthcoming.

BOUND TO DARKNESS

CHAPTER 1

C

Titanium spikes slashed the fighter's face, spraying blood across the floor of the steel cage and thrilling the crowd of cheering spectators inside the underground fighting arena. Gritty industrial music pounded from the dance club upstairs, bringing the din to a deafening pitch as the long match between the pair of Breed males built toward its finish.

Carys Chase stood near the front, among the throng of avid spectators as Rune's fist connected with his opponent's face again. More shouts and applause erupted for the undefeated champion of Boston's most brutal arena.

The fights were technically illegal, but highly lucrative. And since the outing of the Breed to their terrified human neighbors twenty years ago, there were few sporting events more popular than the outlawed gladiator-style matches pitting a pair of six-and-a-half foot, three-hundred pound vampires against each other in a closed, steel mesh cage.

Blood was essential to Carys and her race, but sometimes it seemed mankind was even more thirsty for it. Especially when the spillage was restricted to members of the Breed.

Although even Carys had to admit that watching a vampire like Rune fight was a thing of beauty. He was dangerous grace and lethal savagery.

And he was hers.

For the past seven weeks—since the night she'd stepped into La Notte with a small group of friends and first saw Rune battling inside the cage—they had been practically inseparable. She had fallen fast and hard and deep, and hadn't looked back for a second.

Much to her parents' dismay. They and her twin brother, Aric, had all but forbade her to see Rune, basing their judgment on his profession and reputation alone. They didn't know him. They didn't want to know him either, and that hurt. It pissed her off.

Which is why, with a full head of steam and a stubborn streak inherited from both of her parents, Carys had recently moved out of the Chase family Darkhaven and in with her best friend, Jordana Gates.

Leaving home to get her own place hadn't gone over well, particularly with her father, Sterling Chase. As the commander of the Order's presence in Boston, he, along with the Order's founder, Lucan Thorne, and the other district commanders, were the de facto keepers of the peace between the Breed and mankind. No easy task in good times, let alone the precarious ones they lived in now.

Carys understood her father's concern for her safety and wellbeing. She only wished he could understand that she was a grown woman with her own life to lead.

Even if that life included a Breed male who chose to make his living in the arena.

All around her now, the spectators chanted their champion's name. "Rune! Rune! Rune!"

Carys joined in, awed by his domination of the fighting ring even as the woman in her cringed every time fists smashed on flesh and bone, regardless of who was on the receiving end. And she could admit, at least to herself, that being in love with him had made her hope for the day he might decide to climb out of the cage for good.

No one had ever beaten Rune—and more than a few had died trying.

He prowled the cage with fluid motion, naked except for the arena uniform of brown leather breeches and fingerless gloves bristling with titanium spikes. The sharp metal ensured every blow was a spectacle of shredding flesh and breaking bone for the pleasure of the crowd.

Also crafted primarily for the entertainment of the sport's patrons was the U-shaped steel torc around the fighters' necks. Each combatant had the option of hitting a mercy button inside the cage, which would deliver a debilitating jolt of electricity to his opponent's collar, halting the match to afford the weaker fighter a chance to recover before resuming the bout.

Although Rune had been the recipient of countless juicings when he climbed into the ring, he had never stooped to using the mercy button.

Neither did his opponent tonight. Jagger was one of La Notte's crowd favorites too, a black Breed male whose own record of wins was almost as impressive as Rune's. The two fighters were friendly outside the arena, but no one would know it to see them now.

Being Breed, Jagger healed from his injuries in seconds. He wheeled on Rune with a deafening roar, plowing forward like a bull on the charge. The contact drove Rune back against the cage. Steel bars groaned, straining under the sudden impact of so much muscle and might. The spectators directly below shrieked and shrank away, but the fight had already moved on.

Now it was Rune on the offense, tossing Jagger's massive body across the cage.

Game or not, the clash of fists and fangs brought out the savage in just about any Breed male. Jagger got to his feet, his lips peeled back from his sharp teeth on a furious sneer. His *dermaglyphs* pulsed with violent colors on his dark skin. He rounded on Rune, amber fire blazing from his eyes as he crouched low and prepared to make another bruising charge.

Opposite him in the cage, Rune stood tall, his massive arms at his sides, his stance deceptively relaxed as he and Jagger circled each other.

Rune's Breed skin markings churned with raging colors too. His midnight-blue eyes crackled with hot sparks as he studied his opponent. Rune's fangs were enormous, razor-sharp tips gleaming in the dim lights of the arena. But beneath the sweat-dampened fall of his dark brown hair, his rugged, granite-hewn face was an utter, deadly calm.

This was Rune at his most dangerous.

Carys's breath stilled as Jagger leapt, catapulting and cartwheeling in a blur of furious motion across the ring. One foot came up at Rune's face like powerful hammer, so fast, Carys could hardly track its motion.

But Rune had. He grabbed Jagger's ankle and

twisted, dropping the fighter to the floor. Jagger recovered in less than an instant, pivoting on his elbow and sweeping Rune's legs out from under him with another smooth kick.

The move was swift and elegant, but it opened Jagger up for sudden defeat.

Rune went down, but took Jagger with him, tackling him into an impossible hold on the floor of the cage. Jagger struggled to break loose, but Rune's spiked knuckles kept the fighter subdued.

Howls and applause thundered through the arena as the clock counted down on the end of the match, with Rune about to claim yet another win.

As Carys cheered his certain victory, she felt a prickle of awareness on the back of her neck. She glanced behind her toward the back of the club. Two of her father's Breed warriors had just come inside.

Shit.

Dressed in the Order's black fatigues, Jax and Eli scanned the massive crowd, ignoring the spectacle inside the cage as they sought to locate her. She was getting used to seeing the Order's babysitting patrol every night, but that didn't make it any less annoying.

Maybe her father's patience had finally reached its end. She knew him well enough not to put it past him to send his warriors out to collect her and eventually bring her home. By force if needed.

Ha. Let them try.

As one of the rare few females of the Breed *and* a daywalker, Carys was every bit as strong as any male of her kind. Stronger than most, given that her mother, Tavia Chase, was a laboratory-created miracle comprised of half-Ancient and half-Breedmate genetics.

But she didn't need to resort to physical strength to avoid Jax and Eli. Carys had another ability at her disposal—this one inherited from her father.

As she stood among the crowd near the front of the arena, Carys quieted her mind and focused on her surroundings. Gathering and bending the shadows around her, she concealed herself in plain sight. No one would see her so long as she held the shadows close.

She waited, watching the pair of Order warriors stroll deeper into the club to scan the hundreds of humans and Breed packed inside. Carys drifted deeper into the throng, unseen by anyone. Jax and Eli gave up after a few minutes of searching. Carys smiled from within her magic as she watched them finally leave.

Meanwhile, the match in the cage was over. Rune and Jagger had taken off their metal torcs and gloves. They clapped each other on the shoulder, both mopping the blood and sweat from their faces as the announcer declared the winner.

Carys let her shadows fall away then. The hatch on the cage opened to let out the combatants. She raced to meet Rune, shouting his name and applauding with the rest of the throng as her man collected yet another victory.

Rune's rugged face lit up with private promise when he saw her. The brutal, fearsome fighter stepped out of the cage and caught her around the waist, hauling her to him.

His dark eyes glittered with need he didn't even try to conceal. Ignoring the cheers and applause that swelled around him, he took her mouth in a possessive kiss.

Then he scooped her up and carried her out of the arena.

CHAPTER 2

Order Headquarters
Washington, D.C.

Lucan Thorne jabbed the disconnect button on his video call with the human politician who'd been chewing his ass for the past half hour. Times like this, he really missed the simplicity of the twentieth century. Back then, an aggravating conversation like the one he'd just had could be punctuated by slamming the phone down and letting the person on the other end know what he really thought about their uninvited opinion.

What he liked even better back then was being able to carry out the Order's brand of swift, effective justice in private, rather than under the scrutiny of human and Breed government types whose endless demands for meetings and board reviews only served to hamstring his efforts and waste precious time.

Lucan shoved his desk chair back on a muttered curse and began to pace across his study.

"That bad, huh?" His Breedmate, Gabrielle, stood in the open doorway.

"The Global Nations Council has called for a debriefing about the assassinations in Italy earlier this week. Apparently, more than one GNC member has petitioned for my removal from the council." Lucan crossed the room to meet his beautiful, auburn-haired mate, unable to resist dropping a kiss on her furrowed brow. "Can't say the council's blame is misplaced since I'm the one who secretly arranged the meeting between the brother of Italy's new president and GNC member Byron Walsh."

"You were only trying to help build an important alliance between two influential members of the human and Breed races. Doesn't the council realize the Order wants peace as much as anyone?" Gabrielle tilted her head at him as he took her hand and led her out of his study into the hallway. "Nobody could've predicted the meeting would be sabotaged. By Walsh's own son, no less."

Lucan grunted. "Derek Walsh was only part of a bigger problem. One that's getting stronger every day the Order allows it to exist."

"Opus Nostrum," Gabrielle said quietly.

The name of the deadly cabal had been unheard of until just a few weeks ago, when the group stole experimental UV technology, then attempted to use it for mass murder at a peace summit gala of Breed and human dignitaries. The Order had narrowly thwarted that catastrophe, killing Opus's leader, Reginald Crowe. But after that very public introduction, and subsequent rumors of chemical and other weapons at their disposal, Opus Nostrum was currently the most feared terror group in the world.

The assassinations of the two high-ranking men earlier this week by a fledgling member of Opus—a member who was also the son of a respected GNC official—would only add fuel to the fire.

And as real a threat as Opus Nostrum was, there was another enemy lurking in the shadows too. One that the Order was only beginning to understand.

For millennia, the Breed had believed they were the only preternatural beings on the planet. Now they had irrefutable proof of another. And this other alien race of immortals calling themselves Atlanteans were apparently plotting a war that would make Opus Nostrum's efforts seem like child's play.

To say the Order had its hands full was beyond understatement.

They had to stop Opus Nostrum and eliminate the deeper, hidden threat posed by the Atlanteans, and Lucan had no intention of doing so with one arm tied behind his back by the GNC or any other meddling entity.

Fortunately, the Order had acquired a few helpful leads and unexpected allies in recent days. For each setback and disaster they narrowly averted, it seemed they were given a small glimmer of hope. Which was a damn good thing. Lucan had a feeling they were going to need all the luck they could get.

Absent of luck, he wasn't opposed to crushing anyone who stood in the Order's way.

As he and Gabrielle turned a corner toward the headquarters' conference room, Lucan heard their son, Darion, talking with Gideon and that warrior's mate, Savannah.

Dare wasn't officially part of the Order yet, but Lucan had to admit the twenty-one-year-old had proven himself an asset both intellectually and in the heat of battle. Tonight, he and Gideon were chasing down a lead on a Breed male in Ireland with apparent ties to Opus.

Lucan and Gabrielle paused to find Gideon seated in front of a wall of computers, with Dare and Savannah poring over reports and schematics on the conference table.

It was a familiar scene that brought back old memories, yet the addition of Darion to the picture made Lucan's chest swell with pride. Gabrielle squeezed his hand lovingly, no doubt feeling the surge of his emotion through their blood bond.

Lucan cleared his throat and Savannah smiled in greeting. Dare's face was intense, all of his focus centered on his work as his parents stepped inside the room.

"We tapped in on Riordan yet?" Lucan asked.

Gideon blew out a curse and tossed his ever-present silver shades onto the workstation. He scrubbed his hand over the top of his spiky blond hair. "Aside from grabbing several hours of basically useless security camera footage of traffic in and out of the place, I haven't been able to find a way into the core of his network yet. The son of a bitch lives in a bloody twelfth-century castle, for fuck's sake. He's got some kind of communications equipment in there, but the connection protocol is closed. I haven't been able to exploit any kind up uplink."

Lucan stared. "Which means?"

Darion was the first one to answer. "Unless we can find a crack in Riordan's communication network, we're at a dead end on hacking into his location."

There was a time—as recently as a few weeks ago—that Lucan would have been surprised, even shocked, at the depth of Darion's knowledge and the breadth of his interests. Add to that his tactical and combat skills, perfected under the tutelage of Tegan, and once Darion was seasoned in the field, he would have few equals. Although Lucan and his son had clashed more than once on the subject of his readiness as a true member of the Order, those concerns were becoming a thing of the past.

"I take it those are Nova's sketches of the Riordan place." Lucan gestured to the hand-drawn blueprints spread out across the conference table.

Darion nodded. "As best she as could recall. Nova said she hasn't been near her family Darkhaven for more than ten years."

Savannah's dark brown eyes were sober as she glanced at Dare. "Calling it a Darkhaven is being too generous. The same goes for calling Riordan her family. Nova didn't have to tell us everything she suffered at her adoptive father's hands, but it's obvious her treatment there was nothing short of brutal."

Nova was Mathias Rowan's Breedmate of a few weeks now. The couple had met while the Order's London-based commander had been investigating a string of murders in his city and a missing shipment of Russian arms.

The tattooed, blue-and-black-haired young woman—whose given name was Catriona Riordan—had been instrumental in providing the Order with most of the intel they currently had on the Breed male who'd raised her. Because of Nova, they had learned that the black scarab tattoos on the dead men had marked them as Fineas Riordan's thugs.

But the Order had no evidence to link Riordan to Opus Nostrum until Derek Walsh's confession about the assassinations in Italy. Derek's boast of his plans to impress Opus's inner circle through the shocking murders was made even more significant for the fact that he also bore the black scarab tattoo.

Lucan glanced at the sketches of the Riordan stronghold and shook his head. "We need something solid to tell us what this bastard is up to now, or what he might've wanted with that container of weapons his thugs tried to collect for him in London." Lucan glanced at Gideon. "How long before we send our little drone out for a fly-by?"

"It went up a couple of hours ago."

"And got shot down only a few seconds into its surveillance," Darion finished, his face grim. "We didn't get any data."

"Jesus Christ." Lucan swung his scowl on Gideon. "Satellite images?"

"We're working on it."

"Work faster. In the meantime, I've got to go assure the GNC and all of the other whining armchair quarterbacks at the Capitol that the attack in Italy was an isolated incident orchestrated by Walsh's mentally unstable son. The last thing we need is word getting out that Opus was even loosely connected to those killings. All that'll do is fan the flames of public hysteria, and we've got enough of that shit to deal with as it is."

Everyone in the room nodded in agreement, but Darion's expression still held an edge of concern. "We can handle scum like Riordan. We can even handle Opus

Nostrum when the time comes. But that still leaves the Atlanteans."

"It does," Lucan said. "And we have to be prepared for that fight too. One thing Reginald Crowe showed us is that his kind can be living right under our noses and we won't even know it. Just like the now-dead owner of La Notte in Boston. No one ever would've suspected Cassian Gray was anything other than human until his Atlantean brethren cut him down."

Gabrielle's hand came down gently on Lucan's arm. "Yes, but where Crowe was evil, Cass's only crime was trying to steal his Atlantean daughter away from his people to give her a better life. There's nothing evil in Jordana. There was nothing evil in her father either."

"It's not any of them we have to contend with," Lucan reminded his mate. "It's their queen who wants a war. Cass lost his head on Selene's command and Jordana will be in hiding from her royal grandmother for the rest of her life unless we find Selene first."

Darion nodded gravely. "If what Crowe said is true, that their queen has been plotting a war to end all others, then we have no choice but to hunt the bitch down and destroy her. The rest of her legion too."

Lucan stared at the man his son had become—the fearless champion. He didn't want to imagine Darion on the front lines of a clash with a powerful enemy race. But the commander in him couldn't ask for a better warrior to one day lead that charge.

"Let me know when you have something on Riordan," he instructed them. "Every minute we let that bastard breathe gives Opus another opportunity to strike."

CHAPTER 3

W ith Carys's jean-clad legs wrapped around him and her mouth locked hard on his since they'd left the arena, Rune strode toward his quarters in the back of the club.

Heavy bass and industrial dance music throbbed all around, the din of the packed club and hundreds of voices muffled to a low drone the closer Rune and Carys got to the fighters' quarters in La Notte's underground level.

Not that he could hear much over the hammering of his blood through his veins.

He kicked open the door and carried her inside. He couldn't wait to be alone with her. To be inside her. Pivoting just as they cleared the threshold, he pressed Carys's back to the closed panel and took her lips and tongue in a fevered, primal kiss.

Twenty-five minutes of hand-to-hand combat in the cage always left him wired with adrenaline and the need to fuck and feed. His post-match ritual had long been to slake both thirsts in La Notte's BDSM dens, but he hadn't stepped foot in that part of the club for the past seven weeks.

Carys Chase was all he craved now.

She'd been the only woman in his bed all this time—on those few occasions they actually made it that far before tearing each other's clothes off.

Sex with Carys had ruined him for any other woman. She brought out the feral side of him like no other, made his veins light up so hot he could hardly stand it, especially when her strong, gorgeous body was clinging to him the way she was now.

Wild and uninhibited, the beautiful Breed female was a raw and powerful force of nature.

As for her blood . . .

Fuck. He couldn't think about the temptation of her blood. Especially not when his cock was as stiff as granite and aching to be inside her.

He needed a shower to soap off the sweat and grime from the cage, but Carys didn't seem to mind. Even though she deserved far better, she welcomed him however he came to her. And damn if that didn't make him even harder.

With one arm looped around the back of his neck, she used her other to work the ties of his leather shorts. They peeled down his bare thighs and she grasped his freed shaft. Rune groaned as she caressed his length. Her mouth was still crushed against his, and with each sure stroke of her hand, she pushed her demanding little tongue deeper into his mouth.

Christ, she truly was his addiction.

He thrust his hips up to grind the ridge of his arousal against her core. The denim abraded his skin, but it was her body's heat that dragged a hiss from him.

"Feel how hard you make me," he muttered against her lips, his voice thick from the presence of his fangs. "You need to be naked. Right now."

"I agree." She smiled, baring the sharp tips of her own as he set her feet onto the floor.

Seeing Carys in her true Breed form still unnerved him at times. Desire made her bright blue eyes glow with amber sparks, as it did his dark ones. Like his, her pupils narrowed to catlike slits in her need.

With eager hands, they made quick work of her black blouse and body-hugging jeans, then Carys shimmied out of her silky bra and barely-there panties. He'd seen her undressed easily a dozen times already, but it didn't keep him from staring in fascination at the *dermaglyphs* that swirled and arced over her shoulders, chest and torso.

The Breed skin markings were more delicate than those that tracked over his body. But her feathery flourishes and lacy patterns churned with deep colors, the same as his, indicating the height of her desire.

She had *dermaglyphs* and fangs, but she also bore the birthmark of a Breedmate. The small scarlet symbol—a teardrop falling into the cradle of a crescent moon—rode the left side of Carys's neck. It was that part of her that allowed her to walk in the daylight, where Rune and the majority of the Breed were creatures of the night.

Rune reached out to touch the tiny mark, tracing the coarse pads of his fingers along her soft cheek, then down to the pretty tangle of *glyphs* that danced across her breasts.

"You're so fucking beautiful," he rasped, stroking the rosy buds of her nipples. He skimmed his big hand down her slender belly to the narrow patch of caramel-brown curls between her legs. She was wet for him, silken and hot. So damn sexy.

He wanted to slow things down, but the adrenaline spike from the cage was still riding him. As was his need for this woman.

Rune lifted her light weight in his hands and held her aloft at his waist. She wrapped her legs around his hips, seating his cock in the slick cleft of her body. Rune thrust inside, the long, hard push seating her to the hilt.

Carys moaned, rocking on him before he could even catch his breath. Fire erupted in her eyes as she held his gaze, her fangs extending even further as desire flooded her *glyphs*. Rune braced himself, his feet gripping the slate floor, one arm holding Carys's weight, his other splaying against the wall at her back as he gave her everything her body demanded of him.

There was no need to hold himself in check with her. Together, their passion was explosive. Immense. As classically beautiful as she was, as delicate as she felt in his arms, Carys was every bit as powerful as any Breed male.

"Yes," she hissed in his ear as he crashed into her. "Rune, yes . . . Fuck me harder."

He growled, happy to obey. As he drove deeper, she cried out. Her fingernails raked his back, scoring his skin, spurring him on. Her *dermaglyphs* were alive and pulsing against his bare chest, her body throwing off heat in waves.

"Come on, baby," he ground out between his clamped teeth and fangs. "This how you want it?"

"Oh, yes," she panted. "Give me more, Rune. Don't stop."

He pumped into her on a thunderous roar as they both began to hurtle toward release. He couldn't slow it down now, even if she wanted him to.

He glanced between them to watch Carys's body tense, her pretty *glyphs* pulsing and wild with deep indigo, wine and gold.

She was close.

Fuck, so was he.

Carys's nails dug into his shoulders as the first wave smashed into her. A scream of pleasure tore out of her, the hottest thing Rune had ever heard. As she shuddered and broke around his increasing thrusts, his own climax rose inside him.

He threw his head back on a jagged shout, hammering into the welcoming sheath of her body, feeling her tight walls milk him with each thrust. When he came, it was on a savage roar, the intensity of his release wracking him.

"Jesus, you feel good on my cock," he rasped, bringing his head back down to look at her. "You keep fucking me like this, and I won't be able to deny you anything, female."

"You mean that?" There was no blue left in her eyes now, only bright amber light. And all of it fixed on his throat. She licked her lips, then glanced up at him, unapologetically Breed.

Even though he could tell she was playing with him, he sobered instantly. He stroked the side of her beautiful face. "You know our rule, love."

She groaned, arching a slender brow. "If I followed everyone's rules, we would never have gotten together in the first place, would we?"

Before he knew what she was doing, she dipped her

head and ran her tongue across his carotid. No fangs, only softness—a swift, wet caress that arrowed through him even more potently than any jolt of electricity he'd ever taken in the cage.

Holy. Hell.

Rune snarled and grabbed her, hoisting her over his shoulder like a sack of potatoes. She squealed, her hands smacking his back, her caramel-brown hair tickling his bare ass as he stalked with her through his quarters to the bedroom. He dropped her onto the mattress, then came down on top of her.

She was laughing, enjoying her harmless little taunt, but Rune was all seriousness now. "The blood bond is unbreakable, Carys. You know that."

Her smile dimmed a bit. "I know."

"What we have together is great, but look around you. Look at me." He shook his head. "Is this really where you belong? The club? The crowd outside the cage every night? It sure as fuck isn't the kind of life anyone wants to see you shackled to for the rest of your life. Not even me."

"Careful, you're sounding an awful lot like my family."

"They're right to disapprove. Of me. Of us, together like this."

"I don't care what anyone else thinks."

No, she didn't. And that was one of the things he respected about her. It was one of the many things he loved about her.

"First time I saw you, I knew you were going to be trouble for me." He speared his fingers into her hair, his palm curving around her warm nape. "You and your little gang of giggling, jiggling friends. I noticed you the second you walked in, you know that?"

She grinned. "I'm sure it was hard to miss us. We were all pretty lit up that night. We'd already hit a bunch of clubs uptown before we ended up down here."

Rune shook his head. "I saw your friends, but the only one I took notice of was you. You, striding in at the front of the group, leading the pack."

His cock stirred at the memory even now. So did his blood, pounding with the same hard need he'd felt the instant Carys had invaded his world like a blast of unstoppable light.

"Every male in here that night took notice of you too, but I knew I was going to be the one to have you."

Her brows arched. "So arrogant."

"Aye," he agreed. "And determined."

"A lethal combination." She smiled as she leaned toward him, until barely an inch separated their mouths. "I never stood a chance."

"Not for a moment," he said. "And when you came back the next night by yourself, neither did I."

As he kissed her and pushed back into her heat, he couldn't help thinking that if they were a normal couple, they'd probably already be mated or well on their way toward it.

If he was a different man . . .

Rune shook the useless thoughts away.

Forever was something he couldn't give Carys.

Hell, he hadn't even given her total honesty. The blood bond would open his ugly past and shameful secrets to her. It would bind her to him irrevocably, and to the darkness he'd been running from nearly all his life.

It would bind Carys to the danger that could catch up to him at any time. As it had already before.

And that was something he would never risk, even if it meant one day pushing her away from him for good.

CHAPTER 4

Seated on a living room sofa next to his mate, Tavia, Sterling Chase did his damnedest to chat with their three houseguests without staring at the clock on the opposite wall every five minutes.

Tried and failed, if the look Tavia slanted at him was any indication.

As soon as he heard the quiet beep of the command center's security system, indicating his patrol team had returned for the night, Chase murmured his excuses and strode out to the mansion's hallway.

The pair of warriors he wanted to see appeared at the far end of the corridor, fresh from their night's sweep of the city. "Anything to report?"

"Just a typical Friday night in Boston," Elijah said in his smooth Texas accent. "Which is saying a lot, based on how things have been going around here lately."

"And my daughter?" Chase pressed.

Jax shook his head, his almond-shaped eyes solemn. "No sign of her at La Notte, sir."

"Was the cage fighter there?" At the warriors' nods, Chase let out a sharp curse. "Then so was she. Carys probably hid from you the instant she spotted you inside the place."

And Chase ought to know his daughter had the skill to evade anyone she had a mind to. The fact that she could bend shadows to her bidding was an extrasensory gift she'd inherited from him, after all. *Damn it.*

As he considered sending the men back out for another fly-by of the illegal sport club, just to get a visual confirmation that his child was still in the city and still in one piece, he sensed a shift in the air behind him.

Tavia had come out to the hallway now.

She smiled warmly at the two warriors, who greeted their commander's blood-bonded mate with deferential nods. "Is everything all right out here?"

"Yes, ma'am," Eli replied.

Jax's head bobbed in agreement.

"They were just reporting in on the night's patrol," Chase said.

"You mean, reporting in on your nightly surveillance of our daughter."

He didn't bother to deny it. Tavia knew how concerned he was for Carys living on her own now. Not simply because she was his only daughter, but because of the dangers lurking in Boston and around the world of late. Dangers few but the Order were fully aware of.

Tavia worried too, but she must have been made of stronger stuff than he was. In the weeks since Carys had moved out of the family Darkhaven, Tavia had reconciled with the fact that their daughter was a grown woman who should be allowed to make her own choices.

As much as Chase hated it, there was nothing he could do. She was an adult, and he had to hope that what he'd taught her in life had not only stuck, but taken root.

He glanced at the pair of warriors and cursed. "Maybe I should send them back out to pick her up and bring her home where she belongs."

Tavia crossed her arms. "And then what? Chain her to the banister? She'd never stand for us dictating her life like that, and you know it. We'd lose her for good."

"We still might if we don't keep her where we can protect her."

"From what I've heard about her friend, Rune—"

"Friend?" Chase scoffed. "Gutter-bred, cold-blooded killer, according to his reputation. She can do a hell of a lot better than some cage-fighting bastard looking for another conquest outside of the arena."

"Carys seems to see something more in him than his reputation," Tavia gently reminded him. "Nathan and Jordana have spent time with Carys and Rune. They both said he appears to care deeply for her. That he's protective of her too. It sounds to me like he loves her, Sterling."

Chase nearly choked on the idea. "He'd better hope nothing happens to our girl—by him or anyone else he might associate with. As for Carys, I still say she belongs with us. Especially now. I'm sure you haven't forgotten what happened to Cassian Gray last week, or the fact that Carys was nearly swept into that whole ordeal with Jordana."

No, of course his mate wouldn't have forgotten. Aside from the fact that Tavia's unique extrasensory gift was a flawless photographic memory, no one in the Order would forget the circumstances of La Notte's club owner's murder by Atlantean soldiers, or the kidnapping of Jordana soon afterward.

Tavia rested her hand on Chase's forearm. "We raised two very strong-willed, hard-headed children, my love. If we wonder where it came from, we only have to look in the mirror."

At his grumbled acknowledgment, Tavia leaned toward him and kissed his cheek. "We have guests in the other room. Come back inside and try to be sociable. Leave that scowl out here in the hallway and let's spend some time with our friends." She smiled at the pair of warriors. "Eli, Jax."

"Ma'am," they replied in unison.

After Tavia had slipped back into the living room, Chase asked, "Have you seen Nathan and Jordana tonight?"

Jax nodded. "They were in the command center operations room with Aric when we came in a minute ago."

Chase had deliberately kept Carys's twin brother off the patrols that would take him to the club where Rune fought. Aric shared his father's opinion that Carys was only going to get hurt. Not long ago, he'd tried to discourage her from seeing Rune and as a result, his children were hardly speaking to each other anymore.

Chase heaved a sigh. "Ask Jordana and Nathan to come see me in about an hour. I have a favor to ask of them."

With the two warriors dismissed, Chase went back to the room where Tavia was chatting with Mathias Rowan and his Breedmate, Nova, who had arrived a short time ago from London.

Chase had known Mathias from their days together

in the Breed's Enforcement Agency in Boston. That was more than twenty years ago, but the two men had remained close friends and both now served the Order as district commanders of their respective regions.

Chase had never seen his comrade more obviously contented than when he was sitting next to Nova. The contrast between the couple was striking—straitlaced Mathias and the tattooed, blue-and-black haired spitfire at his side. Nova's colorful inked arms were encased in a sheer black blouse tonight that made the unusual beauty look both elegant and rebellious. And Mathias was clearly smitten with her. He'd been holding Nova's hand all night, hardly able to take his eyes off his mate.

The Darkhaven's third guest was also from London, and had been visiting Tavia and Chase for the past couple of days. Pretty, sable-haired Brynne Kirkland was an investigator with the Joint Urban Security Taskforce Initiative Squad. While the Order and members of the Breed/human law enforcement group had a prickly relationship at best, Brynne's trip to Boston hadn't been in an official JUSTIS capacity.

She had come to spend time with her half-sister, Tavia.

The women had found each other about a decade ago, both Breed females born in a madman's lab as an experiment in blending various Breedmate DNA with the DNA from the last-surviving Ancient forebear of the Breed. The result had produced the Breed's first females in existence.

There had been several daywalkers like Tavia and Brynne from that experiment who had survived to adulthood, but all were raised apart from one another in secret and most remained lost. Tavia and Brynne had been working to locate their sisters, and in the process had forged a special bond.

Tonight's gathering was supposed to be pleasant, casual. Chase's expression must have resembled a thundercloud.

"Problems in the city?" Mathias asked.

Tavia arched a brow, a smirk dancing at the corner of her mouth. "Some of us are still trying to adjust to parenthood, even after twenty years of practice."

Mathias and Nova shared a look. His grin widened. "In that case, I guess we'd better start collecting tips and advice now."

Chase gaped.

Tavia drew in a surprised breath. "You mean—"

Nova's cheeks flooded with color. Mathias beamed like a son of a bitch and pulled his expectant Breedmate closer. "We've only known for a few days."

"Oh, my God," Tavia exclaimed. "We're elated for you!"

Nova's blush deepened as she murmured her shy thanks.

Mathias looked at Chase. "We'd like you and Tavia to be godparents. That's why we wanted to stop in to see you before we headed on to D.C. to meet with Lucan."

"It would be an honor," Chase said, humbled by the gesture of trust and friendship. He rose to take Mathias's hand, then decided the occasion merited more than the stiff gestures of his upbringing. He clasped the other male in a brief embrace. "You honor us well, my old friend."

Tavia went to Nova and hugged her too, delight shining in her eyes. "A baby is the most wonderful news."

Although Brynne's smile was more reserved, her dark green gaze was warm as she reached out to grasp Nova's tattooed hand. "Congratulations to you both."

As they all resumed their seats, Tavia asked, "Have you told anyone else?"

"Only Eddie," Nova said, referring to the nine-year-old human boy who'd worked in the tattoo shop with her when Mathias had first met her. The couple had taken Eddie in when they mated, and the boy now lived in the London command center with them.

There was a time when no human would have been permitted inside a Breed household. A lot had changed in the twenty years since First Dawn had brought the human and vampire worlds together.

Chase met Mathias's gaze. "How's the boy adjusting to life among the Breed?"

"Very well, actually. Thane and the other warriors have practically adopted him along with Nova and me. If they have their way, they'll probably turn him into an honorary Order member in a few years."

Nova tilted her head. "Not if I have anything to say about that."

Mathias shrugged, chuckling as he stroked his Breedmate's right hand.

Chase couldn't help but notice the Egyptian eye symbol on the back of Nova's hand. He'd been told that beneath that mark was another one—a black scarab forced on her when she'd been just a little girl, branding her as the property of Fineas Riordan, her adoptive father.

The Order was currently conspiring to take the bastard out for his apparent affiliation with Opus Nostrum.

Mathias seemed to follow Chase's line of thought. His face turned grave as he met Chase's look across the room. He wanted to discuss Order business, but there was a question in his eyes—one that Chase caught on to with the subtle flick of Mathias's gaze toward Brynne.

She caught the glance too. "I should allow you all to speak privately. I'm sure you have much to catch up on."

Tavia frowned when Brynne started to rise. "You're not here on official JUSTIS business, Brynne. You're my sister. I trust you the same as I would trust anyone else in this house."

Chase nodded, completely comfortable in Brynne's integrity and discretion. In fact, since he'd come to know Tavia's sister, he considered her an ally the Order would be fortunate to call their own. "There's no need for you to leave. Your word to treat anything you hear as confidential is guarantee enough for me."

Brynne nodded. "Of course, you have my word."

Mathias acknowledged her promise as well. "Lucan has told me to prepare my team to be called in to move on Riordan at a moment's notice," he told Chase. "I'm sure I don't have to tell you that taking down that bastard and everyone loyal to him will be my personal pleasure."

Chase grunted. "We all feel the same way. But we have to make sure every piece of intel is in place first. There can be no room for error. If we move too hastily, or miss the mark in taking Riordan out, we could drive the other Opus members to ground. The Order needs to unmask every last one of them first, if we have any hope of obliterating the organization."

Brynne seemed twitchy at the mention of Opus's other members. She started to say something, then stopped.

"What is it?" Chase demanded.

When she frowned and shook her head, Tavia held her pensive look. "Tell us what you're thinking, Brynne. We're trusting you, so you have to trust us now too."

"I don't have any actual proof, but . . ." She sighed and blew out a curse. "I've had a hunch for some time now. Nothing actionable. Nothing but a suspicion . . . about Neville Fielding."

"The GNC director in London," Chase murmured. "What kind of suspicion?"

Brynne tilted her head. "I have a feeling he's on the take. It's got to be someone with deep pockets, because a couple of weeks ago, Fielding moved into a pricey townhouse that's way above his means."

Seated on the sofa, Mathias leaned forward onto his elbows. "A couple of weeks ago, that container of Russian arms went missing from the Thames docks."

"The container that was supposed to go to Riordan," Chase added.

Mathias inclined his head. "*Would* have gone to him, if Gavin Sloane hadn't double-crossed his and his gang of scarab-tattooed thugs."

Brynne's frown deepened. "Wait a minute. JUSTIS Officer Sloane was killed in the line of duty, according to the official reports."

"He was killed in the line of duty," Mathias said. "By me. After the son of a bitch came after Nova and would've killed me in the process too."

Chase shrugged. "The Order has its own back channels, Brynne. We made sure the official reports didn't shine inconvenient light on Riordan before we have the chance to take him out on our own terms."

She swore under her breath. "I can't say I'm happy

to be hearing this. But it only makes my suspicion about Fielding all the stronger. Opus Nostrum is everyone's problem, not just the Order's. After the disaster they tried to unleash at the GNC peace summit a few weeks ago, they must be stopped."

"Seeing that you're family, maybe you and the Order can start sharing intel," Chase suggested. "Even hunches can prove useful."

Brynne nodded. "I can do that."

"Speaking of family," Mathias said. "Have we been able to get anything promising out of the Order's interviews with Reginald Crowe's ex-wives?"

Chase had to chuckle at the term *interview.* They'd brought in Crowe's widow and all five of his former wives one by one, trancing each human female and culling everything they could from the women's subconscious minds. Only one had provided anything helpful. "None of them had any knowledge of Crowe's involvement with Opus, but one former missus did mention a mistress that Crowe seemed to spend a lot of time with in Ireland."

"Ireland?" Brynne asked. "You don't suppose there's a connection to Riordan too?"

"We don't know," Chase said. "The lead on the woman hasn't gone anywhere. We don't even have a name yet."

"If there's anything JUSTIS can provide you on that—officially or otherwise—just say the word. Opus Nostrum is the biggest terror threat this world has ever known. Anything I can do to help defeat them, consider me in."

Even while he shook Brynne's hand in appreciation, Chase couldn't help thinking that she was wrong about

Opus. They weren't the biggest threat.

He wasn't ready to share the real headline with his sister-in-law just now, but Chase and the rest of the Order knew all too well that there would come a time— and soon—when the threat of the Atlanteans and their vengeful queen would eclipse anything Opus could possibly dream up.

He only hoped the Order would be ready when that time came.

CHAPTER 5

☾

The elevator slowed to a stop at the penthouse of the Back Bay apartment building. As the polished doors started to slide open, Carys took a step forward to disembark—only to be dragged back into Rune's arms for another bone-melting kiss.

"Why don't you come in and spend the night?" she murmured against his mouth. "Jordana's living at the command center with Nathan now anyway. We'll have the apartment all to ourselves."

Rune groaned, amber light still glowing in his dark blue eyes from the hours of lovemaking back at his quarters at La Notte. "I'll come in, but I can't stay. I have things to do back at the club."

"You mean feeding," she murmured, knowing he took his regular nourishment from human blood Hosts, like most other unmated Breed males. Carys's unique metabolism allowed her to eat and drink for sustenance, but she occasionally fed from Hosts too. Still, it was hard not to be jealous of the human women who knew the bite of Rune's fangs and the suction of his mouth on their veins as he drank from them.

"I do need to feed tonight, love." His fingers were tender on her cheek, soothing her sullen mood. "And then Jagger and a few of the other fighters have asked me to meet with them about some club business."

"All right, I'll let you make your escape." She gazed up at him and slowly shook her head. "I hate that we hardly ever wake up together."

He grunted, one dark brow rising. "Waking up together implies we'd let each other sleep."

She laughed. "Well, that's true. We don't even go on proper dates because we never make it out of the club. Or rather, out of your bed."

His mouth curved, a sensual bow of his full lips that barely hid the points of his fangs. "Are you complaining?"

By way of answer, she grabbed the back of his neck and pulled him down for searing kiss. Rune growled with pleasure, his strong arms wrapping around her as his tongue pushed past her lips to tangle with hers. Instantly, her blood roared in her veins, rekindling her desire and hunger for him. She tilted her hips and ground against the rigid bulge of his cock.

Rune drew back on a low curse. "Christ, you are dangerous, woman."

She grinned. "Would you have me any other way?"

"Never." He stroked her face, his eyes crackling with fiery embers. "Let's get you inside the penthouse before we give the old fella down in the lobby a show on the security cameras."

She glanced up at the small monitor in the corner of the lift and laughed. "I have a feeling we wouldn't be

Seamus's first peep show from in here. Jordana and Nathan will have already broken him in."

"I'm sure we could shock him even more." Rune smirked. "Come on. Before you give me a lot of bad ideas."

Lacing his fingers through hers, he stabbed the OPEN button on the now-closed elevator doors. They exited together and walked through the iron gate to the vestibule of the elegant penthouse. Carys's high-heeled boots echoed on the polished marble tiles as she and Rune entered the living area of the expansive apartment.

Her steps stopped short an instant later, when she found Jordana and Nathan waiting inside. It didn't look like they planned to stay long.

No, from the serious looks on their faces, it appeared they'd come there on a mission.

"Let me guess," Carys said. "When Eli and Jax reported me MIA to my father tonight, he sent the captain of his top team and my best friend out to drag me home."

Jordana's mouth twisted in a wry smile. "Not quite as bad as that."

"But don't think it won't come to that eventually," Nathan added, his deep voice low with warning. "Everyone is only concerned with your wellbeing, Carys."

Nathan glanced at Rune as he spoke, giving the other male a curt nod that almost passed as friendliness for the lethal warrior.

Rune flashed a bit of fang, granting Nathan an equally reticent greeting. Not surprising, considering the last time the two Breed males had met in this apartment, Nathan had come right out and threatened to kill Rune if his involvement with Carys ended badly.

Jordana stepped between the two big men. "Your parents would feel much better knowing you were somewhere they could be certain of your security, Car. Things have gotten so dangerous lately, it would be one less worry for everyone while the Order is dealing with everything else right now."

Carys crossed her arms over her chest. "And if I move back home, my father hopes it will minimize the time I spend with Rune."

Jordana gave her a sympathetic look. "I'm not going to deny that's part of it too. You have to know that when you dodge your father's attempts to protect you, it only makes him grip the reins that much tighter."

Nathan grunted. "He wasn't happy to hear you pulled that disappearing act tonight at the club."

Rune glanced at her now, his dark brows furrowed. "What happened?"

Carys shrugged. "Jax and Eli came in during your match. I didn't feel like having my father's watchdogs breathing down my neck all night—"

"So you bent the shadows and avoided them," Rune said, shaking his head. "Jesus Christ, Carys. They were only trying to look out for you."

Her temper flared at all of them now. "I'm a grown woman, for fuck's sake. I'm also Breed."

"Yeah, you are," Rune agreed. "But this is no time to be tempting fate. Or did you forget that just last week you ran up against something none of us were prepared for?"

He was talking about Jordana's abduction during a reception at the Museum of Fine Arts, where Jordana and Carys worked. The man who took Jordana had knocked Carys out when she'd tried to intervene and help her friend.

"I don't know what I would've done if something worse had happened to you," Rune said. "Or if those three fucks who killed Cass and Syn at the club had gotten their hands on you."

Carys embraced him, reaching up to caress away the deep worry that had settled on his brow. "It wasn't me they were after. The only thing that got hurt was my pride. And I was terrified for Jordana too."

"We all were," Nathan muttered.

He put his hands on Jordana's slender shoulders, protective, possessive. The deadly warrior was devoted to his mate, a woman who turned out to be even more extraordinary than anyone could ever have guessed. Carys smiled to see her best friend and the Order's most unreachable warrior so clearly devoted to each other.

"What the hell were those men?" Rune asked, leveling a hard stare on Nathan. "Not human, that's for damn sure. Not Breed either. I've never fought anything like that before. No matter what I did, the bastards kept coming. Two of them got away, but the one I killed? I had to take his head off to stop him. And when I did . . . The light that poured out of his body was blinding. What the fuck are we dealing with, warrior?"

When Nathan said nothing, Carys spoke up. "Rune should know the truth. I trust him to know the truth."

"That makes one of us," Nathan muttered, his face impassive and forbidding.

Jordana lifted her chin, her cascade of long, platinum blonde hair shifting at her back. "I trust him too, Nathan. And Cass trusted Rune. He considered him a friend."

Rune's dark eyes narrowed on Jordana. "The three who came to La Notte after killing Cass . . . They said they were looking for his daughter, but as far as I knew—as far as anyone at the club knows—Cassian Gray didn't have any family."

"I was a secret he'd kept for almost twenty-five years," Jordana said. "He wanted to protect me from the kind of men who came looking for him that night."

"Immortals," Rune guessed.

"Atlanteans," Jordana said. "Like Cass. Like me."

Rune shook his head. "Where did these Atlanteans come from? Where do they live now?"

"We don't have all of those answers yet," Nathan said. "The Order has evidence that suggests the Atlanteans have been in existence on this planet for at least as long as the Breed. Longer, in fact."

"They're linked to us," Carys pointed out. "The Order has known for more than twenty years that Atlantean men fathered children with human women, and those female offspring were all born with the teardrop-and-crescent-moon birthmark."

"Breedmates," Rune said. He considered for a long moment, then let out a low curse. "So, if Atlantean daughters are mating with members of the Breed, why do I get the sense that most of these immortal fucks would like to kill us all?"

Nathan grunted. "That's a discussion for another time. And a higher security clearance."

Rune looked back to Jordana. "Cass never said a word. Never let on for a second that he was anything other than human. Everyone just assumed—"

"Which is how he intended it," Carys added. "Jordana didn't know any of this either, not until after he was killed by the Atlantean soldiers that day outside the club."

Jordana nodded. "Cass smuggled me out of the realm as an infant, after my mother died. He arranged for me to live among the humans and the Breed." She gestured to her Breedmate mark. "He hid me in plain sight as the adopted daughter of a Breed Darkhaven leader he trusted here in Boston."

"Cass never reached out to her, never risked contacting her in any way," Carys said. "Not until the day those men caught up to him."

"He visited me at the museum that day, but even then he didn't reveal himself to me as my father. I wish he had," Jordana murmured wistfully. "Apparently, when he realized he couldn't outrun his past any longer and that his enemies might find me, he contacted someone who could help."

"Another Atlantean," Rune guessed.

"Zael," Carys said, having since been told the name of the Atlantean who'd left her unconscious from a powerful beam of light as he'd stolen Jordana away for her own protection.

Since Zael had helped Jordana escape Cass's killers, and, together, the three of them had defeated the other Atlanteans who had pursued them, she and Nathan now considered Zael to be their friend.

"Zael wanted to bring me to a hidden colony of other Atlanteans who'd defected from the realm, where Cass's enemies would never find me. But I said no." She tilted her head up to meet Nathan's tender gaze. "I chose to stay where my heart was."

Rune cocked his head. "If others have defected to a safe colony as you said, then why were Cass's pursuers so determined to kill him and find you?"

Jordana gave Carys a nod of permission. "Because Jordana's grandmother is the Atlanteans' queen."

Rune's brows rose. "Meaning you're an Atlantean princess?"

Jordana nodded. Carys nodded too.

Nathan glowered and jabbed a finger toward Rune. "No one can know this. If you leak a word of it, I'll kill you myself."

"I'll take the secret to my grave," Rune vowed. "But . . . are you telling me that Cassian Gray was not only Atlantean, but royal blood too?"

Jordana shook her head. "His true name was Cassianus, and he wasn't royal. He was one of Queen Selene's legion. My mother, Soraya, was daughter of the queen."

"Holy shit." Rune fell silent for a minute, holding Carys's gaze in an incredulous look. "This conversation will go no further. I give you my oath."

Nathan and Jordana nodded. Carys snaked her arm around Rune's muscled waist and held him close.

No one mentioned the other secret that came out of Jordana's ordeal—the Atlantean crystal, which Cass had stolen out of the realm at the same time he had taken Jordana away from the royal court. Carys had seen the egg-sized, silvery crystal herself, when Jordana and Nathan presented it to all of the Order at a special meeting upon her return home to Boston.

It was safeguarded at the D.C. headquarters now, where Lucan and the others were trying to determine its powers and how it could be used in what they dreaded was soon to be a war with Selene and her immortal legion.

In the silence that fell over the room, Rune lifted Carys's chin and met her gaze. "If I'd known any of this before, I would have delivered you home to the Order's protection myself. Hell, I would've helped your father lock the door behind you." His deep voice lowered to a private growl. "The dead last thing I ever want is for anything bad to touch you. Tell me you know that, Carys."

She reached up to touch his stern, handsome face. "I know that—"

"Good." He seized her hand in his warm grasp. "Then if you won't do it for your parents or your friends, do it for me."

She frowned and started to protest, but he wasn't having any of it.

"Go home to your family. At least for now." He brought her palm to his mouth and placed a kiss in its center. "Stay where *I* can know you're safe."

She smiled at him, her heart squeezing with emotion. "You're a good man, Rune."

He blew out a sharp breath. "No, love. I'm not. But I'm right. Your family needs to have you close to them now."

She nodded, then glanced over at Jordana and Nathan. "I guess I'd better pack a few things before we go."

CHAPTER 6

C

Carys had only been gone for a week, but it felt like a year had passed since she had last walked into the Chase Darkhaven. Jordana and Nathan left her in the back vestibule of the large mansion while they headed down to the Order's command center and Nathan's quarters, which the couple now shared.

Carys missed them instantly, but it was at her request that they'd left her to face her parents alone. She adjusted the packed tote slung over her shoulder, then took a deep breath and headed through the back of the house to the main living areas.

Her path took her toward the kitchen, where she heard her mother talking with two other females. Carys recognized her aunt's voice. Brynne's smooth London accent called to mind posh society galas and invitations to high tea.

The other feminine voice was also British, but more reserved, even though it carried an intriguing punk rock edge to it. Curious now, Carys stepped into the kitchen.

Her mother stood at the large island in the center of the space, sharing a tray of canapés and finger sandwiches with her guests. Occupying two of the counter's dozen tall stools were Brynne and the other female—a petite, pretty young woman with asymmetrically cut blue-and-black hair, countless colorful tattoos and multiple piercings.

Carys awkwardly cleared her throat. "Hello, everyone."

Her mother spun toward her with a little gasp, her beautiful face lighting up instantly. "Carys! Come in and join us."

No censure. No judgment. Just pure, maternal warmth and affection. Carys all but launched herself into her mother's open arms. They embraced for a quiet moment before Tavia brought her around to greet the other women.

Brynne got up to hug Carys. "How nice to see you."

"You too," Carys replied. "How long have you been in Boston?"

"Just a couple of days. A much-needed holiday from the office."

Carys nodded. "I'm sorry I didn't stop by sooner."

Brynne waved her hand. "You're here now."

Tavia gestured to their other guest. "And this is Nova, Carys. She's Mathias's mate."

Carys's brows rose at the idea. She'd known Mathias Rowan for as long as she could remember. Although she'd heard he had mated recently, she had always pictured the Order's London commander settling down with a female more like Brynne than Nova, but she had to admit she liked the unusual pairing.

Carys held out her hand in greeting. "Very nice to

meet you, Nova."

"You too," Nova replied, her tattooed fingers delicate and warm. As was her shy smile.

When Carys glanced back at her mother, Tavia gestured to the large tote hanging from her shoulder. "Does this mean what I think it does?"

Carys nodded. "It's only temporary. The huge penthouse has been kind of lonely without Jordana there with me, anyway."

Her mother cupped her cheek. "Well, no matter what brought you home, I'm happy you're here. Your father will be thrilled . . . and relieved."

Carys set her bag down, then reached over for the tray of appetizers. "May I? I'm starving."

At her mother's nod, she grabbed a little cucumber sandwich off the tray. Then another. Now that she was home, she realized how long it had been since she'd last eaten. Longer still, since she'd sought out a human blood Host.

As a member of the Breed, she needed to drink fresh red cells from an open vein at least weekly. She'd never given the necessity a lot of thought until she'd met Rune.

Now the idea of feeding from anyone else, even simply for nourishment, only served to remind her of the one thing that was missing in an otherwise amazing relationship.

At some point, she knew she would have to accept that Rune might never be willing to take that step with her.

Carys pushed the sting of that thought aside as she reached for a third helping from the tray. As she ate, she glanced at Nova's intricate body art.

"Whoever did your ink has an impressive talent. It's

really beautiful work."

"Thank you." Nova smoothed one hand over the other, idly tracing some of the art. "Most of it was done by my friend, Ozzy. He owned the shop where I worked. He was killed a couple of weeks ago."

Carys instantly regretted bringing up a sad subject for the other woman. She wasn't aware of the details, but she could see that Nova still grieved for her friend. "I'm sorry for your loss."

"Me too. He was the only family I had, aside from Eddie, the boy Ozzy took in a few years after he saved me from the streets." Her pained expression shifted a bit. "Now, I have Mathias. We've formed a new family together. With Eddie too."

Tavia reached out to squeeze Nova's hand affectionately. "And your new baby on the way."

"A baby!" Apparently, Mathias and his mate were full of surprises. Carys smiled at Nova. "Congratulations."

She murmured her thanks, looking both awkward about it and overjoyed. "I never dreamed I'd have a child of my own one day. I never imagined I'd take a mate either, especially from among the Breed."

The way she said it—the way her pale blue eyes clouded over with an unspoken darkness before she glanced down at her hands again—made Carys guess there had been a lot of ugliness and suffering in Nova's past. But she didn't pry, just let the comment pass in the silence that followed.

"I'm sure you'll have nothing but happiness with Mathias."

"I'm sure of that too." Nova lifted her head, no more dark clouds in her gaze now, only certainty. "I'm thankful every day that Mathias walked into Ozzy's shop. I'll be thankful for the rest of my life that he didn't give up on me, even though I tried my best to push him away."

"Maybe sometime you can tell me all about it," Carys said.

Nova nodded. "Sure. I'd like that."

As the four women fell into an easy conversation around the canapés, footsteps sounded in the hallway outside the kitchen. A moment later, Carys's father strode in with Mathias.

"I thought I heard my daughter's voice in here."

Carys offered him a guilty smile. "Hello, Father."

He crossed his massive arms over his chest, looking every bit the formidable warrior, even in a crisp white oxford shirt and tailored pants. "I'm glad to see you didn't try to ditch Jordana and Nathan tonight too."

Tavia clicked her tongue. "Sterling, don't be difficult."

His frown stayed directed at Carys. "I wasn't aware that's what we're calling a father's concern these days."

She bristled, even though she knew he had a right to be upset. To be worried about her. "I didn't move out to add to your stress or to the Order's problems."

"And yet you have," he informed her. "At a time when all we've got are problems."

A fresh dread crept up her spine at his ominous tone. "What's happened? Has there been anything more regarding Opus or the Order's other missions?"

"Nothing in our favor," he grumbled. "We're still gathering intel. We only have Riordan in our sights now, when we need to unmask all of Opus's members if we stand any chance of bringing down the organization."

Mathias nodded. "Too bad Reginald Crowe didn't leave behind anything solid to lead us to the rest of his associates."

"Only a cold trail to a rumored lover who may or may not exist," Chase said. "Gideon hacked into all of his business and personal accounts, but Crowe took precautions with his interests. Nothing to implicate anyone as a member of Opus. And if Crowe did have a mistress, he was careful to keep his relationship with her out of the spotlight. Which is saying something right there, based on Crowe's lack of discretion in all the other areas of his life."

Carys knew of Reginald Crowe, of course. Anyone alive in the past twenty years was familiar with the billionaire business magnate who was as famous for his numerous, progressively younger ex-wives as he was for his limitless ego. He'd put his name on everything he could, from high-rise hotels and casinos, to enormous grants for art and science institutions.

Even Boston's Museum of Fine Arts where Carys and Jordana worked had a large exhibit of masterworks on loan from Reginald Crowe personal collection.

As Carys listened to what the Order and her family had been dealing with in her absence, she felt guilty for the strife she'd caused in her need to spread her wings. She should have been helping her family and the Order however she could.

Instead, she'd been preoccupied with Rune, and unintentionally causing everyone more problems and distress.

"I'm sorry," Carys said, looking at her father. "I didn't realize everything that was going on right now. It was selfish of me to leave the way I did."

"You're damn right it was." He was still frowning, still terribly upset with her. "I'm just glad Nathan and Jordana were able to talk a little sense into you where no one else could. I'm glad someone was able to convince you that you belong at home right now, not running around with that fighter down at La Notte."

Carys walked toward her blustering, bristling father. She didn't stop until she was standing directly in front of him, close enough to see the tightly leashed fury glittering in the blue eyes that were the same shade as her own. He stared at her mutely, nostrils flaring.

He rarely showed this side of himself to his family: the explosive Breed male. The lethal warrior. Protector of the entire city of Boston for the past twenty turbulent years and then some.

Carys stared up at him for a long moment, seeing the concern of a devoted parent in his hard-held expression. She saw the bone-deep fear she'd been causing all of her family by distancing herself from them when the dangers surrounding the Order demanded that they keep the ones they cared about closer than ever.

"I love you too, Father." She raised up on her toes and kissed his cheek. "And you should know that it wasn't Jordana or Nathan who convinced me to move back home tonight. It was Rune."

His face went slack, utterly stunned.

He didn't say anything, just swung a silent, dumbfounded look toward his mate.

Tavia's broad smile lit her face, amusement dancing in her gaze. "Well, isn't this a night for surprises?"

Admittedly, Carys probably took a little too much satisfaction in her father's rare descent into mute shock. He was a difficult man to rattle, but he seemed totally at a loss for words.

Smiling, Carys picked up her tote and murmured that she was going to get settled.

CHAPTER 7

C

Rune sat at the long bar in La Notte's underground arena, reviewing the night's receipts. The last of the club's patrons had left more than an hour ago. Few of the Breed lingered in public past the city's nightly feeding curfew, and the humans tended to stagger home once the band on the main floor upstairs packed up and the drinks stopped flowing.

From out of the back of the club where Rune worked now, a group of La Notte's employees drifted through the arena, chattering as they headed for the exit. The men and women were humans—payrolled blood Hosts and sex workers from the BDSM dens.

Rune nodded to them and murmured goodnight as he continued to work on the books. The woman who fed him a short while ago gave him an inviting smile he hardly noticed. Although his Breed genetics demanded he drink fresh red cells from an open vein every other day at least, his hunger stopped there. For the past seven weeks, the rest of him had craved only one woman.

The one woman he would never be able to take between his teeth and fangs.

Not when bonding to her would mean letting her see the ugliness inside him, the stains on his soul. The shame and horror he'd left far behind him.

And which he damn well meant to keep banished there for good.

Rune cast the dark memories aside. He studied La Notte's receipts, reconciling the digital reports to the cash and credits taken in tonight. With Cass and Syn dead, the day-to-day management of the club had settled onto him.

As he flipped to the liquor invoices and consumption accountings, Jagger and two other Breed fighters—Vallan and Slade—strolled into the bar area of the club. They were dressed in street clothes, their arena garb left behind in the dressing rooms out back. "You got time to talk now, Rune?"

He nodded and closed the ledgers to avoid curious eyes on La Notte's business, then pivoted on his stool to give the men his full attention. "Tell me what's going on."

Jagger took the lead. "It's the club, man. We've all been talking for the past few days. Any idea what's gonna happen to it now that Cass is dead?"

Before Rune could say anything, Slade piped in. "One of the girls working the dens says the assholes who came in here the other night and killed Syn were asking about Cass's daughter."

The third fighter, Vallan, blew out a curse. "If he did have a kid, I doubt Cass knew about it. He wasn't exactly the doting daddy type."

Rune let them talk, more interested in what they

knew—or thought they knew—than in helping to clear up any confusion. None of the club's fighters had seen the Atlanteans who killed Syn. The club was closed after Cass's murder.

Syn and Rune had been the only ones there, aside from a handful of human employees, when the Atlantean soldiers had infiltrated the club and started digging through Cass's office and private rooms on the floor above the arena.

In search of Jordana, or information that would lead them to her, Rune now understood.

Once he'd been alerted to the intruders' presence, Rune had sent the straggling employees out of the place for their own safety. It had been only seconds later that he had smelled Syn's blood spilling upstairs.

"If Cass does have family," Slade said, "I wonder how long it will take before they start sniffing around the club. The fights may be illegal, but they bring in serious cash. Too much cash to just walk away from."

Jagger lifted a shoulder. "What's to say they don't decide to close down the arena instead?"

Vallan grunted. "Or convert the whole building back into the pseudo-Goth dance club it was twenty years ago?"

Slade swore under his breath. "Could be worse. What if they decide to turn the place into one of those damn sim-lounges instead?"

Jagger chuckled. "Trade the real fights for virtual reality shit, so all the tourists and wannabe hardasses in this town can sit in their simulation rooms and pretend they'd last more than half a second in the cage."

Rune wasn't amused by the possibilities either, although he doubted Jordana would do any of those things to La Notte. He had to admit, the future of the club was nothing if not uncertain. And given what he knew about Jordana now, he couldn't imagine holding on to a business that profited from violence and debauchery was high on her priority list.

The other men were right. They needed to know where La Notte stood now that its proprietor was gone.

Vallan's face was grave. "Been nearly a week and no one's stepped forward to take the place over or shut it down. We've all been talking that maybe we should make other plans before someone else makes them for us."

"What do you mean?" Rune asked.

"Move on," Jagger said. "Go find another arena, or start a new one of our own."

Rune shook his head as he came up off the barstool. "No one's leaving. No one's going off to fight somewhere else so long as I'm here."

Vallan crossed his arms over his massive chest. "You've been acting as manager since Cass's death, but how long are you gonna look out for a business that doesn't belong to you?"

It was true, the club didn't belong to him. Never had. Rune had never aspired that it could.

He and Cass had built it together—one providing the venue, the other providing the spectacle that would keep the crowds coming back for more. It had been a profitable arrangement. Rune had managed to accumulate close to a million dollars from his fights and shares of the gaming proceeds Cass took in every time Rune climbed into the cage.

The money was his future. His escape plan, should he need it, earned through sweat and blood and broken bones.

He'd never intended to put down roots in La Notte, but a decade at the club, and he felt an obligation to look after it now that he was the only one left to do so.

He met the questioning gazes of his fellow fighters and shrugged. "Someone has to keep an eye on the receipts and make sure inventory and supplies stay stocked. Someone's got to pay the employees, including you three meatheads."

They all chuckled. Jagger gave him a smirk. "Yeah, and someone's got to keep one hand tight on the kitty for himself too."

Jag was only joking, but Slade's laugh held a sharper edge. "His hands are too busy with another kind of kitty. Kinda greedy, ain't it, Rune? Keeping all that exotic daywalker tail to yourself? Save some for the rest of us before you get bored and—"

Rune lunged at Slade. He seized him by the throat, fangs bared, eyes blazing. "Say something stupid like that again, and those'll be the last fucking words to leave your mouth."

Slade choked, struggling for air. He grasped at Rune's hand, his own fangs emerging.

Rune squeezed harder.

Neither Jagger nor Vallan made a move to intervene. Everyone on the club's roster knew Rune hadn't claimed his place as the most lethal motherfucker ever to enter the cage by demonstrating an iota of mercy for someone who'd earned a thorough beating.

Fury rode him, and before he realized he was moving, he had Slade pinned against the wall, his feet dangling three inches off the floor. The Breed fighter struggled for all he was worth—which wasn't much when Rune was crushing his neck, mere seconds from ending the bastard.

Slade's face turned purple. Spittle foamed at the corners of his mouth as he tried—and failed—to suck in precious air.

"Jesus," Jagger finally muttered. "You're gonna kill him, Rune."

"Aye," he growled. "I'm thinking about it."

But at the last moment, he decided to let Slade go. The Breed male sagged, coughing and choking, sputtering as he wheezed in ragged breaths.

Rune stared at him, murder simmering in his veins. "Go back to the dressing room and pack your shit. Then get the fuck out of here."

Slade swung a dark scowl on him, fangs bared. "W-what?"

"You're done here," Rune said. "If I see you back inside this club for any reason, you're dead."

"Fuck you," he rasped, rubbing his injured throat. "You can't kick me out."

"I just did. You want to go on your feet, or you want me to drag your broken corpse out of here to wait for the morning sun to rise in a couple of hours?"

Slade looked to his fellow fighters for support, but got none. Glaring, he collected himself and stormed out, knocking over a table and chairs as he went.

After he was gone, Rune rounded on his two colleagues. "Anyone else got something stupid they want to say to me right now?"

Vallan raised his brows. "Uh, we still don't have any answers about the club. Why should any of us hang around waiting for the new management to come in and fuck us over?"

Rune ran a hand over his jaw as his decision settled

on him. "No one's going to get fucked over."

"You can't be sure of that," Jagger said, looking less than convinced.

"I am sure. Because I'm going to buy the damn thing myself."

CHAPTER 8

L ucan Thorne carried a small titanium box into the
archives room at the Order's D.C. headquarters.
The container was slightly smaller than his palm, simply
crafted, but inside was a treasure of legendary
proportions.

And unknown, potentially lethal, power.

As he set the box on the work table in the spacious
records room, Gabrielle held him in a troubled stare.
"Are you sure this is a good idea?"

"Far from it." He swung his frown on the other
members of the Order gathered there that day. "No
one's gotten close to this thing since Jordana brought it
to us in Boston last week. I'd feel a hell of a lot better if
we keep it that way until we know for certain what it can
do."

"Maybe Jenna can give us that answer," Darion said
from the other side of Lucan.

Dare, Gideon and Savannah had paused their intel
collection on Riordan as soon as they heard the warrior

Brock had arrived in the predawn hours from Atlanta with his extraordinary mate.

Visits from the couple to D.C. were frequent, due to Jenna's work on the growing collection of Breed archives, yet her appearance at headquarters was always an event. It was hard even for Lucan not to gape in wonder at the genetic miracle that was the former Jenna Tucker-Darrow.

Born human and fully mortal, it wasn't until she'd been attacked by the last living father of the Breed race—an otherworldly Ancient—that her incredible metamorphosis began. Instead of killing her, the alien creature implanted her with a minuscule bit of biotechnology.

That chip, to this day residing under the skin at Jenna's nape, contained the Ancient's memories and his DNA. As it took root inside her body, the genetic material began to transform the woman from basic *Homo sapiens* to something . . . other.

Impervious to injury, illness or age, Jenna was also inhumanly fast and strong. But her transformation had not stopped there.

Soon after the chip had been implanted in her, a small *dermaglyph* had appeared on the back of her neck. Now, twenty years later, her pale skin was covered in intricate *glyphs*. They even tracked up the back of her skull, faintly visible under her shorn brown hair.

Brock stood beside her on the other side of the long table, the black warrior's dark hand stroking his mate's shoulder. "You're not the only one with heavy doubts about this, Lucan." Brock's lips flattened as he shook his head. "I don't want anything to happen to you, babe."

Jenna tilted her head. "Believe me, neither do I. But

the dreams—the memories—have been getting more vivid, more intense, all week." She gestured to the closed titanium box in front of her. "I can't help feeling that this is the reason why. I have to know."

Lucan had to give the former Alaska State Trooper credit. Jenna never shrank from a challenge, and fear didn't seem to have any place in her vocabulary. That didn't mean she wasn't making every person in the room more than a bit nervous on her behalf.

"May I?" she asked Lucan, reaching out for the lid of the box.

At his nod, she lifted the clasp and opened the container. Her slow exhalation joined several others as the Atlantean crystal was revealed. All of the Order and their mates had seen the unusual, egg-sized object at the Boston command center upon Jordana's return. But seeing it again did nothing to dim the reaction again now.

Just looking at it, no one would mistake the crystal for anything found on Earth. It was silvery, yet clear. Smoothly polished, yet it seemed to sparkle with thousands of tiny facets beneath its surface. Where it sat in the center of its titanium box, the crystal seemed to pulse with mysterious life.

"There are really four other crystals like this somewhere?" Gabrielle asked, moving closer along with everyone else.

"According to the Atlantean who took Jordana captive, there are," Lucan said. "Two were stolen from their realm ages ago. Only one remains with their queen now. Another is with the colony of Atlanteans who defected from the realm. And this one."

Jenna glanced at Brock. "I have to do this. If the crystal can tell us anything more about the Atlanteans or the Ancients, I have to know. We all have to know."

He nodded as he caressed her cheek with the back of his big hand. "I don't fucking like it, but I'll be right here beside you."

She turned her mouth toward his palm and pressed a brief kiss there. "I'm ready to do it," she said, glancing to Lucan. "I want to do this."

When he gave her a nod, Jenna reached into the box to pick up the crystal. "It's warm." She lifted it into her hands, holding it as if it were fragile glass. "It's getting even warmer. I can feel some kind of vibration in its core. It feels powerful . . . alive, somehow."

She closed her eyes, concentration pouring over her pretty face. Only seconds passed before the *glyphs* on her hands and arms began to pulse and fill with color.

"I don't like what I'm seeing, Jen." Brock's warning was grave, full of dread for his beloved. "You'd better put it down now, baby."

She gave a faint shake of her head, but didn't speak. Lucan wasn't even sure she could speak in that moment.

Her hands closed tighter around the crystal as she sank deeper into whatever had a hold of her now. Light began to emanate through the gaps between her fingers.

"Jesus Christ," Brock growled. "I've never seen this happen to her before."

Lucan agreed. Everyone gathered there fell into an uneasy silence, but Jenna seemed oblivious to everything but the crystal. Lucan muttered a low curse. "Okay, we're done here."

Brock was already reaching for his mate. "Baby, let it go."

The instant he touched her, energy arced out of her body and sent the massive warrior flying across the room.

Holy. Hell.

Brock came up to his feet with a look of horror on his face. "Jenna!"

He raced back to her, but was stopped a foot away as if a wall of steel stood in his path. Lucan tried to grab for her then, and he too was blocked by an impenetrable field of energy.

Jenna's *dermaglyphs* started to glow. Her eyes remained closed, but behind her lids they moved rapidly, caught in a dreamlike state.

The light inside her swelled. Her hands glowed as if on fire.

With no further warning, the energy erupted outward. Streaks of light shot out in all directions, as bright as the sun.

Every Breed male in the room shielded their eyes from the blast of pure white energy. Lucan and Gideon grabbed their mates close, while Brock roared Jenna's name.

And then, just like that, the light was gone.

Lucan lifted his head to find Jenna calmly placing the crystal back inside its box. Brock flew to her, pulling her into a frantic, protective embrace. "What the fuck?" he rasped thickly. "What just happened?"

She was breathless, her *glyphs* still churning and alive on her skin.

Brock ran his hands over her. "You're not in pain."

It wasn't a question. The Breed male had the unique ability to absorb human suffering into himself with a touch. His talent would tell him if Jenna felt any kind of distress.

He glanced at Lucan and the others, then shook his

head. "She's unharmed."

"I saw it again," she murmured. She drew out of Brock's arms her big hazel eyes wide. "I saw the night of the attack on the Atlantean realm again."

Jenna had seen many glimpses of history through her biotech link to the Ancient's memories. Twenty years ago, she'd first seen the destruction of Atlantis, which had been the first the Order had learned of the violent war between their otherworlder fathers and the second alien race that had inhabited Earth in secret for an even longer period of time.

"They used Selene's crystals against her," Jenna said now. "The night of the attack on her realm, the Ancients used the power of two Atlantean crystals like this one to destroy them. They weakened the realm's defenses, then they unleashed the explosion that washed away everything in its path."

"The Ancients had crystals like this too?" Gideon's mate, Savannah, asked.

Gabrielle turned to Lucan. "Jordana told us that two of the five had been stolen a long time ago. Did the Ancients take them, Jenna?"

"I don't know," she said. "My memories haven't told me that yet, but it seems likely now."

Gideon's blond brows lifted over the rims of his pale shades. "If the Ancients were able to defeat Selene and her legion using two crystals like the one we have now . . ."

Brock picked up the thought, his arms still wrapped around his mate. "And we know there's another one with the colony—"

"Hell, yeah," Darion interjected, his mouth spreading in a broad grin. "And we happen to know someone with ties to that colony now."

Lucan nodded. The pursuit and elimination of Opus Nostrum was paramount, but if what Jenna just reported was accurate, they had gotten a crucial—possibly game-changing—bit of information on an even more insidious adversary.

But first, they needed to determine if they would be alone in their fight against Selene when that day came.

"I have to talk to Jordana," Lucan said. "I want a face-to-face introduction with Cassian Gray's Atlantean friend, and I want it yesterday."

CHAPTER 9

C

Carys scribbled her name on the museum worker's tablet, noting her approval of the exhibit's rotation and the time the pieces were removed under her supervision. It was hours past closing at the Museum of Fine Arts, but she had hardly noticed the time. This exhibit had been the last of her day's duties—a job that normally would have fallen to Jordana, had she not been on temporary leave following her ordeal the week before and her more recent mating.

Carys had trained under her friend for months since Jordana had gotten her the job at the MFA, and although she had never expected to be called upon to fill in, Carys had made it her mission to study every facet of Jordana's position. She never wanted to be a disappointment to her friend, and felt the need to prove her worth.

It didn't hurt to have been born with not only her father's Breed ability, but her mother's unerring photographic memory as well. If she had to, Carys could complete any task or recall any bit of information she'd ever seen or heard.

As the last of the paintings were crated and wheeled away to other secure locations in the building, she took a moment to stroll the now vacant floor.

Something had been prickling her senses since her return to her family's Darkhaven last night. All the talk about Reginald Crowe, and the Order's inability to penetrate the man's secrets and shadowy connections hadn't left her.

It nagged at her now too, as she walked toward the gallery containing many impressive masterworks on loan to the museum from Crowe for the past several years. More than a dozen priceless paintings in this exhibit belonged to him, Carys recalled as she glanced at the collection. Some dated back many hundreds of years. Others were more contemporary, yet still important, valuable works of art.

She exhaled a short breath, shaking her head as she looked at the pieces now, with the knowledge that Reginald Crowe had been no mere human with a taste for fine things and the deep pockets to go along with it. As an Atlantean—an ageless otherworlder—he would have been amassing his wealth and treasure for centuries. If not longer.

He must have thought he was invincible. For a while, he had been. But the Order had thwarted him before he'd had the chance to unleash his worst.

Now, the Order needed to stop the rest of his Opus Nostrum associates.

Carys's curiosity was piqued as she studied Crowe's private collection of art more closely. Something was different here. The inventory codes on the placards of each painting had been modified since she had seen them a couple of months ago. That was . . . odd.

Carys opened her tablet and brought up the museum's donor database. Her security access level to that kind of data was limited, but she'd once been in a meeting with Jordana and the MFA's chief curator as they'd reviewed another private collection. It took only a moment's focus to recall the tap pattern of the curator's access ID and password.

With no one to see her now, Carys entered the credentials and watched as the database opened for her. She scanned in the inventory code from one of Crowe's paintings—a rare little Renoir. The catalogue record was locked, but the date on it had been recently updated.

She tried another code. Another locked record, also updated recently.

The dates on those two records—and on every one of the half-dozen catalogued pieces she now pulled up—had all been modified. The date stamp read two weeks ago.

Immediately after Crowe had been slain by the Order.

Footsteps echoed in the gallery promenade. Carys's head snapped up at the intrusion. Her instincts automatically stirred the shadows around her, but she held her ability at bay. She gave the strolling security guard a pleasant smile as he poked his head into the exhibit gallery.

"Working late tonight, Ms. Chase?"

"Not too much longer." She held her tablet close to her chest. "Just a few more things to wrap up, then I'll be heading out."

The uniformed human nodded, returning her easy smile. "You have a pleasant evening. If you need anything before you head out, just let me know."

"Okay, I sure will. Goodnight, Frank."

After his steps faded down the other end of the museum floor, Carys casually left the Crowe collection and returned to her office. She shut the door and locked it behind her.

Seated at her desk, she went back to the catalogue records on her tablet. There had to be a way to find out why those items had been modified. There had to be a crack somewhere.

It took a couple of hours, but she kept digging, utterly absorbed in her search for answers. She scoured the item entries for every priceless painting, sculpture and artifact on record that belonged to Reginald Crowe.

With no luck at all.

Not until she realized there was another item she recalled was on loan from the billionaire that wasn't among those on active exhibit. There was a piece missing from the count. On a hunch, Carys tapped over to the restoration catalogue and found the very crack she'd been looking for.

One of Crowe's paintings had been flagged for conservation maintenance several weeks ago. It was still out of circulation, and not part of the locked-access catalogue.

Carys brought the painting up on her tablet and immediately noted the same date of modification recorded on the piece. The change to the catalogue record referred to a transfer of ownership. No doubt, she'd find the same notation on all of the other, locked records as well.

The new registered owner of Reginald Crowe's entire collection was a private trust, not his widow or any of his five ex-wives.

What the hell was going on?

Either someone was looking out for Crowe's interests, or had stealthily moved in to claim some of his most valuable assets for their own.

Excitement zinging through her veins, Carys called her father's private number in the command center. He picked up immediately. "Is everything okay? Tell me where you are."

After being home again last night, hearing the concern in his deep voice now didn't annoy her in the least. Just the opposite, in fact. "I'm fine, Daddy. I'm at the museum."

"So late?" Still a note of caution in his tone. "It's going on midnight."

"Is it? I didn't realize how long I'd been here." The time had sped by in the thrill of her pursuit of information. *Shit.* She'd planned to be at La Notte by now to watch Rune's match. If she didn't leave soon, she was going to miss the first few rounds. "I ran across something interesting here tonight. Does the name Hayden Ivers mean anything to you?"

"No. Why, should it? What's this about, Carys?"

"I'm not sure, but that's the name of the manager on a private trust that controls Reginald Crowe's art collection on loan to the MFA. A trust that just assumed ownership the day after Crowe was killed. Do you think this person could be useful to the Order?"

Her father blew out a curse. "I think it's a damn good start. Seeing as how we've turned every other lead inside out and come up empty on Crowe, this could be our best break yet. Excellent work, Carys."

At his praise, she couldn't hold back her smile. "I

hope so. I saw something strange on some of the catalogue references for Crowe's art down here, and I decided to dig a little deeper."

"Excellent work, Carys. I want to hear all about it. Lucan will be pleased to hear this too. Why don't you head home now, and you can be the one to relay the intel to him personally when we call headquarters with the information?"

She bit her lip, hating that she had to disappoint him. "I'm, uh . . . I'm actually just on my way out for a while . . ."

He kept his answering grumble low, as if it took some effort for him not to demand she report to the Darkhaven because he said so. Instead he cleared his throat. "Very well. I'll bring this to Lucan now, and we can talk some more tomorrow, then."

"Okay. Goodnight, Daddy."

He grunted. "I suppose one of these nights I'm going to have to meet this fighter of yours."

"I'd like that," she said. "And his name is Rune."

Another grunt. "What kind of name is that, anyway?"

Carys smiled. "I'll see you when I get home."

She ended the call, then closed up her equipment and office and raced out of the museum to head for La Notte. Rune would already be in the cage, but she'd only miss the first couple of rounds.

Except when she got to the red-brick, former church that housed the underground club, instead of hearing the pulsing throb of music the place was quiet. Instead of seeing excited crowds bursting at the seams of the building and spilling out onto the street, people were leaving. Most didn't look happy about it.

Carys wove her way through the thinning streams of exiting patrons at street level, then headed to the arena below. Only a handful of stragglers remained in the cavernous space, and even those were focused on making their way out.

The cage was empty too. And through the dark of the arena, she spotted Rune crouched in front of a sobbing blond woman seated on one of the couches in the lounge. He glanced Carys's way as she came inside, a brief but intense look to say he knew she was there and that his business with the other woman was just that.

Carys recognized the human female—one of several who worked the BDSM dens. Tonight, Lexi wore a thick robe over her obviously torn leather outfit. Heavy black mascara ran down her cheeks with her tears. A nasty bruise was forming under her left eye, and dried blood caked the corner of her lipstick-smeared mouth.

Carys glanced toward the bar and saw Jagger and Vallan standing there. "What happened?"

Jagger pressed his lips together and shook his head. "Bunch of human punks thought they could come in here and get rough with some of the staff, now that Cass isn't here to enforce his house rules. Rune stopped his match and shut the place down for the night, kicked everyone out."

Carys was surprised, but then it wasn't the first time Rune had stepped in as the de facto law of the place since Cass's slaying. The other Breed fighters seemed to naturally look to him as their leader too, and not only because he was the most feared, most lethal of them all.

Rune commanded respect because in spite of how dangerous he was, he would be the first to defend someone weaker and the last to back down from a fight, even if it wasn't his battle to win. He was a warrior at heart, a good man, even if few took the time to see it in him . . . including himself.

Carys watched him talk to the injured woman, trying not to feel the pang of jealousy that arced through her at the focused attention he was giving another female. Instead, she walked behind the bar and collected some clean cloths from the cabinet to help tend to the battered employee's contusions.

As she wet the cloths at the sink and folded some ice into one of them, she scanned the arena for the other fighter. "Where's Slade?"

The two Breed males exchanged a look. Vallan shrugged. "He and Rune had a disagreement last night. Slade's been encouraged to look for employment elsewhere."

"Rune threw him out too?" At their nods, she frowned. "Why? What did he do?"

Neither one of them seemed eager to answer. Finally, Jagger spoke up. "Maybe you'd better ask Rune about that."

CHAPTER 10

Rune murmured a gruff reassurance to the shaken woman that she would never get hurt in the club again. As he stood up, he sensed Carys drawing near.

His blood was still drumming hot and aggressive through his veins after the scuffle in the arena before she'd arrived. Now that she was there, his veins began to throb for an altogether different reason.

"Here, these should help." She carried a couple of clean cloths and a cold compress, things he hadn't thought to provide. Carys turned a concerned look on the woman and sat down beside her on the couch. "Are you all right, Lexi?"

"I think so. Asshole about knocked me out when he hit me, though."

"Let me see your eye." Carys gingerly inspected the injury. She put the makeshift ice pack against the purple bruise. "Does that feel a little better?"

The woman nodded, and Carys smiled. She took one of the cloths and gently dabbed the blood on the female's split lip, then cleaned the dark streaks of makeup and tears from her cheeks.

Rune watched her work, relieved that she seemed to know exactly what needed to be said and done to comfort someone. His own nurturing skills were somewhere between pitiful and nonexistent. God knew, he'd had little experience with tenderness in his life. He'd survived his youth by being tough. Deadly. He'd made his living that way too. Softness and affection had never had a place in his life—until Carys had stepped into his orbit.

When she finished, Rune cleared his throat. "That's gonna be a hell of a shiner in the morning. Why don't you take the rest of the week off, Lexi, give yourself time to recover. Tell everyone else to go home for the night. I'll see to it that you all get full pay."

As she thanked him and got up to do as he asked, Rune glanced at Jagger and Vallan at the bar. "You both can clear out too. I'll lock up."

In the quiet moments after everyone left the arena, Rune found Carys's gaze on him. Her expression was questioning, concerned. "Sounds like you've had quite a day."

He made a wry sound in the back of his throat. "Had better. What about you? Working late tonight?"

"Yes, we rotated some of the exhibits, so I wanted to make sure everything went smoothly in Jordana's absence. But I actually stayed longer than I'd planned because I was trying to track down some secured information on Reginald Crowe for my father."

"Covert intel-gathering for the Order?" Rune couldn't hide his surprise. He reached out to take the soiled cloths from her hands and pitched them in the nearby trash bin. "I didn't think you were interested in warrior business."

"I'm not. My family's always looked to my brother to pick up the torch for the Order, not me." She gave a no-big-deal shrug, but Rune could see the excitement still glowing in her face. Her bright blue eyes were charged with enthusiasm and pride like he'd never seen in her before. She looked exuberant, a lioness who'd just run her first prey to ground.

Carys might be a rebel at heart, but inside, she was also an intelligent, stubbornly determined woman who could accomplish anything she set her mind to. Why she had let herself fall for him, he would never understand.

"You'd be a hell of an asset to the Order, you know." Stepping closer, he reached out to lift her chin on his fingertips. "And you'd make a hell of an adversary to anyone who crossed you."

She grinned at him. "Then you'd better hope you stay on my good side."

"Baby, from where I'm standing, all I see are good sides," he said, drawing back to take a long, appreciative look at her.

She laughed, then slipped off her heels and ducked around him to walk toward the open cage at the center of the arena. "So, what happened with Slade last night?"

Without waiting for him to answer, she gave him a longer view of her tempting backside as she stepped into the cage in her black dress pants and wine-colored silk blouse. She bent to pick up his spiked gloves and steel torc from the floor where he'd dropped them after halting the night's match.

"Jagger and Vallan said you and Slade had a disagreement."

"Slade's an asshole. I got tired of seeing his face around here, so I told him to get lost or I'd help him get dead."

She swung a look back at him, eyes widened, caramel waves sifting over her shoulders. "That must've been some disagreement."

"It was." Rage still simmering in his veins when he recalled the fighter's words and the offending intimation that he would even think for a second that he could put his hands on Carys.

Rune followed her over to the cage now, disturbed by the sight of her inside the steel mesh ring. She didn't belong in there, and not just because she was dressed for a day at the museum.

Hell, in truth, she didn't belong with him either, but that hadn't stopped him from pursuing her all those weeks ago. Seducing her right into his bed that first night.

"Are you going to tell me what happened, Rune? What did you and he argue about?"

"You."

"Me?" She pivoted, sparks lighting in her eyes as she looked at him through the wire. "What about me?"

"Slade said some things I didn't like." Rune all but growled his reply. "He was under the deluded impression that I might ever let him near you while I was still breathing, so I had to set him straight."

"Oh." Her brows knit as she walked slowly back to him. "You set him straight, did you? And what do you mean by that?"

Rune watched her hips sway with each gliding step. Hips his hands itched to touch them—to grasp onto them and drag her close. "I explained—not in so many words—that you were off-limits. I made sure he knew you were mine."

"Am I?" A smile danced at the corners of her mouth. She was toying with him now, enjoying his possessiveness. "You know you are."

"Mmm, but I always like hearing you say it."

"You're mine, Carys."

As she stood there, holding the accoutrements of his brutal profession in her hands, for an instant he was gripped with a dread he couldn't justify or explain. Nor could he shake it.

Scowling, he blew out a low curse. "Come out of there, now. You shouldn't be handling those things."

When she didn't obey him, he stepped inside and took them from her loose grasp. The urge to smash the gloves and torc against the nearest wall was almost overwhelming.

Carys's hand came up to his face, caressing his rigid jaw. Fire glittered in her irises, and her smile turned a little wicked. "You defended my honor."

Oh, she was enjoying that fact all right. The sparks in her eyes intensified, desire lighting them with a heat that Rune's body responded to like dry tinder.

Looping her arms around the back of his neck, she tilted her head up to brush her mouth against his. "You're my knight in shining armor."

He scoffed. "Hardly that."

"You are. You just don't know it." She held his gaze, studying him. "I would defend you too, Rune. No matter what. To anyone. To the death, if that's what it came down to."

The very thought froze the blood in his veins. "Christ, don't say that. Don't ever fucking say that."

"Why not? It's true."

"Even worse," he growled.

He wanted to feel anger when he stared into her fiery blue gaze, but it was need that spiked through him instead. Need so deep and strong, it rumbled out of him on a ragged breath through his emerging fangs.

He couldn't stop her from caring for him. She could even love him if she didn't have the good sense to give her heart to someone more worthy. But to say she would die for him? Christ. No man would ever be worth so much, least of all him.

She deserved to know that.

She deserved to understand that she was pledging her life to a merciless killer. Not only in the cage, but all aspects of his life. From the time of his hideous beginnings, to the half-truth he lived now. He wasn't worthy of the love she gave him so freely.

Eventually, unless he found the will to walk away from her, Carys would one day learn all of the shame that clung to him even now.

If he had any honor at all, he'd have told her everything already. Before he'd let himself care whether or not she stayed. Before he'd let himself fall in love with her.

The words were right there now—poison at the tip of his tongue.

All he had to do was spit them out.

But then Carys kissed him. Her tongue thrust into his mouth, past his teeth and fangs, greedy and demanding. The erotic sensation of it arrowed straight to his balls. His fangs throbbed in time with the pulse now hammering in his cock, and what little honor he had was swallowed up by the consuming heat of her mouth on his.

He groaned, suspended between torment and ecstasy as she tightened her arms around his neck and her kiss took on a more fevered urgency. Their tongues tangled, fangs clashing as Carys pressed herself against him.

The leather shorts he wore from the halted fight barely held his raging arousal. His sex was hard as stone and starving to get loose. To get inside the temptress who was swiftly stoking him toward madness with her hot little mouth and merciless curves.

He slid one thigh between hers and ground against her, growling at the pleasurable friction of his shaft riding her hip as her tongue thrust in and out of his mouth.

It took all he had to keep a leash on his Breed instincts. It would be so easy to give in to the primal urge to take her plump lower lip between his teeth and bite down, hard enough to draw blood. It would be the act of an instant to break away from her mouth and sink his fangs into the soft flesh of her throat.

So goddamn tempting . . .

She had no idea how often he fought those urges with her.

Nor could she know. Because if she did, his beautiful, headstrong rebel would make certain he gave in to them.

Her mouth still joined with his, she dropped her hands to his bare shoulders and chest. Her fingers skated over his skin, tracing the swirls and flourishes of his *glyphs* as if she knew their patterns by heart.

No doubt, she did. Of her two Breed gifts, it was her photographic memory that was her most powerful where he was concerned. She knew exactly how to touch him, precisely how to bring him to the edge of oblivion.

When she reached down beneath the loose ties of his shorts to grasp his sex, Rune sucked in a tormented moan. His blood raced through his veins, most of it already heading south to meet the demand of his engorged shaft.

Carys palmed the blunt head of him, slicking her fingertips with the wetness that beaded there. Her caress glided along his length, a sure and steady motion that built swiftly toward an unbearable ache. She showed him no mercy, her touch leaving him taut as a bowstring and panting with need.

Rune still held his fighting gloves and steel torc in one hand. With each sure stroke of her fingers over his stiff cock, his fist tightened, driving the titanium spikes deeper into his palm. He barely felt the pain for all the pleasure of her touch.

And he needed to touch her too.

But not here.

The fighting pit was for pain and destruction, not anything he shared with her, no matter how hungry he was to take her beneath him regardless of where they were. But not in the cage.

He would never let that brutal part of his life brush too closely against what he had with Carys.

He pulled away from her kiss on a harsh curse.

Her touch stilled, confusion dimming the bright embers of her transformed eyes. "What's wrong?"

He didn't answer. He didn't have words, only need.

Taking her hand from his chest, he laced their fingers together and led her out of the cage.

CHAPTER 11

He brought her through the vacant corridors of the arena to his private quarters, tossing aside his gloves and torc as soon as he entered his chamber with her. Carys sighed as his hands found her face and held her steady for his kiss.

Breathless, weightless on her feet, she melted into his touch, into his fevered claiming of her mouth. He stopped only long enough to bring her with him into his bedroom, saying nothing, even as he pulled her into his arms with another searing kiss.

He hadn't answered her back in the cage. She knew part of his brooding silence could be blamed on need. She felt it too—the flashfire heat that ignited between them whenever they came together.

But something was troubling him. Had been, even before his abrupt exit with her from the arena. She couldn't pretend she hadn't noticed.

When their kiss finally broke, she rested her forehead against his and stared into his smoldering eyes. "What happened, Rune? Because if I did something, or said something that bothered you—"

He scowled and reached up to caress her cheek. "You're doing everything right. All you have to do is look at me now to see that."

It sounded like a line, something he'd never fed her before. But his eyes were blazing with desire. His fangs were enormous, filling his mouth as he spoke. Need had turned his deep voice to gravel.

Whatever shadows she had thought she'd seen in his eyes out in the arena were gone now, burned away by the twin glowing embers that locked on her now.

"But back there, in the cage . . ."

He drew her close, his large hands framing her face. "This is where I want you right now, Carys. In my arms. In my bed." He bent his head and let his lips brush against her ear. "I want you on my tongue. On my cock."

The words cleaved into her senses, conjuring mental images of the two of them naked and sweating and wild for each other. Whether he had planned to distract her like that, she didn't know, but it was damn hard to hold on to doubts and misgivings when Rune was whispering wicked promises in her ear.

"The club is empty, just you and me now," he murmured, his hands moving down to her shoulders, then around to grasp her backside. "So tonight, I plan to take my time."

As if to prove his point, he dragged her into a slow, bone-melting kiss. Her pulse kicked into a faster beat. Her blood raced, sending rivers of fire through her veins.

He drew back, and her gaze fell to the bulge of his erection where it pushed against his leather shorts. She knew well enough that Rune's cock was as impressive as the rest of him, but the thick outline of his shaft made her mouth water and her fangs erupt further out of her gums.

"Christ, the way you look at me," he rasped. "Those eyes could ash a man in seconds."

She smiled, meeting his own hot gaze. As he unfastened her slacks, she ran her fingers through his thick brown waves, gasping at the rush of cool air against her bare legs. Her skin was hypersensitive, eager for his touch.

Her panties went next. As he slid them off her hips, he ran his hands along her thighs, then slid his fingers into the slick wetness of her sex. She sucked in a sharp breath as he teased her sensitive flesh, then moaned in protest an instant later when he took his wicked touch away.

"So responsive," he uttered, his voice thick with desire. His hooded eyes crackled with carnal intent. "Sit down on the bed and I'll give you some more."

Oh, God. She couldn't obey him fast enough.

With her perched on the edge of the mattress, he came over and took off her blouse. His hands were gentle, but shaking with barely restrained desire as he pushed her bra straps down her arms. A kiss warmed the crest of each shoulder, his mouth tender, breath hot against her skin.

It was slow torture, but she loved it. Couldn't wait for him to ease the impossible ache that was blooming in her core.

With deft fingers, he unfastened the clasp of her bra, freeing her breasts and revealing the *dermaglyphs* that hid beneath the lacy cups.

He growled, his broad mouth curving in a smile as

he looked at her. "So pretty. I don't know what's more perfect, your breasts or these sexy-as-fuck *glyphs* that decorate them."

His praise quickened her blood even more. But then he crouched onto his haunches to kiss her breasts and the tremors of arousal began to vibrate through her.

She wrapped her arms around him, her head dropping back in pleasure as he suckled her nipples. The suction of his mouth and tongue sent streaks of fire into her veins. The fleeting graze of his teeth and fangs put the heat inside her on a boil.

Need raked her, made her writhe and squirm for more.

And as Rune promised, she could tell that he meant to give it to her.

He drew back and placed his palms on her inner thighs. He spread her wide, baring her to his fevered gaze as he lowered his head toward her sex. A low purr rumbled deep in his throat even before his lips touched her.

"I love the scent of you, Carys. Sweet, honeyed nectar and exotic spice twined together." He glanced up at her then, his eyes hot and his sharp fangs gleaming. "And I know you taste even better."

His dark head dipped between her parted legs. His mouth closed over her, his tongue cleaving her folds. When he found the aching knot of nerves nestled between them, she cried out at the sudden, searing pleasure.

He licked and suckled her without mercy. It didn't take long before she shattered against his tongue, wave after rippling wave coursing through her.

Rune kept his eyes on hers as she came, his mouth

still working its wicked magic, sending her spiraling toward another peak. She couldn't bear any more. She needed to feel him filling her. She wanted to feel him coming with her now.

"Rune," she gasped, her hands clutching at him. Her fingers dug into his shoulders, into his hair, and she wasn't sure if she wanted him to stop or give her more.

"I'm addicted to the taste of you." He groaned against her, lapping up all of her juices. "But my cock's addicted to you too."

He rose and yanked the ties of his leather shorts. They fell away, unveiling the heavy spear of his erection. If he thought she was beautiful, that was the only word she could use for him too.

No matter how many times she saw him naked and fully aroused, Carys marveled at the sheer size and power of her formidable lover. Like the man himself, his cock was breathtaking.

His veined shaft and the glistening plum at its crown jutted long and thick from a nest of dark hair. *Glyphs* tangled around the base and curled like admiring fingers around his girth. Those Breed skin markings were dark with pulsating color, as were the others that tracked over the rest of his body.

He pushed her back onto the bed. But instead of following her as her body was dying for him to do, he advanced slowly, delaying long enough to kiss her hip bones and belly, his hands roaming over her, driving her wild. He followed the pattern of her *glyphs* with his lips and tongue, tracing each arc and swirl.

Carys writhed beneath him, that unbearable pool of heat building between her thighs, reaching for its crest again. She arched up as he stroked her slick cleft. No teasing touches now. He played her masterfully, knowing just what she liked, just what she needed.

She hadn't been a virgin when she'd fallen into his bed the first time, but having been with Rune all this time made the handful of her other sexual experiences blow away like dust.

When she thought she couldn't take another second of agony, he stretched out alongside her and took her mouth in a deep kiss while fluttering his fingertip against her clit, making her quiver and snarl with a pleasure that bordered on savage.

"I can't take any more," she panted. "I need you to stop this ache. I need you to fill me, Rune. And I need it now."

He made a low, approving sound in the back of his throat. His fangs were bared and enormous, his eyes searing her with amber heat as he positioned himself between her parted thighs.

Her body was drenched, starving for him. "Now, Rune. Please."

He moved into place and she felt the delicious pressure of his blunt head at her body's opening. Hunger and desire raking her, she grabbed his shoulders and pulled him down for a hard kiss as she shifted her hips to seat him more fully at her core.

He pushed inside, stretching her tight, and—*oh, God, yes*—driving in all the way to the hilt. She cried out in pleasure and relief at the overwhelming invasion. Her fingers clawed his shoulders as he plunged deep, then withdrew with achingly perfect slowness.

"You're so hot and wet," he ground out, pushing their rhythm to a more urgent tempo. "Fucking you feels so damn good."

She could only nod in agreement, her words fleeing her as she spiraled toward another shattering orgasm. She clamped her legs around him and held on as he drove harder, deeper.

When her release slammed into her, his name was a raw cry on her lips. He followed a moment later on a sharp, vicious shout.

It took a long while for them to drift back down from their peak. Carys held Rune close, his body a heavy comfort on hers as the aftershocks of orgasm rippled out of them.

They were as intimate as two people could get, but she couldn't help feeling that tonight, somehow, he'd been distant. He'd been pulling away from her.

If she was being honest with herself, Rune had been holding something of himself back from her for weeks.

Maybe even from the very beginning.

As he rolled off her and drew her against his warmth, Carys tried to tell herself she was imagining things. But the small, gnawing coldness that settled in her heart seemed to warn her otherwise.

CHAPTER 12

It felt strange waking up in her own room, in her own bed, back home at the Darkhaven that next morning. Strange, yet comforting too. Her time with Rune had been incredible as usual, a blissfully exhausting gauntlet of pleasure and release that never failed to leave her sore in all the right places and longing for the next round.

But as she showered and dressed, it was the other persistent ache that clung to her.

Was she anything more than just a good fuck to him? Did she even know him?

She knew he cared for her. More than once in the weeks they'd been together, he'd even told her he loved her. She believed him. Even now, she wanted to believe that what they had together was real.

But there were missing pieces to the puzzle that was Rune.

There were secrets.

Last night, she saw for the first time that there were walls built up around him too. Steep walls she hadn't even realized she needed to climb. Walls he obviously wasn't ready to let her get close to, let alone begin to scale.

Rune came from dubious beginnings; she knew that. He'd told her that he'd grown up on the streets, a denizen of Boston's underworld. He'd scraped by most of his life, making his living on his fists and other dangerous means.

He'd told her all of that the first time she had asked about his past. He hadn't seemed proud of where he'd come from, but he hadn't seem bothered by any of it either.

Now, however, she wondered . . .

Those heavy thoughts followed her as she left her room and walked to the main living area of the Darkhaven mansion. The place was quiet, no one around. Then again, at nine in the morning, her father would be deeply entrenched in Order business with his warrior teams down in the command center.

Carys strolled toward the kitchen, following the aroma of fresh baked goods and brewing coffee. She found Brynne seated at the island counter, enjoying both by herself. She wore jeans and a crisp white button-down shirt, with her long sable hair twisted up into a messy bun on the top of her head.

Carys smiled as her mother's half-sister glanced up. "Good morning."

"Morning." The Breed female's expression turned sheepish as she chewed a big bite of blueberry muffin. "I know, I really ought to go find a blood Host this morning, but honestly. How am I supposed to resist temptations like this?"

Carys laughed. "Just one of the benefits of being

winners of the genetic lottery. Not only can we walk in daylight, but we can eat and drink anything we like."

Brynne lifted her coffee mug in salute. "And not a bit of it ever goes to our hips."

Carys walked over and took a muffin off the serving plate. She popped off the top and began nibbling at the crispy edges. "I suppose everyone is down at the command center already?"

"For about an hour now."

"My mother too?"

Brynne smiled. "She left me with muffins and coffee, so I can hardly complain."

It wasn't unusual for Tavia to be part of patrol reviews and mission strategy meetings. She'd been involved in Order business since her mating to Carys's father, and it was obvious Tavia was at her happiest when she was working at her mate's side. But her impeccable manners would balk at abandoning a guest—family or not—for so long by themselves.

"Today's meeting must be important," Carys mused out loud.

"Must be," Brynne said. "Lucan's called in personally this morning, from what I understand. Something about a new lead on one of the ongoing operations."

Carys nibbled on her muffin, her mind running a hundred miles an hour. It couldn't be *her* lead they were discussing, could it? Had the information she'd found last night proven useful? Had it possibly led the Order to another Opus Nostrum member? The very idea spiked her veins with a jolt of adrenaline, the thrill of the hunt.

"Why don't you go find out for yourself?"

"What?" She blinked at Brynne.

"If you want something, sweetheart, you have to be willing to reach for it."

She gaped. "What are you saying? That I want to be part of the Order?"

"I didn't say that at all. But you just did."

Carys shook her head, but the denial didn't quite make it to her lips. "They haven't asked for my help."

"Just because you don't have an invitation to the party doesn't mean you don't belong."

Brynne picked up her empty plate and coffee cup, then carried them to the sink. As she washed both, her phone chirped on the island countertop. Murmuring her excuses, she dried her hands and took the call into the other room.

No sooner had she gone, than Carys set down her half-eaten breakfast and headed for the command center.

She didn't have to guess where everyone was because a low rumble of voices carried out from the war room at the far end of the corridor. Carys slowed her pace to a stroll as she approached the interior windows and glass-paneled door.

Her father saw her immediately. She waited for his questioning look or even a scowl, but instead, his handsome face eased into surprise. His blue eyes bright under the crown of his trimmed blond hair, he motioned for her to come inside.

She opened the door and stepped into the room.

"Carys," he said. "Is anything wrong?"

"No, nothing's wrong. I just . . ." She felt awkward suddenly, but would have felt even more so if she gave in to the urge to turn around and leave now that everyone was staring at her.

Seated around the long conference table with him were her mother and the Boston team of warriors: Nathan and Rafe, Elijah and Jax. Her brother, Aric, was there too. Mathias and Nova sat together across from her parents. Jordana was there too, seated beside Nathan.

And on the video wall opposite the table was Lucan and Gideon.

Her father stood up. "Come in. We were just talking about you."

On the huge monitor, Lucan's stern mouth curved into a smile. "Excellent work, tracking down that information on Crowe's associate, Carys."

Heads nodded in agreement, both in D.C. and around the conference table in front of her.

Even Aric seemed pleased and impressed. Despite their personal cold war of the past week or so, his green eyes were warm on her. As she stepped farther inside, he pulled out the empty chair beside him.

Carys sat down. It was the first time she'd seen the war room from such an angle—at the table as one of them. Part of the group. It felt surprisingly comfortable.

It felt pretty damn good.

"Gideon's been putting Hayden Ivers under the microscope since you gave us his name last night," her father informed her from his seat at the head of the conference table.

"That's right," Gideon said on the video screen. "Ivers is human. Runs a private law practice in Dublin, but for more than a couple of decades, he's only handled confidential clients. Two, to be exact. Anyone care to guess who the second one is?"

"Riordan?" Carys's father practically spat the name.

"You've got to be fucking kidding me."

Mathias Rowan stroked Nova's hand as a murmur of outrage traveled the table. "Do you think Ivers could be a member of Opus too?"

"If he is, he's covered his tracks well," Lucan said. "Gideon's hacked into his computers and found a whole lot of nothing."

"I scoured Ivers's computers and email accounts," Gideon added. "I can't find anything to implicate him in Opus or anything even remotely suspect."

Carys frowned, finding it hard to hide her disappointment. "What about Crowe's trust?"

"I could only find a handful of references to the trust document—all taking place after Crowe's death. But no trace of the document itself. I couldn't find digital files of any kind pertaining to Crowe or the trust or any other aspect of Ivers's relationship to Crowe."

Nathan glanced at Carys and the others at the table. "Ivers knew to leave no trail, even after Crowe's death."

Chase grunted. "Given Crowe's true identity, he obviously warned all of his business associates to be meticulously cautious with his affairs."

Aric smirked. "Too bad no one warned Crowe to be cautious with his head around helicopter blades."

Jax, Eli and Rafe all chuckled with him at the reference to the Atlantean's demise the night of his attempted attack on the GNC peace summit.

Carys looked up at the D.C. group on screen. "There has to be some record in Ivers's possession. Printed documents, if nothing else."

Across the table from her, Mathias nodded. "My team in London is assembling at nightfall to pay a visit to Ivers's residence in Dublin. If he doesn't prove cooperative, we'll bring him in for a thorough questioning."

Lucan flashed the tips of his fangs. "If the human doesn't want to talk, I'll be there to persuade him personally."

"What if he isn't part of the organization?" Carys blurted. "What if the trail to Crowe's Opus colleagues goes cold again with Ivers?"

"Then we keep looking," her father said.

Lucan nodded. "Right now, we're farther ahead than we were yesterday. We have you to thank for that, Carys."

"I just followed a hunch," she murmured, but the validation felt like warm sunshine on her face.

"Keep following your hunches," Lucan said. "We need them. We need everyone following every lead and working together if we want to flush Opus's members out of the bushes and take them down. That goes double for our bigger adversary."

Lucan's gaze swung to Jordana now. "Have you been able to contact the Atlantean?"

Jordana's white-gold hair flowed over her shoulders as she shook her head. "I wish it were that easy. When my father, Cass, summoned Zael to find me, he apparently was able to reach him through the power of his mark. This mark."

She held up her hand now, and the center of her palm began to glow. A symbol emerged, illuminating in the shape of a teardrop and crescent moon. A Breedmate mark, the symbol that had, in fact, originated with the Atlanteans.

Being one of that immortal race, Jordana carried the same hidden mark in the center of her palms since her twenty-fifth birthday several days ago. She had the same extraordinary powers, which she and the rest of the Order were still attempting to fully understand.

She lowered her hand as the glow dimmed. "I don't know if Zael's received any of my attempts to find him, but I'll keep trying."

"Good," Lucan said. "I need to meet this immortal face-to-face as soon as possible. I'll be ready on a moment's notice to make it happen."

Aric frowned thoughtfully, then leaned away from Carys, toward her friend. "Do that again with your hand, Jordana. I want to try something."

Chase and Tavia exchanged a hesitant look. Even Nathan's face was grave with caution. "Be careful, Aric. We're still trying to assess the full scope of Jordana's new powers."

As her mate spoke, Jordana lifted her palm. The symbol in the middle of it began to appear again, gradually lighting with an otherworldly, internal fire.

Aric moved closer, studying it. "So, this is some kind of Atlantean communication device?"

"I guess so," Jordana said. "Among other things."

He grunted, and put his face near the ember-bright glow. Then he chuckled. "E.T., phone home."

Carys punched the muscled bulk of his shoulder. "You're an idiot."

But she laughed anyway. So did Jordana. God, Carys thought, how long had it been since she'd smiled with her twin brother? How long since she'd laughed with him over stupid jokes only the two of them could appreciate?

If her coming down to the command center today had done nothing else, it had at least thawed some of the ice that had gathered between her and Aric over her relationship with Rune. She'd missed him since their falling out.

Lucan cleared his throat and all eyes returned to the Order's leader. "Speaking of following hunches, I'm interested to hear more about Brynne's suspicions concerning Neville Fielding. If there's reason to believe the London GNC representative warrants a closer look, I want the Order heading things up and I want to move on that as soon as possible. I'll need Brynne to tell me everything she knows or suspects about Fielding, if she's around."

"She's upstairs," Carys volunteered, looking to her parents. "Shall I go get her?"

At their nod, she rose. Jordana did too. "I'll go with you."

Carys and her friend stepped into the corridor and began the walk back up to the Darkhaven mansion.

Jordana blew out a soft breath. "I never would've thought to look into Crowe's portfolio records at the museum, Car. Was his collection listed in the general inventory catalogue?"

"Ah, not the general one, no."

Jordana's eyes widened. "The chief curator's account? How did you . . . Never mind, I'm sure I don't want to know."

"Probably better that way." Carys smirked. "You'll have plausible deniability in case anyone notices the after-hours login on her account. And anyway, I only started with the curator's files. I found Crowe's trust listed in the conservation department files."

Jordana slowly shook her head. "With sleuthing skills like those and your steel-trap mind, what are you doing assisting me with exhibits and patron receptions? You should be putting your talents to use in more important ways. Have you ever thought about—"

Carys slanted her an arch look. "Working for the Order? That seems to be coming up a lot lately."

"Does it sound that awful to you?"

Carys shrugged, wishing it did sound awful. "I'm not in the market for a new job. I enjoy what I do at the MFA with you. Besides, I like having my nights off. I'm sure my family would love nothing more than to make sure I never had time to be with Rune."

"No one wants to see you get hurt, that's all."

"I'm a big girl. I know what I'm doing." Except even as she said it, the small prickle of her growing doubts about Rune came to life again.

Was she heading for broken heart with him? She didn't want to think so. She wanted to think she was as important to him as he was to her. In the time they'd been together, she'd all but convinced herself they had a future together, and that someday his need for her—his love for her—would overrule his determination to avoid any long-term entanglement.

Too often, her heart had entertained a fantasy that someday Rune would climb out of the arena and leave the brutality of the fight club behind him for good. Then they would make a life together—maybe even raise a family of their own—as a mated, blood-bonded couple.

This morning, when she had reached for those slender threads of hope, they'd disintegrated through her fingers like elusive wisps of smoke.

"I heard what happened last night," Jordana said as they rounded a corner in the long corridor.

Confused, Carys looked at her in question.

"Last night, at La Notte. The rowdy patrons and the woman who was injured?"

"Oh. Yeah, things got out of hand and Rune shut everything down for the night and sent everyone home."

Jordana nodded. "I'm glad he did. Rune was right, the club can't go any longer without proper management in charge."

"He told you that?"

"When I spoke to him earlier this morning," Jordana said. "When he called me to make an offer to buy the club."

Carys wasn't sure if her feet had stopped moving in reality, or if it only felt like they had suddenly turned to lead. Her heart sank with equal heaviness. "He . . . He told you he wants to buy La Notte?"

"You didn't know?" Jordana looked at her, aghast. "I just assumed—"

Carys waved her hand dismissively. "Of course, I knew. Yeah, he told me he was thinking about it. I just didn't know . . . I didn't realize he was ready to . . ."

She was rambling, hoping to hell she sounded convincing when her veins had gone cold and her entire being had gone numb with shock and disappointment.

With bitter heartache.

While she had been foolishly dreaming he might trade in his brutal lifestyle for her one day, Rune was busy putting down roots.

And he hadn't even cared enough to tell her.

CHAPTER 13

Rune knew Carys was in the building even before he saw her. Still, he was surprised to find her seated alone at the bar in the arena around noon as he carried a box of cage equipment out of the back room. A shot glass and an open bottle of Jameson sat in front of her. Rune's nostrils flared at the scent of the Irish whiskey and the faint, but lingering salt of her spent tears.

He didn't have to see her face or get any closer to sense that she was fuming. Anger radiated off her long, lean form.

Christ, she was livid. Trembling with fury and something else that stabbed at him even harder. Sadness. Pain.

Without looking at him, she poured a shot of whiskey into the short glass.

His voice rasped in the quiet of the arena. "What's this about, love?"

"I hear there's cause to celebrate." Lifting the shot, she pivoted toward him with a brittle smile.

"Congratulations on buying the club."

"Shit." Of course. He didn't mean it to be a secret between them. God knew there were enough of those without this one. "Jordana told you."

"At least someone did." Carys lifted her shoulder in a move that was anything but blasé. "In her defense, she thought I knew. I suppose that should've been a safe assumption, seeing as how you and I have been fucking nearly every night for the past seven weeks."

When she threw back the liquor in one hard toss, Rune let out a hissed curse. He set the box of fighting gear down near the cage. As she poured another shot, he walked over to her. "What are you doing, Carys?"

"I've been asking myself that same question all day."

"I would've told you about the club."

"When? After you signed the papers?" Her lips pressed flat. Her blue eyes were shooting hot sparks of anger and disappointment. "Since you called Jordana early this morning, you must've known last night you were going to make an offer for the club. You must've already thought it all out and had your plans in place, but you didn't say a word to me."

"It didn't come up," he said. A lame excuse, but it was the truth. "I didn't think it was important."

Those fiery sparks flared sharper now. "You're making this a permanent part of your life, but you didn't think that was important to tell me?"

"It's always been a permanent part of my life. I thought you knew that."

She glanced away, and he realized she didn't know that at all.

"Fighting is the only thing I know, Carys. It's the only thing I've ever been good at."

"Not the only thing," she muttered quietly. Her velvety voice was dry, simmering with the hurt he was causing her now.

He tried to be gentle. "This is the only way I know how to live. I don't expect you to understand that. I wouldn't want you to understand what that really means."

"What if I want to understand? What if I told you I need to understand, Rune?" She looked at him, holding his stare with a searching gaze that pierced him. Stabbed him. "What if I want something more than this for you . . . for us?"

He slowly shook his head, knowing there was nothing he could say that she would want to hear. "I'm never going to be part of the world you want me in. Not in any way that matters, Carys. I can't be."

"Only because you refuse to be," she said, seeing through him as only she could do.

"Ah, love." Regret made his words hard to summon. "I tried to warn you. I told you not to expect anything from me . . ."

She scoffed now. "Oh, don't worry. I remember the rules. No blood between us, not ever. We'll have a good time together until it's no longer a good time, then we'll go our separate ways. No harm, no foul."

Jesus. Had he actually said something so stupid and callous? He knew he had, and Carys, with her flawless memory, hadn't forgotten a syllable of the asinine terms he'd set down for their relationship.

He reached out to smooth a wild tendril of caramel brown hair behind her ear. "This is what I wanted to prevent from happening with you, Carys. Hurting you. Disappointing you."

"Because you care so much." She said it as if the words were ashes on her tongue.

"Yes, because I care." He slid his fingertips under her chin to draw her eyes to his. "I care more than you can possibly know."

She pulled away from his touch. "Why don't you want a blood bond with me?"

The question made his pulse hammer, even while the notion of binding her to him as his mate sent a coldness into his veins. "I don't have room for that in my life."

"No room for me."

"No, not just you." He shook his head. "Hell, especially you."

"Especially me?" A jagged laugh scraped out of her. "At least you're finally being honest about something."

Shit. He was fucking this all up. Saying the wrong things. He was making everything worse.

In a darkened corner of his conscience, he knew this was the moment when he could do the right thing by her at last. Right here, right now, he could let Carys go.

She was angry with him for good enough reason, already wounded by him. One more hard push and she would probably be able to hate him.

But damn it . . . He couldn't do it.

He didn't want to let her go.

A harsh curse rushed out of him as he looked at the misery on her beautiful face. "You weren't supposed to happen to me, Carys. You were going to be trouble for me and I knew it. I told myself that, the very first time I saw you. I should've fucking listened."

He leaned in to kiss her, but she shoved him away on a broken cry.

"Don't touch me." She was off the barstool and

standing more than arm's length from him in less than a blink of time. Her eyes were glittering with fury now. The pretty tips of her fangs peeked out from behind her lip as she glared at him. "Sex isn't going to fix this, Rune. I'm asking you to let me in. I want to know who you truly are."

In truth, she didn't want to know.

No more than he wanted to go there with her.

He couldn't open that up. He'd buried that part of him in the past where it belonged. And where he planned to keep it.

"You know more than anyone else, Carys." He rubbed a hand over the tight tendons that started to ache in his jaw. "Christ, woman. You know more than you should."

"It's not enough. I can't do this with you anymore. It hurts too much."

"Carys . . ." He moved toward her and she dodged him, using her Breed genetics to elude him in a flash of motion.

She started for the corridor across the arena toward the staff entrance at the back of the building. Rune fell in behind her, but she was already at the door.

"Carys, for fuck's sake. Wait a minute—"

She paused only long enough to throw a searing glare over her shoulder. "Congrats on the club, Rune."

She pushed the door open. The battered metal panel swung wide, into the blinding blast of midday sunlight. Hot rays poured inside the corridor, pushing Rune back into the shadows on a hiss.

He brought his arm up to shield his eyes and saw her stride into the broad daylight, where she knew he couldn't follow her. She was unreachable now. Gone.

He told himself he should be relieved.

He kept telling himself that, even as he stormed back into the arena bar and smashed the bottle of whiskey into the nearest wall.

CHAPTER 14

A fter a long day of talks in the command center with
D.C. on conference call and his own team in
Boston, Sterling Chase still had hours of work ahead of
him that evening. But as he strolled back up to the
Darkhaven with Tavia, he could think of nothing more
pressing than taking a long moment to appreciate his
mate's perfect backside as she walked ahead of him in
the corridor leading into the mansion.

He fell back another pace or two, watching her hips
sway with each long-legged stride. Her firm, fine ass
never failed to captivate him. Wrapped in gray tailored
pants as it was now, or gloriously bared for his every
wicked pleasure. Preferably the latter. As soon as
possible, if he had anything to say about it.

"Stare any longer, vampire, and my cheeks are going
to be scorched from the heat your irises are throwing
off."

He chuckled, but didn't take his eyes off her for a
second. "I know another way to pinken those pretty

cheeks."

"Promises, promises."

Tavia's stride turned into a teasing strut that made his veins thrum and his cock ache with hunger. He caught up to her in a flash of motion, spinning her around on her heels and taking her into his arms. She gasped in surprise as she crashed into his chest, but her eyes were dancing with bright sparks of desire as he kissed her.

Their mouths joined in a tangling of tongues, mingling breaths and rushing pulses. When he drew back from her lips a long moment later, every cell in his body was pounding with the need for more. The need for her—his female. His beloved, eternal mate. "You do it to me every time, you know that?"

Tavia's mouth broke into a grin that revealed the pretty tips of her fangs. "Do what?"

"Stop me in my tracks whenever I see you. Make me think about what a lucky son of a bitch I am that an extraordinary woman like you decided to hang your heart on me."

She made a throaty sound that sent a jolt of lust straight to his shaft. "Maybe we should discuss this in further detail later tonight."

He slowly shook his head. "Not sure I can wait that long, darlin'."

"You'll have to. We do have guests, Sterling. You told Mathias and Brynne you wanted to meet with him twenty minutes ago."

"I don't care. They won't care. Mathias will certainly understand that I needed time alone with my mate." He caressed her face, then skimmed his hands onto the sweet ass he'd been drooling over a moment ago. He brought her against him, against the hard ridge of his erection. "I want you now. And I don't care who knows it."

She giggled and nipped his lip. "You're terrible."

"You're delicious."

He took her mouth in another deep kiss, then pulled her under the shelter of his arm as they headed for the privacy of his open study down the nearby hall.

Which turned out to be not-so-private.

Mathias was seated in one of the guest chairs on the other side of the large desk. Brynne sat in the other one. Their eyebrows quirked at the sight of Chase and Tavia, both sporting amber-lit eyes and emerging fangs.

Mathias cleared his throat and started to get up from his chair. "Apologies. I thought we were supposed to meet and discuss the situation in London—"

"Yes, you are." Tavia disengaged herself from Chase's hold, ignoring the possessive growl of protest he made. "I'm sorry we kept you waiting."

"Not at all." Mathias still looked uncomfortable at the inopportune intrusion. "If you'd rather—"

"I would," Chase grumbled.

But since Tavia was already perched on the far edge of his desk, all he could do was drop into his chair and hope it didn't take too long for his raging hard-on to subside. He rallied his thoughts—and wrestled his focus—onto the business at hand.

"Any word from your team on the ground in Dublin tonight, Mathias?"

He shook his head. "Not since the op rolled out a few hours ago. They should be in the city and heading for Ivers's residence as we speak. My captain, Thane, will call in the status as soon as there's news."

"Good." Chase glanced at Tavia's sister. "I appreciate your discretion with this, Brynne. All of the Order appreciates that we have your trust. Not only with the mission under way in Dublin tonight, but the one concerning Neville Fielding as well."

"Nothing I've heard will go any further, I assure you," she said, but there was a hedging quality to her answer. She gave a vague shake of her head. "And I hope the Order can appreciate what both my discretion and trust—not to mention my active cooperation—may cost me, if things go wrong and JUSTIS were to find out I'm privy to any of this."

"No one wants that to happen," Tavia interjected.

Chase agreed. "The Order will tread carefully with Fielding, Brynne."

"I hope so. I'm sure I don't need to tell you that willfully withholding information from my superiors at JUSTIS about possible GNC corruption could have career-wrecking consequences. If JUSTIS were to find out I'd confided in the Order instead of my own organization? I don't even want to think what that could mean. It won't be merely my career on the line."

Chase could hardly argue any of that. "And if it turns out the London GNC director is dirty—if it turns out that he leads us to within striking distance of Opus and the rest of that sick cabal—then you'll have the satisfaction of knowing that you helped bring down a terror group feared around the world. A victory like that could catapult you to the top of the heap at JUSTIS."

She blew out a dismissive breath. "I'm not aiming for a higher office in the organization. I just want to do what's right. And that means ridding the world of cancerous groups like Opus and all who serve them."

"We appreciate that, Brynne. And your concerns are ours as well."

She glanced between Mathias and him. "How soon do you anticipate Lucan will want to begin his reconnaissance on the director?"

"Soon," Chase said. "Days at most. Right now, Fielding has no idea we'll be watching. We want him to stay that way. We want him comfortable until the moment we're ready to strike."

Brynne nodded. "He won't be paying much attention to anything this week. Fielding's daughter got engaged. The director and his wife are hosting a party for her this weekend at their new home."

Tavia arched a brow. "Their expensive new home they shouldn't be able to afford?"

"That's the one," Brynne replied. "They've invited half of London, including many of us in JUSTIS."

Mathias sent a sardonic look at Chase. "Nothing in my mailbox. I feel slighted."

Chase smirked. "You should be getting used to it. The Order is never on the invitation list for these things."

"More's the pity," Mathias drawled, chuckling. His phone chirped with an incoming call. "It's Thane."

Everyone fell silent as Mathias took the call from his operation's team captain. He mostly listened, and from the expression on the London commander's face, the news wasn't good.

"What do you mean, he's dead? Ah, fuck. Jesus Christ." Mathias went silent again, then a violent curse exploded out of him. "No records at all? Damn it. Any idea where the box might be located?"

Chase didn't like what he was hearing either. It

sounded like the simple data recovery mission in Dublin had gone totally off the rails.

"All right, take what you've got and clear out of there," Mathias ordered. "Leave the body. Let the damn place burn."

Mathias ended the call and looked up grimly. "Hayden Ivers is dead. He popped some kind of poison pill just as my guys arrived and set his damn house on fire."

CHAPTER 15

◑

Some unlucky lady was having a loud, ugly cry in the Darkhaven's media room.

Since misery loved company, Carys left the kitchen and wandered that way, wearing an oversized T-shirt, baggy pajama bottoms and fluffy socks—the wardrobe of a woman in the midst of a good sulk.

She shuffled inside the room and found Jordana and Nova seated on the enormous sectional inside. Both women were riveted to the sappy sob-fest taking place on the large movie screen on the opposite wall.

Carys plopped down with them. "Who died?"

"No one," Jordana answered without looking away from the screen. "Those are tears of joy. She just found out she's pregnant with twins after years of trying, and her husband surprised her with a nursery he'd been building for her in secret with his own hands."

Carys rolled her eyes. "In other words, total fantasy."

"Totally romantic," Jordana countered. "I like my happy endings. Since when don't you?"

Carys blew out a short sigh and dug her spoon into the fresh pint of ice cream she'd confiscated from the freezer.

Now Jordana looked at her. "Is that chocolate?"

"Chocolate with fudge," Carys said around a mouthful of it. "Plus more fudge. And caramel."

Her friend made grabby hands for the container. When she took it from Carys, she peered inside and frowned. "It's almost gone."

Carys shrugged. "I'm using it for medicinal purposes."

Jordana offered it to Nova, who declined with an emphatic toss of her blue-and-black hair. "Ordinarily, I'd be all over that. Right now, just the smell of it is enough for me, thanks."

After Jordana took a big spoonful, she passed the pint back to Carys. "You're not out with Rune tonight."

"Nope. I'm not." Carys stared into the container. "We had an argument today. I think I broke up with him."

"What?" Jordana stared at her, confused and aghast. "No wonder you're medicating with double fudge and caramel. What happened?"

"The thing everyone warned me about—that I was being a fool letting myself get tangled up with him. That I was going to get hurt."

Jordana frowned. "This morning everything seemed fined between you two. What did he do, Car? Wait a minute. Does this have something to do with the club? You didn't know he wanted to buy it, did you?"

Carys shook her head. "It's not about the club itself. It's the fact that he won't let me into his life. Not all of it, anyway." She looked around Jordana to include Nova in the conversation. "I've been seeing this guy for a while now. A Breed fighter in one of the cage arenas in the city. Of course, my family doesn't approve."

"Those are dangerous places," Nova remarked. "A lot of dangerous people there."

"Rune's not one of them," Carys said, feeling the need to defend him. A little. "I mean, he's definitely dangerous, but only in the cage. Outside of it, with me, he is . . . amazing. He's tender and kind and exciting. We've been practically inseparable these past several weeks. I've never felt more wanted, more *alive*, than when I'm with him."

Nova listened, a smile at the edges of her mouth. "Doesn't sound like a problem to me so far."

No, it didn't to Carys either. But that *was* part of the problem. "Everything is great between us, except he's holding back. He's been keeping me at arm's length and I never saw that until today. I fell so fast and so deep for him, maybe I didn't want to let myself see it."

"It sounds like he cares about you," Nova pointed out.

Carys nodded, but it was a weak effort. "I want to believe he does, but there's a steep wall between us and I can't reach him. I can't help feeling that if I try to scale it, he might be the one waiting to push me off once I reach the top."

Jordana reached over and squeezed her hand. There was a gentle understanding in her best friend's eyes. "Everyone's afraid of what's waiting at the bottom of the fall, Car. Someone once told me that the safest path isn't necessarily the best one. That sometimes you have to be willing to leap into the unknown. Into the storm."

Carys recalled that conversation she'd had with

Jordana. It had been only a couple of weeks ago, when Jordana was having doubts about risking her heart on Nathan.

"Do you love this male?" Nova asked.

"Yes." The truth jumped easily to her tongue, in spite of her misgivings about where things were heading with Rune. But she couldn't deny what she felt for him. Not to her best friend, nor to the new friend she felt she had in Nova. "I love him with all my heart."

"Then you have no choice but to try to reach him."

Carys nodded, less certain now. She knew Nova's advice was sound, but the sting from her argument with Rune was still fresh. So was the fear. If she gave him any more of her heart and he broke it, would she ever be able to piece it back together again?

She wasn't sure she was ready to take that chance.

"Is this how it was with you and Mathias?" she asked Nova.

The tough-looking Breedmate held Carys in a tender, vulnerable gaze. "Yeah, it was like this for us too. But I was the one surrounded by high walls. Mathias showed me that the only thing strong enough to tear them down was love. I'm grateful every day that he was stubborn enough not to give up."

CHAPTER 16

F or the third time in the past hour, Carys went back to her exhibit design diagram and reversed the placements of a pair of John Singer Sargent paintings. She drew back from the virtual reality monitor to see how the change would look from the exhibit room floor.

Yes, that works better. Or not.

Dammit, maybe their placements had been right the first time. . .

She moved them back with a huffed sigh. Normally, she wasn't so indecisive, but too many things on her mind had made it difficult to focus on her work at the museum.

The late-night news from Mathias Rowan's warrior team about the mission that had ended so badly in Dublin had cast a grim mood over everyone at the Darkhaven. As she'd left for work, the command center had been abuzz with activity and back-and-forth communications with the D.C. headquarters, and more than once during the day Carys had to stifle the urge to call home and find out what was going on.

That was, when she wasn't even more distracted thinking about Rune.

Thinking about the fact that he hadn't tried to call or message her since she'd left him at La Notte yesterday.

It should have been a small relief, that he had apparently decided to let her go. If it truly was over between them, she would rather it be now than down the road—after she let herself fall any deeper in love with him.

She was still hurting from their argument, still trying to tell herself that she'd done the right thing in walking away.

Work helped. She focused on that with renewed resolve, determined to have the exhibit plan finalized and ready for approval before she quit for the day. Half the department was working into the evening with her on the special project. They were getting closer to wrapping it up, but Carys still had a few items on her list that she needed to handle.

She was on the phone checking in with a colleague about one of her key pieces when her department assistant knocked on the door. Carys waved the young woman in.

"Someone's downstairs in the lobby for you."

She covered the phone and murmured, "Great. It's probably the lighting fixtures I ordered for the exhibit. Will you please sign for them, Andrea?"

"It's not the lighting order," the assistant said. "And I don't think there is anything I can sign for . . ."

"Then what is it?"

"Not *what*," Andrea said. "It's a *who*. A very large, hot-looking who. I can't say for certain, but I think he's one of those Breed fighters from down at that club, La Notte."

Rune. He was here? He'd never come to the museum before. He'd always been so careful to keep their worlds separate. Just one more way he'd been holding her at arm's length.

What was he doing here now?

Adrenaline surged into her veins—along with a shot of hope that sent her heartbeat racing.

Carys held her expression neutral as she made her excuses to her colleague on the phone and ended the call. She smiled politely at the department assistant. "Thank you, Andrea. I'll be right down."

After the woman left, Carys grabbed her mirrored compact out of her purse and checked her appearance. *Ugh, not good.* She hadn't touched her makeup or hair since she'd arrived at work that morning. She looked wilted at best, except for the flush of color filling her cheeks from the news of Rune's arrival.

On a resigned sigh, she snapped the compact closed and tossed it back into her purse. He'd seen her looking more disheveled than this before, and she wasn't about to race to the restroom to freshen up for him before finding out what he wanted. No matter how tempting the idea was.

Walking out of the office at an unrushed pace, she headed for the open central staircase that led down to the museum lobby.

The sight of Rune standing down there made her breath catch.

He waited in the center of the lobby, dressed in black jeans and a basic black shirt that clung to his broad, muscled shoulders and massive chest and arms. His wavy, shoulder-length brown hair was brushed off his ruggedly handsome face, exposing the striking cut of his cheekbones and his firm, square jaw.

Power radiated off him, even more when he was wearing casual clothes and standing in the middle of a quiet lobby than when he was in full fighting garb in the center of the cage.

Carys stopped at the top of the stairs. She had been telling herself all night and throughout the day that she was fine without Rune, that the hours since she'd last seen him hadn't been some of the slowest, most empty hours of her life. All of those little lies burned to ashes as she gazed down at him now.

He turned her way and looked up at her on the stairs. His dark eyes seared her with their familiar heat, but his face remained unreadable.

She descended at a measured pace, even though her stomach felt as if a hundred butterflies had been turned loose inside it.

"What are you doing here?" The words blurted out of her, sounding more like an accusation than a greeting. "Shouldn't you be back at La Notte, getting ready to open?"

He shook his head. "Jagger's overseeing things tonight. I told him I had other plans."

Carys stepped off the final stair, but stayed put at the bottom, hesitant around him now. She crossed her arms, mostly to keep herself from giving in to the urge to touch him. "What kind of plans?"

"A proper date." The hint of a smile tugged at his sensual mouth. "At least, I hope that's where I'm heading."

"A proper date?" She exhaled a soft puff of air.

"Because you want to, or because that's what I said to you a few nights ago?"

"Both." He closed the distance between them, making every nerve ending in her body tingle with awareness. With longing. "I'm trying to apologize to you, Carys. I'm trying to make it right between us."

She couldn't summon words. God, she could barely breathe for the sudden chaos of emotions stirring up inside her. She wanted to forgive him. She wanted to throw herself into his arms, never mind that they were standing in the middle of her place of work.

And they weren't without an audience either. From the corner of her eye, she noted the handful of people who had gathered at the promenade railing overlooking the lobby. Andrea and a few other colleagues from their department stood there, watching with avid curiosity.

Carys lowered her voice to a private level. "I'm working, Rune. You should've called first."

He tilted his head in nonchalant acknowledgment, but his dark blue eyes stayed locked on her. "I didn't want to give you an easy way out. I'd hoped it would be harder for you to say no to my face."

It was, and the last thing she wanted to do was refuse him now. But she couldn't make it easy on him. He had hurt her, and one gallant gesture wasn't going to fix things between them any more than a tumble in his bed would. Not that she expected she'd have the strength of will to refuse him that either.

"I can't leave right now," she murmured. "I have to finish what I was doing, and it could take a while—"

"I'll wait."

The determined look on his face didn't leave room for argument. It also stole some of the indignation and stubbornness from her sails.

She shrugged. "Suit yourself, then. I'll finish up, and if you're still here when I'm done, maybe we'll talk about a date."

"I'll be here, Carys." He tenderly stroked her cheek with the back of his hand—in front of the museum staff watching above them. "I'll wait as long as it takes."

Heaven help her, but that simple touch nearly incinerated her on the spot. She had to force herself to step back, to move out of his reach before she did something stupid, like fling herself into his arms.

"Fine," she murmured. "I'll be down . . . in a while."

He gave her a sober nod.

She pivoted away from him and marched back up the long flight of stairs, trying not to feel the weight of his eyes on her as she went.

Impossible, of course.

From the beginning, Rune had been a presence she felt in her blood, in all of her heightened senses. Her body had no qualms reacting to all that primal, masculine heat even if her heart and mind wanted to pretend otherwise.

He was still watching her as she reached the top step and as she breezed past the cluster of people who only now began to disperse.

"Andrea, please call on that lighting delivery for me, will you?"

"Of course." The assistant nodded and hurried off to take care of it.

Carys forced herself to walk leisurely back to her office, despite the urge to run there and put all of her work aside for him. But she truly did have things to do.

And while she couldn't deny her elation that he had

come to take her on a date tonight, damn it, she was going to make him wait for it.

CHAPTER 17

S he kept him waiting almost an hour.

Rune didn't comment, and he had no room to complain, since he'd kept her waiting a lot longer for this date. He had pulled some strings with the owner of one of the most popular restaurants in Boston, one of La Notte's regulars in the arena. The human had raked in a lot of winnings off Rune's blood and sweat in the cage, so he'd been more than willing to help with a favor by giving them the best table the place had to offer.

Apparently, the owner wasn't the only fight fan in the place. A trio of young men walked past the table twice since Rune and Carys had arrived. They poked each other, whispering in obvious recognition.

Rune ignored them. He ignored everything except the beautiful woman seated across from him.

She smiled in awe when the waiter brought her plate of seared scallops and some kind of brightly colored, artfully arranged vegetable accompaniment. Even Rune had to admit the dish looked and smelled delicious. Not that he would be partaking. Unlike Carys, the rest of the Breed could only consume human food in minute quantities.

"Why take me to dinner if you can't enjoy it too?" She took a sip of her chilled wine and all he could do was stare at the delicate working of her throat.

"You'll enjoy it, so that's enjoyment enough for me."

He watched her cut into a scallop, then spear it on the end of her fork. Her lips closed around it and a slow smile spread over her face. "It's amazing."

She moaned in quiet pleasure as she chewed, and his groin went tight under the drape of the white tablecloth. Fuck. Had he really thought he could watch this sensual woman eat a decadent meal without it making him think how hungry he was to put his mouth on her?

"I'm sorry I kept you waiting so long at the museum," she said after a moment. "I'm working on an American painters exhibit and I really needed to get it wrapped up before I left."

Rune smirked. "Here I thought you were punishing me for yesterday."

"Maybe some of that too." She glanced down and picked at some of the fancy vegetables with her fork. "Is this date your idea of an olive branch? Wine and dine me at one of the hardest restaurants to get into in the city?"

"I was hoping it could be a start." He reached across the table to settle his hand over hers. "I'm sorry I didn't tell you about the club."

She shook her head. "That wasn't it, Rune—"

"I'm saying I don't want to lose you, Carys." He swore under his breath. "I'm saying I want to try again. Can we do that?"

When she didn't answer right away, a coldness began

to infiltrate his chest.

"You have to be willing to let me in."

"You are in. You were in before I even knew what hit me."

She smiled, but he could see that she was also wary of him now. Damn it, he could see that she was afraid to get hurt again.

Part of him wished she didn't care so deeply for him. But a stronger part of him couldn't deny how his blood roared through his veins, knowing that this extraordinary woman wanted to be with him when she could have her pick of any man she set her eyes on.

"I'm willing to start again, but I've got questions, Rune." She exhaled a dry laugh. "I'm not even sure that's actually your name."

"It is," he said.

"Your first, or your last?"

A tendon pulsed in his jaw. "My only name."

"But not always." She stared at him, and he knew she saw the tell.

He forced himself to hold her sharp gaze, even when she seemed to look right through him. "No, not always. But it's the only name I've used for a very long time."

She didn't say anything. Her silence measured him, and he knew he owed her more than that.

"I was given a different name at birth, but when I left my father's Darkhaven, I left behind everything he gave me." And he would never utter that man's name again, unless it was to curse the bastard to hell as he took his hideous life. "My name is, and will always be, Rune."

Tenderness softened Carys's gaze as she listened to him. She sat very still, compassion written across her face. "It must've been difficult, being on your own at such a young age."

A young age? He'd been a grown man by the time he had finally cut ties with his past, not a child. He frowned, unsure what to say. Not quite certain where she was going.

"I've heard a bit about your background from the other fighters, from things I've picked up here and there. You know, how you grew up on the streets here in Boston, all alone. Doing whatever you had to in order to survive. It couldn't have been easy for you."

Rune felt himself nodding absently. He'd told a lot of different stories about his past over the years, some of them more or less true. But leave it to him to get tangled up in one of those tales with a woman gifted with photographic memory.

"I never expected life to be easy," he murmured, and that much was the truth.

As he spoke, the group of guys from before circled back and began to approach the table.

The one in the lead awkwardly cleared his throat. Rune ordinarily might have scattered them with a glower, but given the uncomfortable path of his conversation with Carys now, he was actually grateful for the interruption.

When he glanced their way, the three young men gave him eager looks. "Excuse us, uh . . . We just wanted to say, uh, really great match between you and Jagger the other night."

Another nodded enthusiastically. "You were awesome, man."

Rune smiled blandly and murmured his thanks, but they weren't leaving. "We know you're kinda busy here, but, uh . . . could we maybe get a picture with you real quick?"

Carys grinned over the rim of her wine glass as Rune nodded and waited for the men to crowd in with him and snap the photo. He made sure to turn his head at the last moment, a subtle dodge of the camera's eye.

Or not so subtle.

Carys's knowing stare held his gaze as the fans finally moved on. "You don't like the attention, do you?"

He grunted. In fact, he hated the attention. "I didn't get into fighting for the fame. Not for the money either."

"Then why did you?"

A dozen different answers rushed to the tip of his tongue, every one of them a lie. Shit he'd casually tossed out to deflect interest or get rid of anyone who started digging around in his past.

But Carys wasn't just anyone. He hadn't set out to deceive her, no more than he wanted to now.

"First time I ever took a real punch, I was eight years old. My mother had died that spring. I didn't take it well. Not long after, my father started bringing me to the pit. To toughen me up, he'd said. To teach me how to be a man."

Just speaking the words brought the memories back in vivid clarity. The cold stone of the old circular fighting pit. The soft dirt floor beneath his small, bare feet.

The sudden, unexpected crash of an adult Breed male's fist connecting with his child-sized jaw.

He could still smell his own blood, then the sharp, pungent stench of his own vomit as the pain had rocketed through him and turned his stomach inside out. He could hear his father's laughter above him, followed by the stern command for him to get up on his feet and take the next blow like a man, not a whimpering little girl.

"I learned quickly under the old man's training. Pain didn't frighten me. My gift made me impervious to it. In the beginning, that's how I withstood it. After a while, I didn't need to rely on that ability. Injury could slow me down, but it didn't stop me. I became fearless, relentless. Merciless. By the time I was ten, I was handing my adult Breed cousins and uncles their asses in the pit. That's about when my father decided to make things interesting. He started bringing in opponents from outside to fight me in the pit. A few of them came willingly. Stupidly. Others weren't so willing. My father's message to me before each match was plain enough: Fight to the death. He didn't care who came out on top."

Carys had stopped eating now. She'd stopped moving at all, her gaze riveted on him with a look hovering somewhere between horror and heartbreak. "Rune . . . my God."

"I fought to stay alive," he said, pushing on, before her softness made him retreat behind the lies and remoteness that had long been his shield. "I got brutally good. Lethally good. I survived. Then, eventually, I left. And I never looked back."

Her brows knit, pain swimming in her gaze. "Wasn't there anyone who was there for you during all that time?"

"To do what? Save me?"

"Yes. Or, I don't know," she murmured. "To show you some kindness. To give you some kind of hope, or . . ."

He shrugged, about to deny there was. But the unbidden image of an impish face framed in pale blond hair sprang into his mind, refusing to let him erase her with a lie. A face that still haunted his memories more than he cared to admit. "There was a little girl. My father and his second mate adopted her many years after my mother had died. She was . . . sweet. She was the only innocent thing in that place."

"What was her name?"

"Kitty." He shook his head on a low curse. "She didn't know about the pit. And I'd have killed anyone who brought her down there to see that, to see the monster I had become."

"What happened to her?"

"I don't know," he said, and it was hard to keep the regret from his voice. "I left in the middle of the night. I didn't tell her I was going, or that I would never be back."

He didn't want to be forced to explain it to her. Or shatter her innocence by letting her see the monster he'd become. So, he'd simply gone.

"I regret the way I abandoned her like that," he murmured quietly. "She deserved better. She must've hated me for abandoning her the way I did. For a long time afterward, I wondered if I should've gone back for her, or taken her with me. Not that I could've provided a better life for a child. Hell, in those early years, I hardly provided for myself. But maybe I should've tried."

Carys was studying him in silence now. She reached out to lace her slender fingers through his larger ones, then drew his hand to her and pressed her lips gently against his knuckles. A kiss to each one, whether to heal or absolve him, he wasn't sure.

He didn't tell her how those early years in his father's fighting pit had nearly devoured every scrap of his humanity. He didn't tell her how he'd hardened himself

127

to the violence, until it became just another facet of his life. Just another condition of his existence.

He didn't tell her how he struggled, even to this day, to imagine being anything but what his father had conditioned him so ruthlessly to become.

He didn't have to tell Carys any of that. Her tender gaze said she could see it all without the words.

Rune stroked the pad of his thumb over her soft skin. He intended to keep his voice low, private, in the middle of the crowded restaurant. But when he spoke his words came out clipped, almost strangled. "My past is behind me, Carys. I don't talk about it. Not to anyone. Not until you. I can't change what I've done or who I am. There's blood on my hands that won't ever wash clean."

She nodded faintly, blinking hard. "It's okay, Rune. I understand."

No, she didn't. Not fully. And for now, that was how he preferred it. He'd already seen the sympathy in her eyes tonight. He didn't think he could bear to see her pity.

The waiter came by in the heavy silence that followed, asking Carys if her meal was to her liking. She'd only eaten half of it, and since her brief glimpse into Rune's past, she'd barely picked at the dish.

"Dessert, perhaps?" the waiter asked hopefully. "We have an incredible strawberry flambé prepared tableside this evening."

Carys shook her head. "No, thank you. Everything was delicious, but I'm finished."

"The check, please," Rune said. After the human scurried off, he tightened his grasp on Carys's fingers and leaned forward. "I have something sweeter and hotter in mind for my dessert. What do you say we get out of here?"

She smiled, tenderness and compassion backlit by a flicker of desire. "Yeah. Take me out of here, Rune."

CHAPTER 18

They hailed a taxi and Rune gave the driver the penthouse address. Carys hadn't told him that's where she wanted to go, but he seemed to understand as well as she did that the club and the weight of what it represented to Rune would not be allowed to invade any more of their time tonight.

She was still trying to process everything he'd told her. His past, his childhood, the trauma he'd been subjected to by the father who was supposed to love him. Her heart broke for the boy who'd endured that kind of hellish upbringing, and for the strong, complicated man who still carried the wounds, even if he did so stoically, unbroken from everything that had been done to him.

His remoteness made sense to her now. His walls were steep for good reason, yet he'd allowed her to peer through a tiny crack tonight. She saw darkness and pain on the other side of Rune's walls, and a solitude that would have wrecked anyone weaker than him.

I survived, he'd said. And, yes, that much was true. But would he ever be able to leave his past behind when he couldn't let go of the cage that still confined him?

Carys knew the answer to that, and as she walked out of the elevator on the top floor of the apartment building with him, she hoped that, in time, Rune would see it too. Either way, she intended to be at his side. But tonight, there would be no more talk of his past or the club.

Tonight, she needed to feel his arms around her as much as she needed to wrap her arms around him. Tonight, she just needed . . . him.

There were no words as they walked into the penthouse, fingers threaded together. No words as she led him to her bedroom at the end of the hallway. Nothing but quiet breaths and slow-burning gazes as they undressed each other in silence and slipped between the cool sheets of her bed.

They kissed for a long while, lying on their sides, facing each other. Caressing each other. A delicious, unrushed exploration of each other's lips and skin and contours that was somehow even sexier—more erotically intense—than any of the frenzied, ferocious, need-you-now matings they'd experienced before.

Rune's loving touch heated her as he traced her shoulder and arm, then circled her taut nipples and the swell of her breasts. Each slow skate of his fingertips over her sensitized skin melted her, made her insides twist with delicious need.

His mouth roamed over hers, claiming her without demand, coaxing her into a tighter coil of yearning. His tongue tangled with hers, testing, not taking, his sweeping strokes putting her blood on a heated boil in her veins.

God, she wanted him. Needed him like never before . . .

She broke their kiss and leaned forward, pressing her lips to the hollow at the base of his strong throat. He groaned as she slid her tongue over his skin, then along the column of his neck.

Her fangs filled her mouth, but she kept them in check as she dragged her parted lips over his drumming carotid. The hard beat called to everything Breed in her.

It made her blood answer with equal demand: *You are mine, as I am yours.* She felt the declaration in her bones, in her marrow. Her veins clamored for confirmation of their bond. For consummation of it.

But she knew his rules, and tonight she would not test him.

On a shudder, Rune exhaled a jagged sigh as she moved away from his neck and on to the muscled bulk of his shoulder. She kissed the rounded curve of hard flesh, then moved lower, across the broad, *glyph*-covered slabs of his chest. He moaned as she teased the flat disc of his nipple, sucking the tiny bud between her teeth and flicking it with the tip of her tongue. His arms came up around her as she guided him onto his back to lavish the same attention on the other nipple.

His cock was hard, and had been since the moment they entered the bedroom. The steely length of it pressed against her hip where she was draped over him now. She reached down to stroke him as she descended farther, kissing and licking and suckling her way toward his lean stomach.

She loved the feel of his skin beneath her fingertips, and beneath her questing mouth. The dark flourishes of his *dermaglyphs* felt alive under her tongue as she traced their beautiful patterns.

She nipped his hip bone and Rune's thick cock surged even harder, even fuller, in her grasp. "Ah, Christ, Carys . . . you're killing me."

She knew what he wanted. Her mouth was watering for it too. Drifting down into the thatch of dark hair at his groin, she licked the *glyph*-ringed base of his erection. He was so large and enticing, steely power encased in velvet softness. She explored the length of him with her tongue, teasing the engorged vein that ran under his shaft, lapping the bead of fluid that wept from the tip of its plum-shaped crown.

With a strangled groan, he arched off the mattress, hips thrusting in plea for more.

She was only too eager to oblige.

Wrapping her lips around the silky smooth head of his cock, she slid him all the way into her mouth. She could barely contain him, he was so immense, so thick and rigid, crowding her throat. But the taste of him, the powerful feel of him, only made her hungry to take more. To take all of him.

"Ah, fuck," he ground out tightly as she withdrew nearly all the way, then plunged back down. His arms clutched her tighter as a shudder rolled through his massive body. "Oh, yeah, baby. Fuck, yeah."

She kept her rhythm slow, but steady. Sucking him deep. Savoring his taste, his heat, his power.

His palms held her head now, his hips rocking with every long slide of her mouth. On her tongue, his shaft pulsed and twitched. Salty juices flowed out of him, slickening her rhythm as she caressed his balls and sucked him deeper.

And with each thrust and groan that shuddered

through him, Carys's body burned hotter, wetter. Her sex clenched with the need to have him inside her, but she couldn't pull her mouth away from him. Her thirst for him consumed her now.

"Carys," he gritted out harshly, his cock stiffening even more.

Tension wracked him. His fingers closed into fists in her hair. She picked up her tempo when she felt him coil tighter with each stroke. He was close, so close. She wanted to push him over the edge. She wanted to leave him room for nothing but pleasure, nothing but the two of them.

He raised his head to look at her, his dark eyes ablaze with amber fire. His fangs gleamed bright white, sharp as daggers. She'd never seen anything so magnificent. And he was hers.

"You're mine, Rune," she murmured against his throbbing flesh. "Tell me you know that. I need to hear you say it now."

The strangled groan that wrenched out of him was somewhere between pleasure and pain. "Fuck yes," he rasped. "Only yours."

She took him deep, brought him to the point of no return. A low growl exploded out of him. He bucked hard against the back of her throat, then the sudden, hot and glorious rush of his seed filled her mouth.

CHAPTER 19

H oly hell, this woman owned him.
Rune couldn't hold back his raw shout of pleasure as his release tore out of him. Wave after wave, tremor after tremor. An inferno he couldn't have held back if he'd tried. Nor would she have allowed him to. No, Carys was in complete control of his body in that moment and damn if she didn't know it, revel in it.

The sheer force of his climax was staggering, but it was the hot suction of Carys's mouth that undid him even more. He hadn't lost a bit of his hardness, even as the last aftershocks of his release shuddered out of him. Carys milked him with her lips and tongue, sucking him deep, then slowly drawing back, showing him no mercy at all. He held her head in his palms, his fingers sifting through her silken hair as she licked him clean of every last drop.

"Christ," he hissed through clenched teeth and throbbing fangs. Heavy-lidded, firelit amber eyes lifted to meet his gaze, and the sly smile she gave him sent an arrow of lust straight to his balls. "Keep that up any longer and I'm going to come again."

She moaned in approval and took him all the way to the back of her throat. The pleasure was staggering, nearly impossible to resist. But he was hungry too.

On a growl, he seized her shoulders and rolled her onto her back. "My turn now."

They'd experienced each other virtually every way possible in the weeks they'd been together, but tonight it was different. Still raw and carnal and consuming, but Rune had never felt more intimate with Carys than he did right now. Never more naked. He loved this woman, and it didn't take an exchange of blood to cement his feelings for her.

But he couldn't lie to himself by pretending the need to claim her in that irrevocable, eternal way—to bind her to him by blood—wasn't pounding in his veins like a war drum.

No.

He pushed the temptation away with a snarl as he rose over her and drank in the sight of her beauty. His hands actually trembled as he skated his fingers along her cheeks, across the plump softness of her lower lip.

The pulse points in her neck throbbed as he followed the delicate lines of her veins. That hard pound beneath his fingertips was torment, almost more than he could resist. His own heartbeat jackhammered in his temples. In his chest. In his painfully erect cock.

His transformed eyes felt like fiery coals in his skull, his thinned pupils fixated on the delectable prize that lay spread out before him, his for the taking.

He crushed her mouth to his in a fevered kiss, thrusting his tongue past her parted lips that still tasted of him. He wanted to devour her, starting with that wicked mouth that had given him no quarter. Caging her head between his bent forearms, he delved deeper with his tongue, thrust harder, with a greed for her he could barely contain.

She was gasping as he drew away from her, fangs bared and gleaming behind the swollen cushion of her lips. He licked the sharp points, groaning at the erotic graze of their tips against his tongue.

"You're amazing," he uttered thickly, his voice taking on the otherworldly timbre that was pure Breed. "I can never get enough of you."

He palmed the rounded swell of her breasts, a low, possessive rumble building in his chest as she arched into his touch, writhing and moaning in eager response. He bent his head and took her nipple between his lips, sucking it hard, tweaking it with a sharp nip of his teeth.

He released the tight bud with a kiss, then lifted his hungered gaze up to hers. "You're mine, Carys."

"Yes." She reached to caress his face, breath racing out of her in shallow pants. "Only yours."

The same words she'd wrung from him in pleasure a few moments ago. He wanted to hear her scream those words before he was finished with her now.

He shifted his position and cupped the warm mound of her sex. Silky wetness met his fingertips on contact, and he slid inside her folds on a ragged breath. He stroked her cleft, reveling in the impossible slickness, the beckoning heat.

The walls of her sheath seared the two fingers he pushed into her. Tiny muscles rippled under his shallow thrusts, making his cock jerk in envy. He penetrated deeper, feeling her plush walls grasp for him with each slide of his fingers.

Her clit was a hard pearl that quivered as he ran the pad of his thumb over it, coating it with her juices. He flicked and teased and massaged it while his fingers continued to slide in and out of her.

He glanced up to find her watching him. Her amber eyes were scorching, so hot and wild with need. Her *dermaglyphs* danced with rich colors across her breasts and the slender planes of her abdomen. Passion swamped her face.

"Harder," she rasped, demand in her husky voice. "Go deeper."

He chuckled low under his breath. "Oh, not so fast, love. We're only getting started."

Her head dropped back on a thready groan, stretching that pretty column of porcelain skin and the delicate blue veins that beat frantically beneath its surface. Rune had to look away and he did so on a vicious curse.

Pumping his fingers into her, coaxing the bundle of nerves into an even tighter knot of pleasure for her, he bent his head to kiss and suckle her breasts. He was ravenous for her, but he wanted her mindless with need before he gave in to his own cravings.

Some primal, selfish part of him wanted to know that he was branded on her senses, stamped deep in her marrow. That she could never belong to another.

He drifted down the length of her body, kissing and nipping, tonguing every taut curve and valley. He shifted so that his face loomed over her sex, which glistened under his gaze, flushed dark pink and ripe for the eating. The sweet, musky scent of her was a drug to his sanity, but he was already addicted to this woman.

His woman.

"Show me," he growled, sounding more savage than man. His fangs ached as painfully as his cock, twin hungers that demanded to be sated. "Let me hear you, baby."

She answered with a throaty moan that nearly undid him on the spot. Her creamy juices drenched his fingers, making slick, wet sounds as he picked up his tempo. Her clit felt like a hot pebble as he rolled and stroked it with his thumb. She bucked under his touch now, her legs falling wide apart, moving restlessly as he commanded the last shreds of her control.

A cry built in the back of her throat, raw and untamed. It drove him on, turned him savage with the need to feel her shatter. She moaned his name, a shudder traveling the lithe arc of her body.

"Oh, God. It's too good." Arms flung up over her head on the mattress, her fingers twisted in the coverlet as she writhed and quivered under the relentless rhythm of his hand. "Rune, I'm going to come. Please . . . let me come now."

He growled his approval and took his thumb from her clit only long enough to cover her with his open mouth. He took the bud deep, his tongue doing the work now, his lips buried in her sweet nectar, his fingers fucking her fast and deep. He stroked and sucked and savored, holding her against his face as her orgasm built to a frenzy. She came on a roar that nearly undid him. Vibrations wracked her strong, lean body, one after another.

He needed to taste more of her. He wanted to feast on her. Cleaving his tongue through the plush folds of her sex, he speared deep into the molten honey of her core. He lapped her up, just as she had done to him, greedy for every creamy, sweet drop.

His cock couldn't take the denial of her heat a second longer. Rune snarled as he pulled away from her, incapable of speech now. Lust raked him, and there was no gentleness in his hands as he cupped her ass and angled her high for the first hard thrust of his hips. He drove inside on a coarse grunt, then fell into a furious, rolling tempo. Crashing into her. Slamming deep. Rocking in and out like a piston.

Carys started to come again. Her moans built toward ragged cries. The soft, grasping walls of her sheath rippled around him as he lost himself to the intense, unstoppable pressure of his own mounting release.

He'd never felt anything as addicting as the way their bodies fit together. So primal, so goddamn perfect. He tucked her beneath him and folded his body atop hers, watching her face, holding her fiery gaze, as her orgasm swamped her. Her fingernails sank into his shoulders with her pleasured scream.

Fuck, yeah, baby. He was right behind her, release rolling up on him fast. He wouldn't be able to hold it back more than another second.

His muscles went rigid. His blood turned electric in his veins, roaring in his temples, throbbing in his shaft with every driving thrust of his body into hers.

His pace turned furious now, beyond his control. His fangs ached to penetrate too. Breed instincts fired up like sparks as his climax coiled into a tighter knot, ready to blow. His pupils homed in on the frantic tic of Carys's carotid.

Christ, he could hear that rapid beat drumming in his ears. Echoing in his veins. Calling to his blood and everything Breed in him.

He wanted to claim her completely.

He wanted her bound to him forever, whether he deserved that gift or not.

In that dangerous moment, his control slipping, he'd never wanted anything more in his life.

Instead, he clamped down with everything he had. He shut his eyes and threw his head back on a raw bellow, then sank in all the way to the hilt as her tiny muscles milked him into a blinding haze of pleasure and the oblivion of a staggering release.

CHAPTER 20

They made love again, and eventually worked their way into the shower in the large en suite bathroom. After washing each other under the steamy overhead spray, they lingered there, kissing and caressing, neither one eager to let go of the moment, or each other.

Sex between them was always incredible, but there was a raw honesty to it tonight—an unspoken vulnerability—that had intensified everything. Carys's entire being still thrummed with an electric awareness of him, with a craving that would never be fully sated.

As his large palms skated over her back and shoulders, massaging her in slow circles, she ran her wet hands over the muscled slabs of his strong chest and the elegant tangle of his *glyphs*. From the first time they'd lain together, every inch of him had been emblazoned into her memory, into all of her heightened senses. Tonight, she explored him with new eyes. With a deeper understanding of the solitary, unreadable man she loved.

She dipped her head to press a kiss to his sternum,

directly over his heart. The powerful drum of his pulse vibrated against her lightly parted lips and the tip of her tongue.

He groaned deep in his chest, a contented, pleasured sound.

She smiled in response, delighting in the fact that she had something to do with his current satisfied state.

Of course, she'd enjoyed all of the ravenous, wickedly carnal states that had preceded it too. She'd enjoyed everything about the past several hours, and could only bask in the peace she felt as Rune held her in the wet quiet of the shower.

"Thank you for tonight," she murmured, glancing up to meet his heavy-lidded gaze. "For coming to the museum and taking me out on our date. For letting me in. For all of this."

"You don't have to thank me—"

"I do," she said. "Because I know it probably wasn't easy for you to go there—back to your past. You want to leave it behind. I understand that. I just want you to know what it means to me that you trusted me enough to let me see what you've been through. Where you've come from."

"Carys." He slowly shook his head, looking uncomfortable with her praise. His hand came up to cup her cheek, his thumb smoothing over her lips. "You deserve more than I can ever give you."

"You're all I want, Rune. Like this, tonight. This is all I'd ever need."

His sensual mouth quirked wryly. "Then the pressure is on now to deliver no less than four orgasms a night."

She laughed. "Careful, I might hold you to that."

"With pleasure, love." He tilted her chin up and took her mouth in an unhurried kiss.

His lips were tender and affectionate, and it was all she needed for the banked embers of her desire to kindle with renewed heat. Arousal stirred to life, and she clung to him, her body beginning a slow melt with every brush of his mouth on hers, every light stroke of his tongue.

She would always crave this man. She knew that in her bones, in her blood.

She'd meant it when she'd said she was his. Only his.

When their kiss broke, Carys reached up to hold his handsome face in her hands. "God, I love you, Rune. So much it hurts."

His head swiveled slowly, but there was raw emotion in his stark, midnight blue gaze. "And I love you. More than you can know. More than I should."

He drew her into his embrace and kissed her again, deeply this time. With a need that drenched her senses and left no doubt that he'd meant every word.

Yet a small, insidious whisper seeped through the bliss, reminding her of the hunger she'd seen on Rune's face earlier tonight when he'd been caught in the throes of release and his fevered amber eyes had been locked on her throat.

This was a truth he hadn't shared with her yet. His rejection of her blood. His torment and denial that he wanted that kind of bond with her. With anyone.

It seemed to have taken all of his will to resist, but he had. And for the first time, she'd glimpsed fear in Rune's eyes.

Fear that he would regret binding himself to her? Or fear that she would one day?

As desperate as she was to have that answer, she

couldn't work up the courage to spoil what they had right now.

She was afraid to know the answer. She, who had never backed down from a challenge in her life. Who had never allowed any obstacle to stand in the way of something she wanted.

But this was too important. Too consequential. Because she knew that if his answer wasn't what she wanted to hear, she might never recover.

So she kept her doubts to herself, too entranced by the feel of Rune's hands moving over her soap-slickened body, his kisses making her delirious with desire.

He guided her farther under the spray, his palm skating down the underside of her thigh, toward her knee. He lifted her leg up, settling her foot on the marble bench built into the wall of the large shower.

"Put your arms around my neck, love. Hold on to me."

She obliged, draping herself against him as he continued his sensual assault on her mouth. She gasped against his tongue an instant later, when his fingers delved into the sensitive cleft of her sex.

"Just for you now," he murmured against her lips as her hips began a faint rotation with his caress. "That's it. All for you, baby."

She moaned as her pleasure raced up on her and sent her reeling. Rune's mouth took her possessively, kissing her so deeply and passionately she could have come from that alone. Combined with his touch, the ecstasy was electric, overwhelming. He stroked her relentlessly, masterfully, until the need for release was so intense, she couldn't hold back for another second.

She came on a cry, shattering in his arms. Rune held

her with one arm, while his other hand slowly brought her back down to earth with gentling strokes of her blissfully spent flesh.

Then he soaped her all over again, taking his time, even washing her hair. She felt revered, worshipped. Safe, protected. And so deeply loved by this dangerous, powerfully lethal male.

Rune cut off the water and they stepped out of the shower together, kissing some more. He wrapped her in a fluffy towel and helped her dry off, smoothing her wet hair off her face, his amber-flecked gaze lit with tenderness and desire.

He groaned as though weighing a difficult decision. "I want to take you back to bed, but I should get you home. Your family will be concerned."

"They would've been," she said. "But I called before I left the museum tonight and told them I was going out on a date and they shouldn't wait up."

Rune drew back, a sardonic look on his face. "They know you're with me?"

"Of course."

He smirked and playfully smacked her bare backside. "In that case, we'd better get dressed before Nathan or your brother comes beating on the penthouse door to rescue you."

Carys laughed and shook her head. "Things are different at home now. Better since I went back. My father even told me I should bring you around sometime to meet him."

Rune nearly choked. "He said that?"

"Not his exact words, but the point is, he's open to it." Leaning against him, she arched a brow. "I'm not sure which of you is more opposed to the thought of being in the same room together. Does meeting my family sound so awful to you?"

"A male like me, walking into the Order's command center to meet your parents? Not exactly my idea of a good time." He exhaled a short breath. "Wouldn't be your father or brother's idea of a good time, either."

"Why don't you let them be the judge of that?" When he started to dismiss the idea with a chuckle and a shake of his head, she reached up to touch the side of his stubble-shadowed cheek. No teasing or laughter now, but utterly serious. "What if I asked you to? Would you do it for me?"

He didn't speak for a long moment. His dark eyes studied her. Contemplative, conflicted. "That's what you want?"

"You're what I want, Rune. And I need my family to understand that. I want them to see what I see in you."

That silence fell over him again, and the pensive look in his gaze went distant, almost unreachable. She resisted the urge to bring him back to her, but only barely. She was so prepared to hear his refusal, that when he finally spoke, it took her a moment to register the word.

"When?"

"You mean it?"

"Tell me when," he said again, his voice gruff. "Before I come to my senses."

Her heart leapt in her breast. "Let's go now."

He barked out a laugh. "In the middle of the night, with your mouth still bruised from my kiss—not to mention other things—and my cock still hungry for more of you?" He shook his head and brought her naked body against his. "I may be undefeated in the cage, love, but I'm not suicidal. Every male in that compound would want a piece of my ass. Hmm, speaking of . . ."

His hands slid down to cup her backside. Heat licked through her veins as he kneaded the muscled rounds and dragged her into a bone-melting kiss.

Carys put her hands on his shoulders and levered herself away from what would be an easy conquest. "Tomorrow night, then. You can come by before you have to open the club. Then we can go to La Notte together, after you meet everyone."

"Tomorrow night." He groaned as if regretting the decision already. "I'll do it. For you. But you're never going to convince me that this is a good idea."

She grinned. "Oh, I think I probably can."

Grasping his strong nape, she pulled him down for a searing kiss. His big body tensed against her, vibrating with the force of their shared desire. He was hard and ready. She was molten and aching to be filled.

"We're gonna need another shower before I'm finished with you tonight," he murmured thickly over her parted lips.

Carys smiled as the head of his cock slid between her slick folds. "Oh, yeah. Maybe a couple more."

CHAPTER 21

There should have been a track worn into the rug in Lucan's study at the D.C. headquarters, given how many miles the Order's leader had clocked in his pacing of the room since the news two nights ago from Mathias Rowan. The report of Ivers's death had been a headache the Order didn't need. But it had also opened up a whole new set of questions they hadn't known to ask.

What had Hayden Ivers been hiding?

Had he known the Order was on to him? Had he been tipped off before Mathias's team descended on his residence the other night? Or had the surprise of their arrival been the trigger that had made him pop his lethal pill?

Had it been slavish loyalty that made him choose death over discovery and capture? Or was it fear that had motivated him to take his own life before the Order had the chance to question him?

A hundred questions and so far, no answers.

Lucan cursed, his thoughts churning as he began

another circuit around his desk. "Not a single goddamn file or document in the place," he grumbled. "Nothing but sanitized hard drives and empty cabinets. What secrets had the bastard been hiding for Crowe and Riordan?"

"Hopefully we'll have that answer once we figure out what that safe deposit key unlocks," Gideon said, leaning against the millwork wall on the west side of the room.

Also standing in wait with them were Brock and Darion. Gabrielle, Savannah and Jenna occupied the chairs and sofa in the study's sitting area near the floor-to-ceiling bookcases.

Lucan grunted and glanced to Gideon's Breedmate, Savannah. "You think your ability can help us determine where the box is located?"

Her dark brown eyes glittered with confidence. "I'll know the key's history when I touch it. I'll see whoever handled it, and where they were when they used it." She nodded. "Yeah, I can figure out where the key will take us."

"Good. I'll tell Mathias to have one of his team hand-carry the bloody thing over from London ASAP." Lucan rubbed a hand over his tense jaw. "What I'd prefer to do instead is strangle the answers out of Riordan with my bare hands. How soon before you're comfortable that we can move in on that son of a bitch, Gideon?"

"Not long. I'm trying a new approach with his network protocols. I should know if I'm in or not in a matter of hours. Maybe a day."

"Too fucking long." Lucan felt the heat of his anger flash in his eyes. "Now that Ivers is dead, we've lost part of our window of surprise. Riordan's either going to get nervous or he's going to get bold. Either way, we need to be ready. We need to hit the bastard before he decides his next move. We know he's Opus, damn it. We have him directly linked to the assassinations in Italy last week."

"Only on the word of a dead man," Brock cautioned.

Gideon nodded. "We'll need more proof than that if we go in and take Riordan out on our own."

Lucan's fangs punched out of his gums. "If we need to answer any GNC or JUSTIS inquiries, I'll present his rotting corpse as evidence."

Gabrielle gently cleared her throat from across the room. "The GNC is already looking for reasons to remove you from the council, Lucan. The Order needs you there. The GNC needs you there as well, but they're too blind to see that right now."

He grumbled, but his mate had a valid point. As much as he despised the bureaucracy of the human/Breed governing bodies and their frequently inept—or corrupt—law enforcement arm, it was crucial to preserve some amount of trust and cooperation between them and the Order. Especially while the Order was covertly dealing with other threats unknown to any but the warrior members seated in the room now as well as in the various command centers around the world.

"Get us what we need to make our move on Riordan," Lucan said. "I don't know if my patience has another day left."

As he finished speaking, a chime sounded in the foyer of the expansive mansion.

Gabrielle's brows rose. "Was that the doorbell?"

It was. At barely six in the morning. At the Order's heavily secured world headquarters.

Lucan tapped a monitor on his desk and a visual of the front door filled the screen. "What the fuck?"

A tall, muscular man stood outside, wearing a loose, white linen shirt and faded jeans. Shoulder-length, golden-blond hair shot with copper crowned the face that filled the camera's eye. Despite his angular cheekbones and squared jaw, his features were fine. Elegant. Not quite human. But since he was standing outside in the full light of morning, the odds of him being Breed—even a daywalker—were slim to none.

Lucan shot a glower in Gideon's direction. "How the hell did someone get past the gates?"

"Without getting roasted by close to a hundred thousand volts of electricity, even if he tried to jump all eight feet of the perimeter fence?" Gideon shook his head. "Impossible."

"Then how do you explain him?"

Outside the door, the stranger held his hands behind his back, waiting patiently. Politely, for crissake.

Lucan didn't possess quite the same set of manners, especially when things were going from bad to worse in his domain at the moment. He jabbed the speaker button on the security system. "You wanna tell me who the bleeding fuck you are, and what you're doing here?"

The man's expression barely changed. "I've been summoned. My name is Zael."

~ ~ ~

Carys's mood was so light, she could hardly feel the floor beneath her feet as she strolled through the Darkhaven that morning. Grabbing an apple from a bowl on the kitchen island, she bit into the juicy red flesh and followed the muffled sounds of Jordana and Nova's voices coming from outside on the courtyard patio.

The two women turned from their breakfasts to glance her way as she headed out to join them. Carys knew her grin was practically ear-to-ear, but there was no dimming it as she flopped onto the nearest chair in her loose pajama bottoms and camisole tank top.

Jordana's pale brows lifted. "You look exceptionally happy this morning."

"I am." Carys took another bite of the apple, slurping the sweet nectar. "I had an amazing night."

Jordana smirked. "That goes without saying."

"I had a date."

"With Rune?"

"No, with Hector from accounting." Carys rolled her eyes. "Yes, with Rune. He came to the museum to take me out for dinner."

"He *what?*" Jordana gaped. "Rune came to see you at the MFA? To take you out on an actual date?"

"Uh-huh. In front of Andrea and everyone else working late on the exhibit last night." It was probably going to be the talk of the workplace for the next week or more.

Carys went to take another nonchalant bite of her apple, but Jordana snatched it out of her hands on an exasperated laugh.

"Stop eating, and spill the details, woman!"

"He took me to Ciao Bella—"

"Only the most popular place in town," Jordana informed Nova, who was also listening raptly. The tattooed Breedmate's pale blue eyes were lit with interest under the asymmetrical fall of her ebony-and-sapphire hair, her pierced lips curved in a smile. Jordana took a bite of Carys's apple. "You can't even get near the door of that restaurant without reservations three months in advance."

Carys gave a mild shrug. "Rune said he pulled a few strings, and the owner was a fight fan, so . . ."

Nova arched a brow. "I guess he wanted to impress you."

Jordana nodded. "I think it worked."

"He did impress me," Carys admitted. "But it wasn't because of the dinner or even the incredible time we spent together afterward. And I do mean *incredible*."

"Don't think we're going to let you skimp on that part either," Jordana warned around another bite of fruit.

Carys shook her head on a laugh. It wasn't long ago that she'd been the one prodding for all of the romantic details about her best friend and Nathan. The steamy parts of Carys's time with Rune had been beyond amazing, but this morning she was floating on air for another reason as well.

"Last night, Rune opened up to me like never before. About his past, his life, a lot of awful things he's survived." Her heart tightened now, just recalling all he'd shared with her. "I needed him to let me in, and he did. It was a really big step for him. For us."

Nova studied her. "Sounds like he probably needed that talk as much as you did."

Carys nodded. Rune hadn't trusted her with all of the secrets and demons that still haunted him, but in time, she hoped he would. After last night, she felt confident there was little that could stand between them now.

"I'm glad it's working out," Jordana said. "It's good to see you like this, Car."

"I've never been happier," Carys admitted. "Now, I only hope nothing goes wrong tonight."

As she said it, her mother breezed outside accompanied by Brynne. "What's going on tonight?"

Not exactly the way she wanted to announce the news, but what the hell? "I've invited Rune to come to the Darkhaven tonight before the club opens. It's time that you all meet."

"Tonight?" An uncertain look swept over her mother's face. "Your father may not be ready for that, with so much going on in the command center and at headquarters now that Zael has arrived there to meet with Lucan."

The newsflash about Jordana's Atlantean friend was a surprise. Carys turned a questioning glance on her friend. "You were able to locate him, after all?"

"Yep. I think I'm starting to get the hang of this thing." Jordana held up her hand and the center of its palm flashed with a soft glow, then went out again. "Zael says my control over its power will keep improving over time."

Carys wanted to hear more, but it would have to wait. She clasped her mother's hands in hers. "This is important to me. Rune is important to me. I want him to know my family. And I want all of you to know him. I want you all to like him."

Tavia gave her fingers a reassuring squeeze, love shining in her eyes. "How can anyone argue with that?"

"Thank you." Carys wrapped her in a hug. "I told Rune to be here at nine tonight."

"I'll make sure your father is aware. And I'll tell him I expect him to be on his best behavior too."

"That goes double for Aric," Carys added. "I want

them both to be nice to Rune. Give him a chance."

Tavia nodded and hugged her close.

Carys breathed a bit easier, knowing her mother was on her side. Now, she just had to trust that her father and brother wouldn't greet Rune at the door with the rest of the Boston warriors, armed to the teeth and fangs.

She wanted nothing to ruin what she had now with Rune.

And she could only hope that nothing went wrong.

CHAPTER 22

☾

At the D.C. headquarters, Lucan sat across from Zael in a conference room usually reserved for visiting statesmen and other diplomats.

In the past two decades, the sumptuous, yet comfortable, chamber had hosted presidents, prime ministers, decorated generals, religious leaders, world-renown scientists and countless other important guests. But Lucan was hard-pressed to name a single meeting that had carried the same weight and potential lasting consequences—good or bad—as the one taking place with this immortal today.

Darion, Gideon and Brock had joined them a few minutes ago, after Lucan and Zael had gotten acquainted and decided if the visit should proceed beyond cursory introductions and politely couched mistrust. Lucan had since put out calls to each of his district commanders to report to headquarters later that evening to meet the Atlantean in person and hopefully set a path toward a mutually beneficial alliance between Zael and the Order.

So far, he had been forthcoming and engaging, answering all of Lucan's questions about Jordana and her Atlantean father, Cassianus, AKA Cassian Gray, as well as another deceased immortal, Reginald Crowe. His azure gaze was shrewd and measuring, but not unfriendly, as Lucan and the other Breed males studied him from around the big table.

"And you're certain Crowe had no ties to the colony?" Lucan asked, after the other men were seated and the conversations resumed. "No one who might know about his activities with Opus Nostrum?"

"None." Zael gave a slow shake of his head. "Crowe was dead to our people long before the Order killed him. He belonged to the old guard—one of the royal legion, like Cass and me—before he decided to make his fortune in the human world. He was loyal enough to our queen, but his real interest had always been in conquest, whether that was business, pleasure, or war. His views went against everything the Atlantean people believe in."

Lucan acknowledged with a nod. "What about the names Riordan or Ivers? Do either of them sound at all familiar to you?"

"I'm sorry, no." Zael leaned back in his seat, getting more comfortable. He cocked his head to the side. "I assume our meeting today isn't merely to discuss Crowe or his unsavory associates."

"No," Lucan admitted. "I wanted to meet because I need to know if our interests are in alignment."

"That depends on what your interests are, Commander Thorne."

"Peace. True and lasting peace between the humans, the Breed and your kind."

Zael's broad mouth pursed slightly. "A simple

concept, but a thousand ways for it to fail. Or worse, end in irreparable catastrophe."

"We'll have better odds without your queen plotting her war in the shadows."

"And the Order won't be opposed to destroying her to achieve it?" Those oceanic blue eyes held steady, unreadable. "How does that make your goal any better?"

A palpable tension poured over Brock, Gideon and Dare at the bold retort. Lucan was taken aback slightly too, but Zael's forthrightness only served to remind him that, although the Atlantean had come to the meeting in peace, he was still a powerful being who would not be cowed. Not even by a room full of Breed warriors and their Gen One leader.

"I'm not interested in a philosophical debate," Lucan said, without heat. "We need to know which side the colony stands on if a war is to come."

"Neither," Zael said. "All in the colony hope for peace, but enough of our lives have been spent already. That's why the colony exists. That's why its inhabitants defected from Selene's rule after the fall of the realm. They want no part of anyone's war or vengeance—yours or hers."

Lucan cursed. "So, you'll all just stand by and wait for the dust to settle around a victor, then determine your course? I'm sure I don't need to tell you what that makes you in my eyes, Zael."

"I didn't say I wouldn't choose a side." Zael's expression was placid, but there was a dangerous gleam in his gaze. "The colony is my people, but so is Selene. And there are others like me—her former legion and a handful of advisors—who feel her rage has blinded her to what is right. Cassianus was one of those people too.

That's why he stole his daughter away, to protect her and give her better a life outside Selene's new realm."

"Is that why Cass stole one of the Atlantean crystals?" Lucan asked. "To keep Selene from using it war against the Breed and man?"

Zael's brows arched. "Jordana told you about the crystal her father was rumored to have taken?"

"She didn't tell us. She showed us."

"Jordana has Cass's crystal?" Zael didn't even seem to try to conceal his astonishment. Or his interest.

Lucan shook his head. "The Order has it now. She entrusted it to us."

"I don't suppose you'd let me see it to substantiate that fact?"

Lucan grunted. "Today is about trust. We hope it's about building an alliance. With you, with the colony. With anyone else who doesn't want to see our world destroyed by an enemy we're not even sure how to fight yet."

Zael narrowed his gaze on him. "Today *is* about trust, I agree. So, help me to trust that what you say is true. How can I be sure you have the crystal if you're not willing to show it to me?"

"Because I told you I have it. We found the egg-sized, silvery crystal hidden in a titanium box. The box was hidden inside a sculpture that sat in a public museum in Boston, right in front of everyone's noses for more than two decades."

Zael smirked as he listened. "Concealed within a sculpture. How like Cass to hide his treasure inside an object of art. What kind of sculpture was it?"

"An eighteenth-century Italian piece called *Sleeping Endymion*. Or rather, an expert replica of that piece.

Jordana said Cass had the original at his villa on the Amalfi coast."

Zael started to chuckle. "Of course. The moon goddess, Selene, and her doomed human shepherd lover."

"You know the myth?"

"The story is myth, but Endymion was a man," Zael said. "He was our queen's consort. He was also her betrayer. He's the one who gave her enemies—your race's Ancient fathers—two of the realm's crystals."

Astonished murmurs traveled between the other men at the table. Lucan stared at Zael. "Pity about your queen's poor judgment in men, but what kind of power do the crystals have? We need to understand how it can be harnessed. How it can be unleashed."

"The crystals are a power source. They're meant to protect, to energize and sustain life. Not destroy it."

"And yet that's exactly what the Ancients did with them," Lucan countered. "Somehow, they used the crystals' power against Selene. Against Atlantis. They did something with them to create that massive explosion and the wave that followed."

Zael's golden brows quirked in surprise. "I wasn't aware that the specifics of the attack on Atlantis were common knowledge among the Breed."

"They weren't. Not until recently."

Now the Atlantean's expression darkened to wary suspicion. "And you know this, how?"

Lucan glanced at Brock, whose grim face looked less than amenable about bringing his mate into the conversation. "Today's meeting is about establishing trust and forming a meaningful alliance. That effort has to work both ways, but if you'd rather we don't discuss her—"

"It's all right," the warrior replied. "We need to extend our trust to Zael too. And if telling him puts Jenna in any kind of danger, I'll know who to go to first for explanations."

Lucan nodded and glanced at their guest. "Brock's mate, Jenna, saw the attack on Atlantis take place. In a memory. Not her own, but the memory of an Ancient. One who was there when it happened."

Zael frowned. "I don't follow."

"Before he died in a confrontation with my men, this Ancient had been wounded and on the run. He attacked a human woman named Jenna. For reasons we've yet to understand, he implanted a piece of himself inside her. Now, at the base of her neck, she carries a biotechnology chip that contains his DNA. It's been responsible for some . . . interesting changes in her. It's also given Jenna recurring glimpses into the Ancient's memories."

"Has she seen how your ancestors relentlessly hunted my people before they destroyed our community and killed three-quarters of our population?"

"She has."

Zael nodded. "We were a peaceful race before the attack on Atlantis. We came here to colonize. We lived in secrecy, in harmony, with one another and our human neighbors for thousands of years. We had no interest in war or bloodshed or conquest."

Lucan grunted. "Whereas the Breed's ancestors thrived on all three. We know the Ancients were a violent, predatory race. They hunted humans with the same ruthlessness as they did your kind, Zael. They fed and destroyed and conquered. But they are not us. The Breed should not be judged based on the sins of our fathers."

"I'm afraid you'll have a hard time convincing Selene of that."

Darion blew out a low curse on the other side of the table and met his father's grim stare. "If the Atlantean queen can't be reasoned with, then she leaves us no choice but to meet her in war."

Lucan agreed with that logic, but he'd seen enough war in his long lifetime. He hoped his son, and those of his fellow warriors, would not have to wade through rivers of blood and cities reduced to cinders the way he and his comrades of the Order had done over the centuries.

But Dare was right. If Selene truly was blind with vengeance, then she would leave the Order no choice but to destroy her.

"Crowe said the queen has been plotting her war for a long time. Do you know how she might accomplish it?"

"I do not," Zael admitted. "But if I were her, I'd be looking to recover the two crystals the Ancients stole."

"Do they still exist?"

"I'm quite certain they must. It's not easy to destroy that kind of power source. And I doubt the Ancients would have been eager to let go of such a valuable weapon."

Holy shit.

Gideon's intrigued gaze seemed to echo Lucan's thoughts. "Where would you look?" he asked Zael.

The Atlantean gave a slow shake of his head. "Even if I knew, I'm not convinced that's a secret anyone needs to have."

"Maybe not," Lucan agreed. "But if you did know,

or were to find out, can we count on you and the colony to keep that information a secret from your queen too?"

"As I said, the colony wants peace. I want peace. So long as the Order's actions demonstrate the same, you'll have my alliance. You'll have my trust."

"And you have mine," Lucan said.

He extended his hand to the immortal. Zael grasped it in a firm, strong grip, and the two powerful males sealed their pact.

Zael turned to Brock then, his tropical blue eyes lit with curiosity. "Now, I would very much like to meet your Jenna."

CHAPTER 23

R une checked his reflection in the mirror for the third time that night as he got ready to leave his quarters at La Notte.

Showered and dressed, he'd finally settled on a pair of charcoal slacks and a pale gray Charvet shirt. Shiny black oxfords gleamed on his large feet. As he stood in front of the mirror, he shrugged into a black suit jacket usually reserved for funerals or mating ceremonies—on those rare occasions he'd actually attended either one.

He felt ridiculous, but tonight wasn't about him. It was all about Carys, and he didn't want to disappoint her or her family. He wanted to make Carys proud. And yeah, there was a part of him that wanted her family's acceptance too.

He wasn't part of their world and didn't fool himself that he ever truly could be, but he'd be damned if he wanted to walk into that Darkhaven tonight and feel unworthy. He'd do his best to look the part, if nothing else.

Finger-combing his unruly mane of hair back from his face, he bit off a low curse. Good thing the other fighters weren't there to see him primping and fussing in the mirror for the past half-hour. If they had, they'd bust his ass about it from now until next year.

He glanced at the time. Twenty minutes across town would get him there just before nine. He didn't want to show up too early, but he sure as hell wasn't going to be late and give Carys's father another reason to despise him.

Shit. Maybe the pall-bearer jacket was pouring it on a bit thick.

Rune took it off . . . then froze when the club's sound system in the arena suddenly went from silent to ear-splitting.

What the fuck?

It was still a couple of hours before the first of the staff were due to show up to open the place, so who was there? He stalked out of his quarters and into the main floor of the arena, cutting the noise with a sharp mental command.

A large man leaned on the bar, one foot jacked up on the boot rail below.

No, not merely a man.

A Breed male.

His head was shaved, showcasing a blend of *dermaglyphs* and tattoos that snaked up his thick neck and onto his skull. He wore black pants and a black shirt, the kind of clothes that were standard issue for any urban street thug. A black nine-millimeter pistol was holstered at his hip.

Rune's hackles rose in warning. "Club's not open now. You lost or something?"

"Just lookin' for someone," the guy said without bothering to look Rune's way. "Thought I'd have me a little peek around in the meanwhile."

The gravelly voice, dark with amusement, carried an unmistakable Irish brogue. The sound of that accent turned the warning that clamored in Rune's veins to something colder.

"I think you misunderstood me," he growled at the stranger. "What I meant was, get the fuck out of my place."

Now the vampire grinned. He drew to his full height, and Rune realized he wore one of the spiked cage gloves on his hand. He curled a fist and met Rune's stare across the arena. "Ya know, as efficient as a nine semiauto is, I'll wager slicing into some asshole with one of these is a lot more satisfying."

"Aye," Rune said. "Come back tonight after we open, and I'll be glad to demonstrate for you."

The thug chuckled. "Won't be staying in town that long. Neither will you . . . Rune, is it?"

Rune didn't reply. Although he hardly needed the confirmation, now he spotted the black scarab tattoo that rode on the back of the male's hand. His molars clamped so tight, it was a miracle they didn't shatter as he immediately began calculating the quickest way to kill the bastard.

"You need to come with me," the vampire said. "Someone wants to talk to you."

Rune grunted. "I'm not going anywhere."

"Really? Looks like you are. All polished up and fancy." The vampire gestured toward him, the metal spikes glinting in the low light of the bar. "That shirt made outta silk? Sure as hell hate to ruin it for you." He put his other hand down on top of his weapon, ready to draw.

"Go ahead and try," Rune said. "Only place you're going tonight is your grave."

"Don't be so sure about that."

The thug's fingers twitched. It was all the warning he gave.

Then the gun was in his hand and exploding a fired shot. Rune dodged the bullet's path, realizing as the round grazed his rib cage that the aim hadn't been to kill. Not yet, anyway. No doubt this son of a bitch was saving that honor for someone else.

Blood seeped warm and wet at his side as he rolled to the floor, then came up on the balls of his feet. On a bellow, Rune launched himself airborne at the vampire. The gun fired again—a shot squeezed off in panic this time.

The bullet went wild, missing him completely.

Rune body-slammed him, driving his assailant across the bar and into the large mirror behind it. The gun slipped out of the thug's fingers and clattered across the floor. Glassware and bottles of liquor crashed down. Broken shelving crumbled all around them.

The other male snarled and made a flailing slash at Rune with the glove's spikes. Rune grabbed the fist as it came driving toward him. Titanium teeth cut into his fingers as he immobilized the strike and wrenched the thug's wrist back with a savage thrust of muscle and fury.

Bones popped as they broke, tendons grinding as they severed. The male howled in agony as his hand flopped uselessly in the wrong direction on his arm.

And then, Rune's rage really snapped its leash.

Straddling the vampire on the concrete floor, he

pounded his fists into the other male's face. Blood spurted. Teeth and fangs crunched under Rune's relentless, punishing blows.

He didn't stop hitting the bastard—could not stop—even after the dead man's face was a pulpy mash of pulverized bone and destroyed cartilage.

Rune's breath sawed out of his lungs, wheezing through his enormous fangs. His eyes burned red with rage. His veins hammered with adrenaline and anger . . . and the dawning realization of what he'd done.

He turned his gaze away from the carnage to look at his torn, gore-soaked shirt and pants. His hands were gashed and bruised. The graze in his side licked at him like an open flame. Even with his Breed metabolism, it would take hours, possibly days, for the evidence of this altercation to fully heal.

Fuck.

Carys . . .

He couldn't go to the Chase Darkhaven now. Not like this.

And the thought of calling Carys to tell her what had just occurred—and all of the ramifications that would follow when he'd have to explain why—would be the certain end of anything they had together.

He dropped his head back and let out a roar of anger and frustration.

As his bellow echoed in the cavernous arena, footsteps sounded behind him. Multiple pairs of feet crunched in the glass and fallen debris as they neared him.

Rune tossed a searing glance over his shoulder, then launched onto his feet, braced for battle.

Half a dozen armed Breed males stood there, all

bearing black scarab tattoos.

The big male in front peeled his lips back in a cold smile. "What are you going to do now, boyo? Think you can kill all of us?"

~ ~ ~

He was late.

At five minutes past the hour, Carys had told herself not to worry; Rune would arrive at any moment. Five minutes late wasn't like him at all, but it wasn't cause for worry either.

He would be there. He knew what this night meant to her.

He wouldn't let her down.

At least, that's what she'd been telling herself as she sat beside her mother on the sofa in the Darkhaven's living room, trying not to notice the increasingly impatient expression on her father's face as his long fingers tapped idly on the arms of his chair across the room.

Now, it was eight minutes after nine and still no sign of Rune.

Nor had he answered her call or message.

"He's got about two more minutes to get here," her father said, his deep voice clipped with irritation. "I've got orders from Lucan to deal with, plus a hundred other things I've put off for this meeting tonight. I can't afford to waste any more time waiting for this male to make his appearance."

"He'll be here," Carys insisted. *Come on, Rune. Please, don't do this to me.*

Her mother glanced over in sympathy, and lovingly

squeezed Carys's hand. "Maybe it would be best if we did this another time instead?"

Carys saw slim chance of that in her father's flinty eyes. His disapproval of Rune was deepening with every second that ticked by. After a moment, he exhaled a curse and stood up.

"I think we've all waited long enough now," he said. He walked over to Carys and rested his palm on her shoulder. "I know you're disappointed, sweetheart. I didn't want to be proven right about him. But I can't pretend I'm surprised, either."

Embarrassment flooded her cheeks. Regret put a dull ache in her chest. Rune and her father meant the world to her, and she could hardly bear the idea that the wedge between them had just widened tonight. She could only imagine how her brother would react when he found out she'd been stood up. Aric would likely have to be chained down to keep from going off to confront Rune and defend her honor.

"This isn't like Rune," Carys murmured, hearing the desperation in her voice. "He said he would be here, and he will. I know he will . . ."

But even as she said it, doubts crowded in like dark clouds.

And rising concern too.

Something wasn't right. Rune hadn't exactly been excited about meeting her parents, but nothing would have kept him from making good on his promise to her to be there.

She felt it in her bones now. In her blood.

Something was terribly wrong.

As her parents quietly left the room, Carys tried calling Rune again. He didn't pick up.

His number rang, and rang, and rang. . . .

CHAPTER 24

D read clawed at Carys's stomach when she reached
La Notte's front entrance at street level and found
the heavy chain lock hanging loose. The fact that the tall,
arched double doors were slightly ajar made the fine
hairs on her nape rise in alarm.

She hadn't been sure what to hope for when she'd
slipped away from the Darkhaven to come to the club
and look for Rune. After he'd failed to pick up her
repeated calls or return her urgent messages, she only
knew she couldn't stay there wondering.

And as humiliated and hurt as she'd felt, sitting in her
family's living room, waiting for him to finally show up,
the concern she'd felt had overruled it. Now, that
concern chilled over into bone-deep worry.

No sounds flowed out to the street. The club was
dark. Quiet.

Eerily so.

Her feeling of foreboding deepened, and instead of
entering through the unsecured front door, she went

around to the staff entrance at the back of the old church building.

Before she even stepped inside, the scent of spilled blood and death blasted her senses. Her gums twitched in response as alarm turned to ice in her veins.

"Rune?" Her voice vanished into the silence of the place as she entered the cavernous, underground arena and bar area. "Rune, are you here?"

He didn't answer, but there he was. Standing inside with a group of six large, menacing Breed males, all heavily armed with semiautomatic pistols trained on Rune. Signs of a struggle were everywhere. The broken mirror behind the bar. Toppled chairs. Shattered glass littering the floor like diamond shards in a sea of pooled liquor.

And blood.

So much blood. On the wall and the floor. All over Rune.

"Oh, my God! Rune, what hap—"

When she stepped forward, his stark gaze halted her. There was a warning in his eyes that made her fall silent. Made her quell the spark of her Breed instincts.

One of the vampires moved beside him now, clamping his hand onto Rune's shoulder. "Well, well . . . who have we here?"

The male's angular face had a dangerous edge to it. Under his short dark hair, his piercing gray eyes glimmered with interest. And unmistakable cruelty.

Rune cleared his throat. "Club's not going to open tonight," he said, directing the statement at her. "You and the other girls can take the weekend off."

Carys wasn't sure how to respond. The Breed male standing next to Rune like he owned him didn't give her the chance.

"Not so fast now, boyo. Don't be rude." His mouth split into a leering smile. "Why don't you introduce us first? Didn't expect this dump to employ such a fine piece of ass." His gaze ran over her like an unwanted caress, narrowing when he saw the mark on the side of her neck. "Breedmate, besides, I see."

Rune didn't correct the mistake, nor did Carys. Although everything Breed in her flared with the urge to attack, she held herself in check. Rune's miserable gaze seemed to command her compliance. He was clearly reigning in his own fury too.

"Go on home. Do it now," he said tightly, his eyes pleading for her to obey.

And then she saw the reason for his gravity. Riding on the back of the hand that still gripped his shoulder was a distinctive tattoo. A black scarab. The other men had the same marks.

Holy shit.

These were Riordan's men.

And Rune . . .?

His eyes took on an even grimmer expression when he realized she'd spotted the tattoo. His mouth went slack at the corners as he stared at her in terrible silence. Almost indiscernibly, he slowly shook his head at her in warning. In abject fear—not for himself, but for her.

Do not say anything, his dire gaze implored her. *Do not cross them.*

Beside him, his dangerous companion continued to leer in Carys's direction. "Come on, girl. Step forward and let me have a closer look at you. Let us see what Aedan here is trying to keep all to himself." The Riordan thug sucked in an exaggerated breath and swung a smirk at Rune. "Oh. Sorry, boyo. Would you rather I call you Rune?"

"What's he talking about?" Carys frowned. "Who's Aedan?"

The leader of the pack of thugs chuckled. "The better question is, who's Rune?"

They all laughed at the apparent joke. All but Rune.

"For shame, Aedan. It's obvious you've been fucking this poor girl, but lying to her too?" The Breed male clicked his tongue. "That's no way to treat a lady."

It felt as if a cold vacuum had suddenly opened up in the center of her chest. Everything Rune had told her started to make sense in a different way now. His past, his shame about where he'd come from, who he was.

All the things he hadn't told her.

The walls he refused to let her breach.

How much was he still hiding from her?

Rune's eyes were shooting hot sparks now. Carys could read the murder in his gaze. But he was keeping it under control. Taking the taunts and obvious threats from these men because she was there now. Because he was trying to give her a chance to get away.

"This isn't about her," he muttered low under his breath. His fangs glinted with every syllable. "You came for me. You've got me. Let her leave."

The dark-haired male seemed to consider for a long moment, then he clapped his palm ungently on Rune's shoulder and gave a careless shrug. "The bitch can go."

"Get out," Rune growled at Carys.

She couldn't move. Her feet were rooted to the floor. Even though he'd deceived her, even though she'd just been struck with the fact that possibly everything she thought she knew about Rune had been a lie, her fear for him was greater than her own pain or confusion.

Her veins hammered with the urge to fight, to fly at these bastards with the full fury of her Breed genetics. Every fiber of her being was firing up with the desire to shed blood, to kill.

She felt her fangs start to erupt from her gums. Beneath her blouse, her *glyphs* prickled with the coming surge of her transformation.

Rune saw the slight change begin to come over her. He shook his head and snarled a vicious curse.

"Go," he commanded her. "Goddamn it, get the fuck out of here, now!"

She'd never seen him so enraged. Nor more afraid. It shook her as surely as a physical blow. She backed up so fast, she nearly stumbled. She wheeled around and ran, her heart throbbing in her chest, cold and leaden. Her tears were hot on her cheeks as she pushed out the door and fled into the night, fumbling to pull her phone from her pocket.

She hit the number for her father's private line. He picked up on the first ring.

"Daddy!" Her breath hitched on a broken sob. "Oh, God, it's Rune . . . Please, I need your help."

~ ~ ~

Rune didn't let out his breath until he heard the staff door slam shut behind Carys.

She was gone.

He told himself he was glad. He felt relief, for sure. Seeing her in the same room with men loyal to Fineas Riordan had been the worst kind of terror he'd ever known.

Her confusion and mistrust when they'd called him by his given name had wracked him. When she'd spied the black scarab tattoos on the men, there had been recognition in her keen gaze. She knew the mark, knew what it meant. Who it belonged to.

Which meant the Order knew it too.

Bad enough he had wounded her by standing her up at the Chase Darkhaven. Tonight, he'd lost her for sure. And if the Order found him first, her father would no doubt want to be the one to kill him personally.

Rune had never felt dread like he had when Carys had stood primed to strike tonight—for him. She never would have survived it. Her Breed genetics were powerful, but not even the purest of their kind was bulletproof.

Together, he and Carys might have taken out a few of Riordan's men, but not without risking their own lives. Rune could hardly be troubled to worry about his own hide now, but there was nothing he wouldn't do to keep Carys safe. Sending her away was the only choice.

If they had realized who—and what—she was . . .

If they had made any move to touch her tonight . . .

He couldn't finish the thoughts. The mere idea raked his veins with icy talons. Let them do whatever they would to him, but he couldn't bear the thought of how she might suffer at their hands.

Or at the hands of the bigger monster back in Dublin.

"How long has he known where I am?"

"A couple of weeks." Ennis Riordan, the Breed male leading the pack of jackals, grinned at Rune. "Ever since one of the scouts he sent to Boston to keep tabs on the Order followed a team of warriors down to this hellhole and saw them talking with you and the Breedmate who came here tonight."

Jesus Christ.

The ice in Rune's blood turned even colder. They'd known that long, which meant they could have made their move on him at any time. Any one of the nights when Carys was in the club with him . . . or in his bed.

"Why wait so long to make your appearance? If bringing me back to Dublin is so damn important to him, why not do it as soon as he knew I was here?"

"The Order's been keeping us busy, trying to fuck up our plans. Forcing us to sacrifice pawns along the way to stay ahead of them while we focus on important work." He shrugged. "Finding you in Boston after all this time was a surprise, Aedan. I can't tell you what it means to your father to know you'll be home again soon. Back in the family fold where you belong. He has great plans for you, boyo."

Rune forced himself to keep his fists at his sides, struggled to keep his fangs concealed behind his curling lip as he listened to his uncle speak. He had to maintain his patience. He had to wait for his chance to strike.

Because he hadn't realized until that moment that he had plans of his own too.

He was going back to Dublin willingly. Eagerly, in fact.

He would return to his father's hellish domain . . . and when the moment was right, he was going to kill the bastard and burn his house to the ground.

CHAPTER 25

☽

In his thousands of years of living, Zael had seen vast and astonishing libraries belonging to pharaohs, emperors and kings. Yet as he stood in the archive room of the Order's Washington, D.C., headquarters, he could hardly keep his jaw from dropping in amazement.

The floor-to-ceiling walls of leather-bound journals were beyond impressive. The fact that they represented two decades of handwritten work—of painstakingly recorded memories—from one woman made the collection even more remarkable.

Then again, Zael had never seen anything quite like the woman herself, either.

He'd been told she was human, but the *dermaglyphs* covering her body told another story. The skin markings tracked along her neck and onto her scalp beneath her short brown hair. More *glyphs* ran along the top of her chest, disappearing beneath the collar of her shirt, only to reemerge below the short sleeves, the intricate pattern continuing on her arms and the backs of her hands.

She seemed more Ancient than *Homo sapiens,* and Zael's Atlantean senses were piqued in response to the close proximity of enemy DNA. But her smile was warm and welcoming, her hazel eyes bright with pride as she watched Zael take in the scope and breadth of her work.

"Feel free to look at anything you like," she told him, standing beside her mate, Brock.

While Lucan had left to greet arriving warrior commanders he'd summoned to headquarters that evening, Brock had opted to remain protectively at his mate's side after her introduction to Zael.

Not that Zael could blame him.

Jenna was a beautiful woman, even more so because of her unusual appearance.

And it was obvious that the big warrior adored her, from the way he had responded to questions about her in the meeting room earlier, as well as the way he looked at her now. The way his fingers traced idly on her shoulder as he held her under the shelter of his strong arm.

Zael studied the couple and their unmistakable bond. "Was it difficult going through all of the changes from human to . . ."

"Alien cyborg?" Jenna finished for him when he wasn't sure how to describe her. She laughed and shared a private look with her mate. "It would've been a lot harder, if I didn't have Brock there with me every step of the way. He got me through the initial attack by the Ancient, then afterward, he held my hand through all of the nightmares that followed."

Brock caressed her arm. "Nowhere else I'd want to be, babe."

Zael acknowledged the couple's devotion with a

nod. "The Breed are certainly a better, more caring species than their Ancient fathers." He strolled along the first tall case of journals. "I don't think many of my people realize that about you."

"The Ancients were bred to be conquerors," Jenna said. "Their entire race thrived on violence and domination. There's so much I've come to understand about them in the past twenty years that I've been journaling their history through my dreams and memories."

Zael browsed the volumes on the shelf in front of him, eventually selecting one off the shelf. "Do you mind if I look?"

Jenna gestured to indicate the whole room. "Of course not."

He flipped to a random entry. It recounted an Ancient hunting party in pursuit of Atlantean warriors on foot. The killing of one of Zael's comrades was described in such vivid detail that there was no mistaking the source of the account had actually been there. Had been the one wielding the weapon that took the Atlantean's head.

Zael closed the journal and soberly replaced it on the shelf.

He browsed a different one, reading of the Ancients' sacking of a small village in Eastern Europe. No life was spared, not even the animals in their pens.

On a low curse, he slid the leather-bound volume back into its place between the others. He strolled on, to a case shelving later chronicles. Flipping through the pages of handwritten notes, he paused at a mention of Lucan Thorne.

This record documented a period in time, hundreds

of years ago, when the tables had finally turned on the Ancients, making them the hunted. Led by Lucan, a small army of Breed warriors had waged war on their alien fathers, doing what neither mankind nor the Atlanteans ever could have. They had neutralized the biggest threat to all life on the planet simply because it was the right thing to do.

"That volume covers the founding of the Order," Jenna said as he read the full account in awed silence. "Lucan, Tegan and several others who were first to join the Order eventually chased down and destroyed all of the Ancients. All but one, as it turned out. The one who did this to me before the Order finally finished him too."

"The Order won't allow anyone to terrorize or harm innocents," Brock added, his deep voice grim with resolve. "Whether that's Opus Nostrum or the Atlantean queen."

No, they wouldn't. And Zael could find nothing but respect for Lucan and the Order.

"When I came here today, I was skeptical of what I'd find, and of how I'd be received." He turned to face Jenna and her warrior mate. "This has been a day of many surprises. This archive is another surprise, one that will be a treasure to many Breed generations to come."

Jenna beamed with pride. She tilted her head and studied him in open curiosity. "Are you mated, Zael?"

He shook his head. "No. I spent my youth serving Selene as one of her legion. Back then, I was devoted to my post and little else. After the fall of the realm and things grew more and more unstable in the court over time, I escaped to travel the world. Once I had a taste of the outside, the only thing I was devoted to was pleasure."

"And now?" Jenna asked. "Haven't you ever wanted to find a mate?"

He shrugged. "Life is a feast to be sampled and savored. Why would I want to restrict myself to a single course forever?"

Brock pulled Jenna a bit closer to him now. "Apparently, you haven't met the right woman yet."

"Perhaps not," he agreed. But his thoughts spiraled back to a moment in time when he had known someone special. Someone who'd made him forget all other women during the handful of days they'd had together. "There was one woman, years ago. A mortal, so no matter how I felt about her, our time together would've been short. But she was also married to another man. We spent a couple of weeks together one summer in Greece, before she returned home to America. Home to him."

Jenna had gone utterly silent. She was staring at him, her brows knit in a pensive frown. "You met her in Greece?"

Zael nodded. "One of the Cyclades islands . . ."

"They met in Mykonos."

The feminine voice that said the word came from the open doorway behind him. Zael swiveled his head and found a lovely, flame-haired young woman—a Breedmate—standing there. At her side was a large Breed warrior with shaggy dark hair and a web of scars that marred the left side of his face.

"Yes," Zael murmured. "It was Mykonos."

Something about the young woman's face made his breath catch in his lungs. Her eyes were somehow familiar. And the copper color of her hair . . . it was the same fiery shade as the strands that shot through his blond waves.

Jenna rushed over to bring the other female and her big mate inside the room. "Dylan and Rio, this is Zael."

"I know," said the woman named Dylan. "I knew who he was the moment I heard his name today."

She had a piece of paper in her hand. As she held it out to Zael, he realized it was an old photograph.

He took it from her loose grasp and glanced down at his own smiling face. He could still recall the beach that day. Could still feel the warmth of the sun on his head and shoulders.

He could still hear the laughter of the young, vibrant woman who'd taken the picture of him that afternoon.

Zael glanced up from the photo to look at the Breedmate standing before him.

She met his astonished gaze with a sweet, uncertain smile. "My name is Dylan. The woman you knew in Mykonos that summer was Sharon Alexander. She was my mother."

CHAPTER 26

"I should've stayed with him. I shouldn't have left him there alone with those men."

Carys sat on the sofa in the Chase Darkhaven, flanked by her mother and Brynne. Also in the room with her were Jordana and Nova. Even Aric was there, no doubt to make sure she stayed put.

"You did the only thing you could've done," her mother assured her. "You said yourself that Rune was the one who told you to leave. He didn't want to see you get hurt."

"I should've tried anyway," she murmured, misery running through her veins like acid. "I should have stayed and helped him fight those bastards. I told him I would always stand by him, and I failed him tonight."

She had regretted leaving La Notte as soon as she'd run out of the place. She should have gone back after she'd called her father for help, but his fear for her well-being had been nearly as palpable as Rune's. He demanded she return home as quickly as possible. He'd promised her that he and his team were heading out to the club immediately to handle the situation.

She had been home nearly twenty minutes with no word from her father, Mathias, or any of the Boston warriors who'd gone with them.

"Why haven't they called in yet? They must be there by now." She pushed herself up from the sofa with a moan. "Dammit, I can't sit here any longer. I need to know what's going on."

Aric's strong hands were firm, but gentle, on her shoulders as he guided her back to her seat. "Listen to me, sister. You're tough and you're Breed, but it would've been suicide if you'd escalated things with those men. You saw the scarabs on them. You know what they mean."

Nova's gaze was as grim as Aric's. "It would've been worse than death for you, if my father's men had gotten their hands on you, Carys. Don't think you would've been given any mercy."

Aric hissed a curse. "No matter how I feel about you being with Rune, the best thing he did was make sure you got out of there safely. For that, I owe him. We all owe him."

"I know he did it to save me. He let them believe I was a Breedmate, not Breed. He tried to make them think I worked in the club, instead of revealing who I really am."

Beside her on the sofa, her mother blew out a shaky sigh and hugged Carys close. "My God . . . Knowing what we do about Fineas Riordan, do you realize how close you came to falling into Opus Nostrum's hands tonight? I don't even want to consider what they would do to a family member of the Order."

Carys didn't really want to think about that either, but what would they do to Rune?

"I never saw fear in his eyes until tonight. He knew those men and what they were capable of. They knew him too—apparently, they know more about him than I do."

"You're saying he's one of them," Aric said, not a question. "Rune is one of Riordan's thugs."

She gave a weak nod. "I think he might've been at one time, yes."

She didn't want to admit it, but after tonight it was hard to deny that it was possible. The realization was still cold inside her. It was hard to process the fact that some of the secrets Rune had kept from her had materialized as a pack of terrifying thugs bearing the mark of the very criminal the Order was trying to destroy.

"They knew him," she murmured again. "They said his name was Aedan. He didn't deny it."

Nova went suddenly still, almost wooden, where she stood next to Jordana. Her face lost its color and her mouth fell slack. "Aedan?"

"What is it?" Jordana asked her. "Nova, what's wrong?"

"Aedan is my brother's name. Aedan Riordan."

Carys's stomach bottomed out at the airless revelation. "Oh, my God. He told me there was a little girl . . . that he had a sister. But he said her name was—"

"Kitty," Nova said. "That's what he called me. Not Catriona. Kitty."

Gasps traveled the room. Aric ground out a harsh curse.

As for Carys, she could only close her eyes as the

reality sank in.

Rune wasn't merely one of Riordan's men.

He was his son.

~ ~ ~

"Not counting the debris and the dead scarab behind the bar, there's no lingering imprint of violence here," Mathias said from beside Chase in the vacant arena area of La Notte. "My guess is that they took Rune out of here without a struggle."

"What about duress?" Chase knew his old friend's unique extrasensory ability would be able to pick up on psychic echoes of aggression the way other people would notice a bruise on flesh.

Mathias shook his head. "He went willingly from what I can tell."

"Shit." About the only thing worse than Carys's all-too-close brush with some of Fineas Riordan's men was the possibility that her lover was actually familiar with the son of a bitch too. Familiar enough that he'd walked out of this club with Riordan's thugs on his own volition.

Chase had been staving off his fury and suspicion from the moment Carys called him for help. Part of him had wanted to believe her, that Rune was in danger—in real fear for his life. It was better than the alternative, at least. But even as she'd told him, he'd had his doubts.

That Rune had given Carys a chance to get away was the only thing that had kept Chase's rage in check as he'd assembled his warrior team and raced down to La Notte. Now, even that small consideration for the fighter was beginning to dim under the weight of what they'd found here tonight.

In frustration, Chase raked his hand over his jaw. His gaze connected with Nathan's grim stare where the warrior captain stood with his team.

"If he's got active ties to Riordan, we can't afford the risk. There can't be any mercy for Rune when we catch up to him."

"Yeah," Chase agreed. Nathan wasn't telling him anything he didn't already feel in his gut. As much as it would destroy Carys, the fighter was a dead man if it turned out his loyalty belonged to Riordan.

Even worse, if that loyalty should extend to Opus Nostrum.

To think he'd almost welcomed the bastard into his house earlier tonight.

And Carys . . .

Christ, what would he have done if anything had happened to his daughter? She was terrified and heartbroken now, but if the night had ended differently, she might have been taken along with Rune. She might have been killed—or worse if Riordan's men had realized who she was.

The thought was still an icy chill under his skin when his comm unit signaled an incoming call. It was the Darkhaven, Tavia's private number. He picked up, his greeting tense with stress.

"Sterling." His mate's quiet, stricken voice went through him like a shot. "There's something you need to know . . ."

Rage steamed inside his skull as he listened to her explain the shocking revelation that had just unfolded back home. As he ended the call, he couldn't bite back his anger. It exploded out of him on a curse and a flash of his fangs. "He's Riordan's son."

"What?" Nathan gaped along with the other warriors.

"The fighter. His name isn't Rune." Chase practically spat the words. "It's Aedan Riordan."

"Aedan?" Mathias's mouth pressed flat, recognition flaring in his eyes. "Holy shit. Does Nova know about this?"

"She's the one who confirmed it just now, when Carys mentioned that's what Riordan's men called him tonight. The son of a bitch has been lying to her all along. Using her."

Chase's blood boiled with the knowledge that for all these past weeks, his beloved daughter had been in the bastard's arms. In his bed.

He hadn't liked that idea even before everything that happened tonight. Now, he seethed with the urge to kill the fighter.

Chase started for the club's exit, his team falling in behind him. "I need to make Lucan aware of the situation. And I want his understanding that when we find Aedan Riordan, no one takes the bastard out except me."

CHAPTER 27

Alone in her bedroom, Carys changed clothes for the imminent departure to the Order's D.C. headquarters. The Chase Darkhaven had been abuzz with preparations for the trip since her father had returned from La Notte with his team and Mathias. Lucan had demanded the presence of the entire Boston command center, Carys included.

She knew it didn't bode well that her father was avoiding her. He didn't have to say the words for her to understand that he was furious and disappointed in her.

And there was no mistaking his animosity for Rune—or, rather, Aedan.

Carys was angry and let down too. She was confused and hurt. Heartsick and afraid. Unsure what she should feel, after everything that had happened tonight. The complicated tangle of emotions gnawed at her, leaving her numb.

Bereft.

As she fastened the buttons on her ivory blouse and

tucked the hem into her camel-colored pants, a soft knock sounded on her door.

"Carys, may I come in?" Nova's accented voice was quiet, uncertain on the other side of the panel.

Although she wanted to be alone to process all that had occurred, there was only one person in the Darkhaven who could possibly relate to how she was feeling. Carys walked over and opened the door.

Nova smiled sadly, her light blue eyes dimmed with sympathy. "It's almost time to go. The jet's fueling up and everyone's just about ready to head out."

Carys nodded. "Tell them I'll be there in a minute."

"All right, I will." Nova hesitated, studying her now. "Actually, I came because I wanted to make sure you were okay."

"I am," Carys replied automatically. "Really, I'm fine."

"No, you're not." Nova's words were gentle. She stepped forward and drew Carys into a warm, totally unexpected, hug.

The kindness made Carys's breath catch. She hadn't realized how much she needed the support until she was standing there, trembling in the other woman's embrace.

"It broke my heart when my brother left home all those years ago," Nova said as she released her. "The best part of my world was suddenly gone. I imagine that's only a fraction of what you must be feeling now."

Carys led her inside the room and they sat down on the edge of the bed. "I feel like a fool, Nova. He lied to me. He left me, and now, to make it all worse, my father and the rest of the Order are talking about Rune—Aedan—as if he's the enemy."

"But you don't believe he is."

"I know he's not." Carys saw the same conviction in Nova's eyes. "You don't believe it either, do you?"

The Breedmate's blue-and-black hair swung against her shoulders as she shook her head. "Aedan may be a Riordan by blood, but he's nothing like that clan. The brother I knew was strong and noble. A good man. From all that you've told me of Rune, I have to believe my brother is still a good man."

More than anything, Carys wanted to believe that too. And, in that moment, she felt an overwhelming gratitude for Nova's friendship. It meant the world to know that she had someone to lean on if she needed understanding and support, the same way Rune had looked to his little sister as the beacon of light in his dark existence so many years ago.

She gave her new friend's hand a reassuring squeeze. "He loved you very much, you know. He regretted that he left you behind and never went back for you."

It took Nova a moment before she spoke. "Did he tell you that?"

Carys nodded. "When he took me out for our date, Rune told me a bit about how he grew up. He told me there was a fighting pit at his father's Darkhaven. Rune had been made to fight in it from the time he was a boy. Life or death matches, all for his father's amusement. For years—until he finally worked up the courage to leave—the pit was Rune's own private hell."

Nova closed her eyes as if feeling the pain herself. Her voice was quiet. "I had no idea about any of that. But I know firsthand how monstrous Fineas Riordan can be."

"When Rune told me about the pit and what he'd done to survive, I couldn't imagine how he was able to endure it. I asked him if there was no one in that house who cared about him," Carys said. "And he told me about you. He wanted to protect you from knowing what he was going through. He didn't want you to see that part of his life."

A soft, unsteady breath slipped past Nova's lips. "Aedan made me feel loved when the rest of my existence was fear and pain. He didn't know what had been happening with me, either. I was too ashamed to let him know. God, how foolish we both were, trying to put on a brave face for the other."

"You did what you had to in order to protect yourselves," Carys said. "And, as much as it hurt me tonight to find out the secret Rune was hiding from me, I can't condemn him for it. I only wish he'd trusted me enough to tell me. He could've asked me for help."

Nova's gaze was solemn, sad. "Given what I know about my brother now, I think he would've left Boston for good, rather than ask for help. Neither of us were taught to reach out to someone else. That's why I kept my secrets from Mathias as long as I did. I locked myself behind my own protective walls, thinking my past would never find me there. Hoping I'd be safe if I started over, if I pretended everything that had happened to me was just a bad dream." She let out a humorless laugh. "But you can never outrun your past or the demons that live there. No wall we build is high enough to keep them away. They always catch up sometime. You have to stare them in the face without flinching before they'll ever let you go."

Nova was right, of course. And Carys didn't doubt for a second that if Rune hadn't already understood that truth, he knew it now.

Her fear for him deepened when she considered that possibility. Her dread grew colder, as heavy as a stone.

In her heart, Carys knew that was why Rune had walked out willingly with his father's thugs. He was going with them of his own free will, most likely back to the hell where he'd been raised.

Back to face the monsters of his past.

Carys could only hope Rune survived whatever he intended to do . . . and pray that the Order hadn't already condemned him.

CHAPTER 28

Lucan sat at the head of the table in the Order's massive war room later that night. Seated around him were nine of his district commanders and their mates. Three other command center leaders were dialed in via video displays on the large wall monitors in the room.

As Chase wrapped up his report of what had happened in Boston earlier that night, a few muttered curses traveled the group, but the reaction of the most seasoned warriors was grim silence.

"Poor Carys," said Elise, Breedmate to Tegan, one of the Order's founding members. She was also Chase's former sister-in-law, and a woman who'd endured her fair share of heartache and loss in the past. "How is she handling all of this?"

"I saw her in the drawing room with Brynne and Jordana when we arrived," said Alexandra. She and her mate, Kade, were the last to arrive, having come in from Lake Tahoe. "Carys looked exhausted, and she was pacing the room like a caged animal."

Tavia sighed. "She hardly spoke on the flight down. She's hurt and confused, of course. She's as shocked as we all are, but she believes in Rune. She loves him."

Chase scoffed. "She's blinded by her emotions when it comes to that male. That blindness might've gotten her killed."

"Or maybe it was love that saved her life tonight." This from ebony-haired Corinne, who was seated beside Hunter, her Gen One warrior mate.

He glanced at her tenderly as she spoke, which was a feat in itself, since the former assassin had been raised by his brutal handlers to think that emotion was weakness. He'd overcome that training, just as Corinne's long-lost son, Nathan, had overcome similar abuse through his newfound love for Jordana.

"Corinne's right," said Tess. "And it's obvious that Rune—or Aedan—must care for Carys too. After all, he tried to protect her from Riordan's men."

Chase grunted, clearly unmoved. "If he really wanted to protect her, he never would've taken up with my daughter in the first place. I'd like to kill the bastard for that alone."

Dante glanced around his mate, Tess. "Come on, Harvard," he said, using a nickname he'd given Chase years ago. "You could say that about any one of us at this table when we met our mates—you included. So, don't judge him too harshly on that point, man."

A lot of warriors' heads nodded in agreement, both around the table and on the monitors. Even Lucan had to admit that what Dante said was true.

"And don't be too quick to execute, either," Mathias added. "Let's all remember that Aedan Riordan is not just his father's son. He's also Nova's brother."

The tattooed Breedmate threaded her slender fingers through Mathias's and gave him a sad smile.

As much as Lucan sympathized with the complicated emotional situation in front of them, first and foremost, the Order had a dangerous enemy to contend with.

"We need to get our hands on Riordan, and anyone who stands in the way of that mission will leave us no choice but to take them out. *Anyone*," he said, casting a sober look at Mathias and Nova, and at Chase and Tavia. "We need Fineas Riordan alive for questioning. Between Tegan and Hunter, I have no doubt we'll be able to wring out everything the bastard knows about Opus Nostrum and his comrades in that cabal."

The pair of lethal Gen Ones inclined their heads in agreement. Tegan's touch could siphon out the truth from even the most unwilling subject, and nothing could hide from Hunter's ability to read blood memories.

Wolfish-looking Kade chuckled darkly on the other side of the table and nodded in the direction of the scarred warrior seated near him. "If Riordan doesn't respond to those lines of questioning, let Rio here put his hands on him for a few seconds. Once Riordan feels his life leaking away, I'll bet all of his Opus secrets will start spilling out."

On one of the monitors, the Order's German-born commander, Andreas Reichen, cleared his throat. "If the rumors in Europe are true, it sounds like Opus has been acquiring new chemical technology recently."

Lucan wasn't the only one to mutter a curse at that newsflash. "They already have access to liquid UV light weaponry. What other kind of chemical technology should we be looking for?"

"You won't like it," Andreas said. "There's underground talk about a new, extremely powerful narcotic. Something that turns even the most docile Breed into a mindless, bloodthirsty savage."

"We've been hearing the same thing in Rome the past few days," Lazaro Archer said from his feed on another of the conference room monitors.

"Jesus Christ," Dante hissed. "Sounds too much like Crimson."

Twenty-odd years ago, a red, powder-based club drug had cropped up in Boston and elsewhere. It had spread like wildfire, and had cut a deep gash in the Breed communities, turning good sons into blood-addicted Rogues.

Sterling Chase had been one of the first to go after the drug and its creator. It was that quest that had brought him to the Order in the first place.

And if Opus had a similar narcotic now, they wouldn't be the first to use it as a weapon against those who crossed them. More than one person seated around the table here tonight could attest to that firsthand.

Chase's expression was stark and contemplative now, even after Tavia gently took his hand in hers in a show of affection and support.

"This news is all the more reason we can't delay any longer," Lucan said. "Riordan's our best lead on the Opus brotherhood right now. We may have already tipped our hand by going after that lawyer in Dublin. We can't give Riordan any more time to prepare for a strike."

He glanced to Gideon. "We're going to need all of your recon data on Riordan's stronghold. Start monitoring who's coming and going, how many men he has. We need assessments of his security setup, possible arms, all of it."

Gideon nodded. "I can be ready to brief everyone within the hour."

"Good. I want us mobilized and ready to crash his fucking gates tomorrow night."

Mathias met Lucan's gaze. "I can have my team on the ground in Dublin and ready to meet us with vehicles and any other arms and equipment we'll need. Just tell me what you want, and it'll be there waiting."

"Excellent," Lucan said.

On the third video monitor, Nikolai, the Order's commander of the Montreal team, started to chuckle beside his very pregnant Breedmate, Renata, a formidable warrior in her own right. "It's been a while since we all went out on a mission together. Gotta tell ya, I'm feeling kind of left out over here."

Renata pinned him with a widened stare. "Oh, no, you don't. If I'm grounded from this mission because of your son's pending arrival, so are you, vampire. You're the one who put us in this position, after all."

Niko grinned. "And once he's finally here, I can't wait to get us in a whole bunch of other positions."

Amid the laughter circling the room, Chase turned a serious look on Lucan. "Getting our hands on Riordan is key, but we also need to consider the lead Brynne's given us on the GNC member in London, Neville Fielding. If the human is connected to Opus, then as soon as Riordan is compromised, Fielding and the rest of the organization is going to batten down their hatches. We could drive them all to ground, and lose a prime advantage."

Lucan agreed. "Ideally, we should go after both men

at the same time. Our investigation into Fielding will need to be totally covert. He can't know we're on to him."

"He's going to be preoccupied with other things for the next couple of days," Tavia said. "Brynne mentioned that his daughter is engaged. Fielding is hosting a reception for her at his home tomorrow night."

Lucan grunted. "As much as I'd like to, we can't storm the party with a team of heavily armed warriors."

"No," Chase said. "But Brynne will be there."

Tavia eyed him cautiously. "She's JUSTIS, Sterling. We can't ask her to do the Order's work, even if she would be willing to defy her own organization to help us. She'd be risking her entire career."

"So, we send someone in with her instead. Someone who can slip away during the event and collect whatever intel or evidence there is to find onsite."

Lucan shook his head. "All of the warriors are too recognizable, even in civilian clothes. So are our mates. For that matter, any uninvited Breed male will be conspicuous. They'll be noted by Fielding and all of his security as soon as they arrive."

Tavia exhaled a short breath. "All of this assumes my sister will be open to having an Order presence there with her at all."

"We may not be able to give her that choice," Lucan replied. "She's given us her word that she's allied with us on getting rid of Opus Nostrum. We're going to need her full cooperation on this if we want to get to Fielding before the shit hits the fan with Riordan."

"Speaking of allies," Dante put in now. "Am I the only one just a bit freaked out that we have an Atlantean in the headquarters with us tonight?"

"I doubt anyone's more taken aback by Zael than my Dylan," Rio said, as he wrapped an arm around his mate.

Dylan frowned. A quiet wonder was written across her pretty, freckled face. "I still can't believe it's him— my birth father—after all this time. For the past twenty years, he was only a photo I'd been saving. He was just an intriguing mystery that my mom took to her grave. Now, he's real."

On the other side of Lucan, Gabrielle leaned forward, smiling warmly at the other woman. "It looked like the two of you had a nice reunion today."

"We did," Dylan said. "We talked for hours, about everything. I think I could've talked to him for a week and I'd still have a thousand questions."

"We all have more questions for Zael," Lucan said. "We need to know more about everything. The queen. The colony. The crystals."

Jenna smirked. "Well, he doesn't seem in a hurry to leave. He's been camped out in the archive room most of the day. I think he plans to read the entire library before he goes."

Brock grunted. "I'm sure it didn't hurt that you were in there with him. That immortal has an eye for the ladies. He could hardly keep his tongue in his mouth around you."

Jenna's brows lifted. "You sound jealous, lover. I like it."

Brock grumbled something under his breath, but his gaze was smoldering on his mate.

The meeting started to dissolve into side conversations and chatter. With the rising din of voices, the soft rap on the conference room door was barely audible. It came again, more determined this time.

"Enter." Lucan raised his head, expecting to see Darion or one of the other Boston team members not included in the Order's meeting of elders.

But it was Carys Chase.

She stepped into the room, her head held high with purpose. With a troubling resolve.

Her mother was the first to speak. "Is everything okay, sweetheart?"

"Nothing is okay," she said. "I can't take another second of waiting. I can't take the not knowing. I'm scared for Rune, and I can't sit here doing nothing."

Tavia frowned. "What do you want to do?"

"I want to help." Carys glanced past her parents, directly at Lucan. "I'm not a warrior. I don't have any training. I know that. But I'm Breed. I can do something useful, can't I?"

"Out of the question," Chase interjected. "I won't allow it, Carys."

She turned a pained look on him and slowly shook her head. "I'm not here to ask for your permission. I'm asking to be taken seriously. To be given a chance—"

Her father's gaze narrowed. "Like hell you don't need my permission."

"Would you be saying this to me if I were Aric?"

It was a direct hit, and everyone in the room felt it hit the mark. Chase said nothing, simmering in a dark silence.

For a long while, no one said anything.

Then Tavia reached over and put her hand on Chase's. Her bright gaze traveled to Lucan and all of the other Order members and mates in the room. "Maybe there is something Carys can do to help us."

CHAPTER 29

The assignment hadn't been what Carys expected, but after sleeping on the idea of the Order's proposed mission, she'd woken up in her guest room that next morning in the D.C. headquarters feeling energized and ready to prove her worth.

Knowing that whatever intel she helped to collect from the London GNC official's house this evening could be used to bring the Order closer to defeating Opus Nostrum only made her all the more eager to get started.

"Someone's up early." Brynne sailed into the kitchen, already dressed for travel in a crisp button-down and dark slacks. "Usually I'm the only one awake and walking around before sunrise."

Carys swiveled her head away from her coffee and toast to smile at the other daywalker. "I couldn't sleep."

"Anxious about the party tonight, or about the Order's mission in Dublin?"

"Both," Carys admitted, watching Brynne walk over

and put a kettle on for tea. "What I'm worried about most of all is Rune."

And worry was only part of what she felt for him. She ached without him.

She felt marrow-chilling fear and unbearable dread to think that he was back in the company of the father who'd hurt him, betrayed him. Abused him so hideously.

Brynne leaned against the counter and faced her. "You really care about this male, don't you?" She tilted her head, frowning as if she was trying to make sense of the idea. "You can forgive him even though he lied to you?"

Carys let out a sigh. "I forgave him as soon as it happened. I understand why he lied, and it doesn't make me care any less. Haven't you ever loved someone, Brynne?"

"No. I haven't." She blinked, then lifted her shoulder in a shrug. "Like your mother, for the first twenty years of my life, I didn't even really know who, or what, I was. My handler controlled everything I did, everyone I came in contact with. I grew up thinking I was unwell, some kind of freak. After the truth came out—after the manufactured life I'd been living was exposed as a lie— I felt I needed to start my life all over again. After wasting all of those years, I wanted to do something purposeful, something real. Most of all, I never wanted to allow anyone to control me ever again. I don't ask for permission. And I don't let anyone tell me no."

Carys recalled her advice from the other day in Boston. "As you told me, if I really want something, I have to reach for it."

"And you did." Brynne smiled in acknowledgment. "I'll be glad to have you with me tonight at the councilman's party. With your shadow-bending ability and photographic memory, you couldn't be more perfect for the task."

Carys nodded. "At least I'll have something to keep my mind occupied while I wait for word about the mission to Riordan's place."

"We're going to be kept in constant contact once the Order arrives in Dublin. You'll also be wired to Gideon here in D.C. while you're in Fielding's house. I'm sure everything's going to be fine."

Carys hoped she was right about that. But the simple truth was, no one had been able to promise her that she'd see Rune again. They couldn't make that promise.

Rune's fate was in his own hands now.

And as much as Carys wanted to be with her father and the rest of the Order when they stormed Riordan's stronghold tonight, she knew they would never permit it.

Her thoughts were heavy as she finished her toast and drank the last of her coffee. "Our flight will be leaving soon," she murmured. "I should say my goodbyes and get my things."

Brynne nodded, palming her steaming cup of tea. "We can go as soon as you're ready."

~ ~ ~

The sunrise beckoned Brynne outside. Taking her cup of tea onto the stone courtyard and gardens behind the Order's expansive mansion, she inhaled the crisp morning air as she drifted to the edge of the terraced patio.

Fragrant clusters of roses and peonies perfumed the

gentle breeze, along with another, more exotic scent that drew her attention toward the far left of the sprawling courtyard.

A man stood there.

The Atlantean.

Shirtless, barefoot, dressed only in a pair of faded jeans that hung low on his hips. His eyes were closed and his arms were opened wide, his head tipped back in silent meditation under the peachy hues of the early morning sun.

Amid last night's chaos at the Order's headquarters, Brynne hadn't seen the immortal who'd come to meet with Lucan Thorne earlier that week. But there was no mistaking the golden male now.

His smooth, sun-kissed skin glistened in the warm light. His shoulder-length waves made her fingers itch with the urge to test the copper-shot strands to see if they felt as silky as they looked. She scowled at the thought and gripped her cup of tea bit tighter.

Still, she couldn't pull her gaze away from him. Even motionless, power radiated off his strong, lean body and muscled limbs. Every inch of him seemed lovingly sculpted by a master who appreciated each graceful curve of sinew and velvety plane of skin.

God, he was beautiful.

No other word for him. Brynne's mouth watered as she studied him over the rim of her cup. An uninvited stirring made her sink her teeth into her bottom lip. A small moan began to uncurl in the back of her throat, but she mentally tamped it down.

At least, she thought she had.

Apparently not.

Because at that same instant the Atlantean's squared

chin dropped and his head swiveled in her direction. Tropical blue eyes collided with her appalled and embarrassed gaze.

It was already too late to pretend she hadn't been gawking, but Brynne's feet were in motion anyway. She pivoted to make a hasty escape—and to her horror, she fumbled her cup of tea.

"Shit!"

The cup slipped out of her grasp, smashing onto the patio bricks. Tea geysered upward like a small fountain and shards of delicate china exploded in all directions.

"Shit, shit, shit!" Brynne dropped to a crouch and began collecting the mess.

"Here, let me help you with that."

She did not want to look up and acknowledge the decadently deep voice or the man it belonged to. Although there was no ignoring him—not when he'd stood across the courtyard from her, and most certainly not when he was hunkered down next to her, half-naked and radiating preternatural heat and masculine power.

This close, his unearthly spicy scent licked at all of her senses. And everything female in her responded, no matter how hard she tried to pretend he didn't affect her.

"I've got it," she murmured, her voice coming out of her in breathy rasp. "It's just a broken cup. There's no need to help me."

"I know there's no need," he said, continuing to pick up the errant pieces.

Brynne blew out a sharp sigh. "I'm not usually so clumsy. I don't know how I did this."

"You must've been distracted by something."

Did she hear him correctly? And was that the hint of a chuckle in his voice?

As much as she wanted to get away from him without so much as a glance at his too-close, handsome face, her head snapped up. He was staring at her, a grin tugging at the corners of his sensual mouth. And the arrogant gleam in his incredible blue eyes was unmistakable.

"I wasn't distracted," she informed him tightly. "I don't get distracted."

"No? So, you came out here deliberately to watch me?" His cocky grin widened. "I'm flattered."

Why the hell her stomach should be doing a little flip at his teasing was beyond her. And why her pulse was suddenly hammering in a tempo too eager to be outrage, she really didn't want to know.

Brynne tilted her head at him, frowning. "What you are is mistaken. And I'm perfectly capable of picking up after myself, so if you don't mind . . ."

"I don't mind at all."

Ignoring her protests, he gathered the last of the pieces and held them all in one hand. Then he stood up and reached out to her with his free hand.

Brynne stared skeptically at his large palm and long, elegant fingers. "You're not going to zap me with that Atlantean glowy trick, are you?"

He shrugged. "You might enjoy it."

"Ha. I doubt it."

Humor still danced in his eyes as she stood on her own, bypassing his offered hand. "Are all Breed females this skittish around men?"

"Are all Atlantean males so certain of their own charm?"

He smirked. "This one is."

Brynne snorted a laugh as she took the broken cup

inside to throw it away. He followed.

"I'm Ekizael, in case you're too shy to ask. Friends call me Zael."

She pivoted to face him. "In that case, hello, Ekizael. I'm Brynne."

He made an amused sound in the back of his throat. "Distracted, skittish and dismissive. How intriguing."

"Arrogant, presumptuous and insolent. How predictable."

"Predictable?" He chuckled. "That's one thing I've rarely been accused of."

Why did her body have to react as if he'd just said something sexual? She pushed the sensation aside. "Well, they say there's a first time for everything."

"Hmm," he said. "By the way, arrogant, presumptuous and insolent all mean roughly the same thing."

Brynne smiled sweetly. "Since we just met, perhaps I thought it would be too rude to say annoying."

Now he frowned. "Am I annoying you? I apologize. From the pretty flush of your cheeks and the uptick of your pulse, I thought we were getting acquainted rather enjoyably. Exchanging some friendly banter. Possibly even flirting."

God help her, but the heat in her face flamed even hotter now, and all over, her skin felt too warm, too tight beneath her clothes. She lifted her chin. "I don't have time for banter, and I never flirt."

"Really?" His voice was somewhere between a growl and a purr, a sound that sent her blood drumming in her temples and in several points lower. His gaze drank her in shamelessly before returning to hers. "That is a tragedy, Brynne."

Before she could respond with a searing retort, several pairs of footsteps approached. Carys strode in alongside Jordana and Nova.

The three women stopped abruptly, falling into an odd silence as if they too could feel the electricity in the air.

Jordana smiled brightly. "Brynne, I see you've met my friend, Zael. Isn't he charming?"

Brynne raised a brow in the Atlantean's direction. "Charming doesn't even begin to describe him."

Zael's chuckle was meant for her alone. "Until we meet again, Brynne. The pleasure was mine."

"Yes, it was," she agreed, smiling pointedly. She turned to Carys. "Ready to go?"

"All set."

Thank God. Brynne couldn't get away fast enough from Zael and his disturbing effect on her. Hopefully, it would be a good long while before she ever found herself in the arrogant Atlantean's presence again.

CHAPTER 30

Little had changed in the long years that Rune had been gone from his father's castle Darkhaven.

The musty, cool dampness of the old stone walls and worn slate floor seeped into his bones the instant he was brought inside by his uncle and the other armed guards. Their footsteps echoed hollowly as they progressed down the main passage into the heart of the ancient fortress.

"Fineas is waiting for you down below," Ennis told him. "Reckon you remember the way, eh, boyo?"

Rune didn't have to ask where they were taking him. There was only one thing below the main floor of the stronghold. And, yes, he still recalled the path, down the spiraling flight of stairs, then through the winding corridor of the underground portion of the keep.

He strode ahead of the guns trained on his back, bracing himself as the sound of his father's low voice reached his ears. The guttural chuckle had haunted his dreams for years after he'd fled this place.

Now it was all Rune could do to resist the urge to lunge forward and attack in a murderous rage as soon as Fineas Riordan's dark head and broad shoulders came into view on the catwalk gallery overlooking the pit below.

As much as Rune wanted the bastard's throat between his teeth, there were five semiautomatic pistols poised to open fire on him the instant he showed any hint of aggression. If he meant to get back to Boston after he was finished here—back to Carys, if she would have him—he had no choice but to keep his rage on a tight leash for now.

Thoughts of Carys put a cold ache in the center of his chest.

She had been on his mind every minute since he'd been gone. The terrible way they had parted. Her beautiful face, stricken with worry and confusion as she saw him with his father's men and heard the unfamiliar name they'd called him. She had seen their scarab tattoos, and Rune could tell she knew what those marks meant. She knew who they belonged to, and now she knew that he, too, belonged to Fineas Riordan.

Rune had broken her heart in that moment. He only hoped she'd be willing to forgive him. That she might still love him enough to consider taking him back once he returned to her.

But first, he would have to survive the coming confrontation with the monster who'd sired him.

His uncle nudged Rune forward with an ungentle shove as they drew near the catwalk above the pit. "Here's your special delivery, brother. All the way from Boston."

Fineas Riordan swiveled his head away from a pair

of armed Breed males who were watching the combat along with him. When his dark gaze met Rune's eyes, a brittle chill seeped into their fathomless depths.

"It has been quite a while, son. I have to say, I was very disappointed when you left."

Rune couldn't curb his sharply exhaled breath. "You must've been bored without me here to provide your entertainment."

A thin, evil smile spread across his lips. "Oh, I managed to find other diversions."

Rune's guards guided him out onto the viewing gallery. In the dirt-floored, stone enclosure below, a pair of Breed males were engaged in a tremendous fight.

Sweat-soaked, bloodied, with flesh torn in numerous places, the two combatants fought with fists and fangs. Their eyes blazed with hot amber, and their pupils were so thinned, the vertical slits were hardly discernible. The males' *dermaglyphs* churned like tempests on their bruised and lacerated bodies as they crashed into each other in a blur of gnashing teeth and punishing blows.

The fight was brutal, animalistic. A feral display of Breed strength and savagery.

Worse than anything Rune had experienced in that hellish circle of granite and sand.

It was . . . unnaturally violent.

Rune's question must have shown in his eyes, because when his father glanced over at him, a broad smile broke across his face.

"Exciting, isn't it? Talk about performance enhancement." He glanced back down into the pit. "The drug was only a prototype until a few weeks ago. Soon it will be in every major city across Europe and the United States. How long do you think it will take the humans before they beg for someone to make the madness stop?"

Rune stared at him, abhorred. "About as long as it will take them to declare war on the entire Breed population."

His father shrugged, thoroughly unfazed. "Ah, well. Either way."

He laughed, and was joined by Ennis and the rest of the guards.

Rune's veins throbbed with disgust. He had always suspected Fineas Riordan was insane, but now he realized it was something even worse than that. He was psychopathic. "You really wouldn't care, would you? Not so long as you can get off watching others in pain."

Riordan stared down at the worsening combat below. "You always did have a weak stomach when it came to these things. I blame your mother for that."

"Is that why you killed her?"

He glanced over, brows raised in surprise. "I didn't realize you knew that."

Hatred seethed in Rune. "I didn't until you just confirmed it."

Riordan waved his hand as if to dismiss the whole idea as he returned his attention to the pit. "She was a bad match from the start. I should've known better than to take her to mate. The bitch could take a punch, I'll grant her that. But raise a hand to anyone else and she crumbled. She never approved of my . . . inclinations. Eventually, I simply got tired of her judgment."

Rune listened in simmering fury to his father's admission. He thought about the gentle woman who'd borne him. Her unique Breedmate gift for withstanding extreme pain had been passed down to him. As a boy thrown into the pit, Rune had leaned on that ability to endure his father's training. Over time, he'd learned to fight without calling upon it, and hadn't used it once since he'd left his father's domain.

But his mother . . .

Rune had been too young, too blind. He had no idea she was being abused, as tortured by Riordan as he was. The realization now made a growl boil up the back of his throat.

"You sick bastard. I should've killed you back then."

The guns held at Rune's spine and the back of his head inched closer at the threat, but his father only chuckled. "Don't be such a pussy, son. Life is pain. I'd have thought I taught you that, if nothing else."

"You taught me a lot of things," Rune muttered.

Riordan looked over at him. "Good. That training will pay off for you even more lucratively than it has in Boston all these years now that you're home again. You've been building your little empire over there, but I've been busy building too. My comrades and I have been laying the foundation in secret for years. Now, we're nearly ready to put our plans in motion."

"What comrades?" Rune asked. "What fucking plans?"

His father studied him for a long moment. "You really don't know?" A wicked glint shone in his dark eyes. "Opus Nostrum, boyo. You're looking at its new leader."

Jesus Christ.

His sick fuck of a father was the current head of that terror group?

Did the Order know? If not, he needed to get that information into their hands as soon as possible. What's more, he needed to get as much intel on his father as he could before he murdered the bastard with his bare hands.

"Congratulations," Rune gritted out tightly. "You must be very proud."

"Oh, I am. But I'll be even prouder once the world understands that Opus is the only true power. If they want peace, the world will come through us to secure it. If not, we'll be ready to deliver a war like no one has ever seen."

"How do you intend to do that?"

Riordan wagged a finger. "Patience, son. We'll have time to talk about all of that later. Right now, I want to enjoy the match." He bared his teeth and fangs in a sadistic smile. "We're just getting to the best part."

In the pit below, the combat had escalated. One of the Breed males was finally tiring. His shoulder was ripped wide open, the arm dangling uselessly at his side. His opponent flew at him on a bellow that shook the ancient rafters overhead. The two massive bodies crashed together, and the weakened vampire was slammed onto the dirt floor.

Fangs gleamed like daggers as the pair bit and gnashed at each other, powerful fists striking and connecting in a blur of speed and brutality. Blood sprayed from arteries torn open in the struggle. Howls of anguish and fury rose to a deafening level from the enclosure far below.

The male on the bottom couldn't hope to hold off the other. Disabled, fatigued, he made the fatal error of leaving his throat open for attack. His opponent seized it, hitting as hard as a viper.

Fangs sank deep and shredded the other vampire's

neck in a single strike, all but severing the head from its body.

The victor lifted his head in a shout of triumph, blood and gore dripping from his enormous fangs. There was no humanity left in that face. Nothing but madness and savagery.

Beside Rune, his father and the other Riordan men hooted and applauded the finish. They were giddy with enthusiasm, avid in their enjoyment of the sadistic spectacle below.

The champion seemed to notice his audience for the first time now.

Lips parted, breath sawing out of him, he cocked his head and stared directly up at Rune and the others on the catwalk high above.

He gave no warning of what he was about to do.

One moment he was crouched atop his dead opponent, the next he was airborne—leaping up from the floor of the pit with a feral snarl.

"Holy shit!"

Rune jumped back as the big male vaulted at them. His father and the other men didn't so much as flinch.

Rune understood why less than a second later.

The fighter's escape was stopped by an invisible barrier. The very instant his body connected with it, bright sparks exploded. Pungent smoke and blinding light made Rune avert his eyes—though not before he realized the vampire was dead.

Or, rather, ashed on the spot. Once the stench and sparks had dissipated, the massive body of the Breed male was nothing but a small cloud of floating dust.

Rune gaped. "What the fuck?"

"UV webbing." His father grinned. "I've made some

improvements to the pit since you've been here last."

He waved Ennis away with a pointed nod, then started walking. Behind Rune, the guns at his back encouraged him to follow.

"Come, Aedan. I'd like to talk about your friends in the Order."

CHAPTER 31

Ⅽ

More than a hundred people, Breed and human, filled the ballroom of Councilman Fielding's mansion in London at nine o'clock that evening. A small orchestra played in the background as the arriving guests made their way along a receiving line toward the newly engaged couple and their beaming sets of parents.

Brynne made introductions for Carys to JUSTIS colleagues and other guests, explaining that she was the daughter of a friend back in the States, who was visiting London for a brief summer holiday. Carys, in an elegant black pantsuit and heels, smiled and shook hands as she and Brynne progressed down the line. All the while, she studied the layout of the house and its numerous archways and passages leading off to the foyer and other rooms from the bustling ballroom.

After a Breed dignitary from Africa and his mate stepped forward to greet the hosts, Brynne leaned close to Carys and spoke around a pleasant smile. "Stop touching your ear, darling. We don't want to draw unwanted attention."

Dammit. She wasn't used to espionage, and it was damn hard to ignore the tiny transmitter and GPS tracker she carried in her left ear. "Sorry," she whispered quietly.

Gideon's voice replied, equally covert. "No worries. Just pretend I'm not here. You know what you need to do, right? Locate Fielding's office, search for any kind of hard intel you can find—login IDs, passwords, calendar appointments, anything at all. Then scatter those bugs I gave you and get the hell out of there."

"Mm-hmm." Carys knew her instructions. She also knew to turn on her best smile as Brynne shook hands with Fielding's wife.

"Such a beautiful night for this happy event," Brynne was saying. She brought Carys forward to meet the GNC official and his wife. "Mr. and Mrs. Fielding, I'd like to introduce Carys Fairchild, the daughter of a dear friend of mine from Boston."

Carys didn't so much as blink at the use of her mother's maiden name. She played along, extending her hand to the portly, middle-aged councilman and his wife.

"How nice to meet you," Mrs. Fielding cooed. She turned and made further introductions to their daughter and her new fiancé, and to the Fieldings' adult son, Simon.

The introverted twenty-something human had his father's pear-shaped body and thinning tangle of curly brown hair, but his mother's soft blue eyes. He blinked at Carys from behind thick-lensed glasses, and, with an awkward bob of his head, took her hand in a clammy, limp grasp.

"Carys is from Boston," his mother informed him

cheerfully. "Simon will be speaking at an economics seminar there next month. Perhaps he'll tell you all about it. Would you like that, Carys?"

"Of course," she replied, dreading the prospect already. "That sounds fascinating."

Gideon's quiet chuckle was a tickle in her ear. "Smoothly done. Welcome to the glamour of covert ops."

"Hmm. Now you tell me," she whispered, turning her face aside to mask the subtle movement of her lips.

Brynne had since gone on to gush over the Fieldings' home, which they had only moved into a couple of weeks ago. "Such a lovely property. And so expansive too. Are there eight bedrooms upstairs?"

"Ten," Mrs. Fielding replied, beaming. "And that doesn't count Neville's study and meeting rooms, which occupy most of the entire east wing."

Carys hid her reaction, as did Brynne, who covered the direct hit with a light tease about having plenty of room for future grandchildren. With the receiving line reaching its end now, the women laughed and began chatting about the upcoming wedding and preparations being made for the honeymoon.

Carys, meanwhile, took the opportunity to fade back into the crowd.

She drifted casually through the scores of elegantly dressed people. A passing server offered her a flute of champagne, which she accepted with a smile before continuing on her incremental, yet deliberate path toward the far end of the ballroom.

She wended her way deeper into the throng, slowing to watch the handful of couples who were now moving onto the dance floor as the orchestra began to play a waltz. She moved on, laughing along with a few of the guests, and pausing here and there to feign interest in the mansion's art.

Bringing her glass to her lips, Carys murmured her position to Gideon. "I'm heading for the exit on the east end of the house. As soon as I see my chance—"

"Uh . . . Miss Fairchild?"

The hesitant croak of a male voice drew her attention sharply. She schooled her expression to one of mild surprise. "Oh, hello again, Simon."

"Hello." He fell back into an awkward silence. Standing there, he fidgeted with the buttoned collar of his dress shirt beneath the tight bow tie at his throat. Then he thrust his hand out at her, palm up. She frowned, uncertain what he wanted.

"Would you care to dance?"

Inside her ear, Gideon's laugh sounded choked and far too amused.

Oh, shit. Seriously? "I, um . . ." She glanced around, casting for an excuse.

But she had no plausible reason to say no, and Simon's face was so pitifully hopeful, she didn't have the heart to refuse him. Besides, she was there to blend in with the other guests. If she was lucky, maybe she could wheedle some useful information out of Fielding's son.

"All right. I would be happy to dance with you."

Setting her half-empty champagne flute down on a nearby tray, she placed her fingers into Simon's moist palm and let him lead her out to the dance floor.

~ ~ ~

"I hear you've earned quite a reputation for yourself in

the ring in Boston," his father said, walking behind Rune with his armed thugs in the dank chill of the passageway. "I hear you're unbeatable. A killer."

Rune grunted. "You taught me everything I know."

"Yes, I did." There was a smile in that thin voice. "Glad to know you'll admit it."

They continued on, around a wide bend that led toward the old store rooms of the fortress. The guards yanked Rune to a stop outside a large, iron-banded door. Riordan stepped around them and stuck a key into the heavy lock. He gave it a twist and shot a smirk over his shoulder at Rune.

"Maybe I should be demanding my share of your profits, eh, boyo?"

Rune kept his voice level, his rage on a low simmer. "You don't deserve a fucking thing."

Except an excruciating death, which he couldn't wait to deliver.

Riordan's face hardened, but then he shrugged. "I don't need money. I'm not looking for anything as mundane as that anymore. I trade in something far more valuable now."

Rune scoffed. "Flesh and blood?"

"When it pleases me, yes. But my preferred currency is power."

With the lock freed, Riordan unfastened the latch and pushed the old wooden door open. At his nod, the guards shoved Rune ahead of them into the room.

Scores of sealed barrels, shipping crates and large steel boxes were stored inside. Riordan motioned for a couple of his men to open some. They carefully pried loose a barrel lid, then levered the top off a sealed wood crate and removed one of the small boxes from inside it.

As Rune was guided toward the containers, he saw brick-sized packages of fine red powder filling the barrel. Inside the large crate were cushioned boxes holding hundreds of thin glass cylinders, all of them glowing with a milky blue light in their center. There were dozens of containers holding each type of supply. So many, they filled the large storage chamber.

"As I said, I trade in power now." Smiling, Riordan gestured around him. "My war chest, courtesy of Opus Nostrum. I have enough narcotics to create an army of bloodthirsty savages, and enough liquid UV weaponry at my disposal to eradicate half the Breed population around the world."

"You're sick," Rune spat. "You'll never get the chance to use any of this shit. Not you, and not Opus either."

"Who's going to stop us, boyo? You? Your friends in the Order?" He chuckled as he slowly shook his head. "Imagine my shock when the scouts I'd sent to Boston reported back to me that they'd not only found you in that city, but found you rubbing elbows with warriors from Lucan Thorne's Order. I have to say, it made me curious."

Rune shrugged. "The arena draws a diverse crowd. Everyone loves a good fight, as you well know."

Riordan's expression was darker than skeptical. "What interest does the Order have with you or the club? Have they been asking you questions about me, perhaps? Do they know I'm a part of Opus Nostrum?"

When Rune remained silent, his face impassive, Riordan's questions took on a more impatient tone.

"Are they planning to come after me? They got too damn close the other night, when they nearly had their hands on that idiot lawyer of mine, Ivers. Have they found the information he's been protecting? How much do they know about me and my Opus brothers?"

Rune couldn't help but take some satisfaction in the edge of panic in his father's voice. Despite the power he was so eager to boast about, Fineas Riordan spoke now as if he could feel a noose closing around his neck. Deep down, beneath all of his bravado, Riordan was worried that his twisted little empire could come crashing down around his head.

And Rune was planning to do whatever he could to make that happen.

Rune chuckled, genuinely amused. "Save your paranoia for the Order. Even if I knew, I would never tell you anything."

His father studied him narrowly. "No . . . you don't know, do you? They haven't told you anything. Do they even realize you're my son?"

Rune scoffed. "No one does." Not until Carys found out so harshly last night. "I buried your name when I left here. I'd planned to take the shame of it to my grave."

Cold eyes hardened with the insult. "Careful, Aedan. You know I can easily arrange that. I might even enjoy it."

"Did you enjoy killing my mother too?" Rune's voice was brittle, filled with all the animosity he was struggling to keep inside. "She was your blood-bonded mate, for fuck's sake. Any pain you inflicted on her would've been echoed in your own veins."

His father smiled. "Like I said, your mother could weather a great deal of punishment. It took a long time to break her. And yes, I felt each blow, every skin-rending lash. I savored them, if you want to know the truth."

Rune's answering growl sounded lethal, even to his own ears. His muscles twitched with the need to smash the sadistic grin from Riordan's face. His tension must have been noticeable, because two of the guards with guns trained on his back now moved around to the front, hemming him in from all sides.

"My second mate was less of challenge," his father remarked, so casually, he might have been talking about the weather. "I ended her as soon as she ceased to hold my interest."

At this new admission, a heavy dread settled over Rune. He'd been avoiding asking about his mother's replacement or the little girl who'd followed. Now, he had to know. "What about Kitty? Where is she?"

A spark of evil interest lit Riordan's gaze. "Ah, you remember that tender piece of ass, eh? My men and I had some good times with that one too. But then the sneaky little bitch ran away and never came back. She could be dead for all I care. She was all used up, anyway."

Rage boiled up inside Rune when he considered all the horrors that repulsive answer implied. "She was an innocent child, you sadistic pig."

He couldn't contain his fury now. It erupted out of him on a roar.

Fuck saving Riordan for the Order. Fuck the need for intel on Opus Nostrum. He needed to destroy this monster now, and if it got him killed in the process, so be it.

Rune lunged. Even before he was in motion, he heard the pop of a shot being fired. Something sharp jabbed into the back of his neck. Several somethings.

Not bullets. Darts?

Fire seeped into his veins, instantly sapping the feeling from his limbs. He went down fast. As his body hit the hard slate of the floor, he realized he'd been hit with a massive sedative. His muscles ceased working. He lay there, paralyzed, his vision beginning to cloud over.

He saw Riordan's boots step past his face, tauntingly close.

The last thing Rune heard before blackness closed over him was his father's toneless voice. "Drag him out of here. Dump him in the pit until I decide what to do with him."

CHAPTER 32

The only intel Carys gathered from Simon Fielding was that he knew absolutely nothing of his father's activities or his colleagues. The younger Fielding's knowledge about biflation and fiscal multipliers, however, was seemingly endless.

It had taken three waltzes before Carys had finally managed to get away from him. Apologizing that the champagne had gone straight to her head and that she needed some fresh air, she had evaded Simon's offer to escort her outside and, instead, slipped out on her own.

"I thought he'd never stop talking," she whispered to Gideon on the other end of her transmitter.

"Neither did I. Where are you now?"

"I just saw Simon go back into the ballroom, so I'm headed inside." She reentered the house through a different pair of French doors, emerging in a quiet, dimly lit section of hallway several yards away from the bustle of the reception. "Okay, I'm going stealth now."

Gathering the shadows around her, Carys shrank

back from the rest of the party and headed for the staff stairwell at the back of the corridor.

"I'm going up to the second floor, where Fielding's study is," she whispered to Gideon.

"Got your signal on the move in front of me," he confirmed.

With no one around to see or hear her, she couldn't resist the need for a mission update on the Order. "How long before the warriors land?"

"They're still en route, but they should have boots on the ground in Dublin and wheels in motion about four hours from now."

She didn't know if the news made her feel better or worse. Anxiety had been riding her ever since she and Brynne had left D.C. that morning. The Order had been gearing up and planning to depart a few hours after she had, and the wait for news had been excruciating. "I wish I could be with them tonight instead of here. I need to see him. I should be there for Rune."

"Listen, no one wants this to end badly for him," Gideon said. "Not even your father."

"I hope you're right." She sucked in a breath as the sound of subdued female voices and approaching footsteps on soft wool rugs carried from around the corner of the passage up ahead. "Shit. Someone's coming."

She went still and silent, keeping herself close to the wall as a pair of housekeepers carrying armfuls of used linens to the laundry room rounded the bend and walked right past her, unaware. As soon as they were gone, Carys beelined for the east wing.

Tall double doors sealed off the expansive wing from the guest rooms and the rest of the second floor. She tried the handles and found them locked. A concentrated mental command was all it took to open them.

Slipping inside the vacant, dimly lit chamber, Carys closed the door behind her, then let her concealing shadows drop away.

"I'm in," she advised Gideon.

Ambient light from a handful of wall sconces bathed the enormous space in a warm glow. The large study contained a desk and credenza, with a seating area off to the side. Carys drifted inside, past the sumptuous leather club chairs and Chesterfield sofa that sat before a massive fireplace.

Other rooms branched off the main suite. A conference room with chairs for a dozen people. A huge library with towering bookcases and an elegant reading nook. Even an exercise room filled with gleaming equipment and floor-to-ceiling mirrors on the walls.

Carys headed straight for the councilman's work area. "There's a tablet on the desk," she informed Gideon in a whisper as she opened the computer and woke it from sleep mode. "Dammit. It's password-protected."

"No problem," Gideon replied. "I can get in later. That's why you have the bugs."

She reached into her pantsuit pocket to retrieve one of the wafer-thin, clear strips of technology Gideon had given her. Peeling off the backing, she stuck the bug on the underside of Fielding's tablet. Once applied, the covert device all but disappeared against the metal casing.

"Done," she said. "Checking paper files now."

She mentally unlocked the credenza and began

sifting through the files and folders inside. "I see some GNC contracts in here, three months' of meeting minutes, committee membership lists . . ."

Her voice trailed off as she scanned the documents for names, appointment references—anything that might prove helpful to the Order in establishing the councilman's activities and interests. Not to mention any associations that might give off a whiff of corruption.

Gideon's voice sounded in her ear as she committed page after page to memory. "Better make it quick, Carys. We need to get the rest of those bugs planted in the other rooms in that suite. To play it safe, you can't afford to be gone more than a few minutes."

"Right." She closed the file drawer and hurried to complete the rest of her assignment. With most of them placed in the meeting rooms and other antechambers, she stepped inside the exercise room. "Just one bug left. You want it on the treadmill or the ski simulator? I doubt Fielding gives either one much action."

Gideon chuckled. "Take your pick."

She looked for something that might get the most use. Something the human male might keep nearby if he was in the room. "How about the TV remote?"

"Perfect," Gideon said. "Stick it and get the hell out of there."

She flipped the small remote over and had just applied the bug when something odd caught her eye. She paused, watching the tiny red light from the remote reflect on one of the mirrored panels on the back wall.

Except it didn't quite *reflect* . . .

No, it seemed to shoot right through the glass.

"Huh. That's strange."

"Talk to me, Carys. What's going on?"

"I'm not sure," she murmured, setting the remote down and walking over to have a closer look. "I think there's something behind the glass . . ."

She reached up and felt around the edges of the panel. Her fingertips grazed a small bump along the right side—a button. She pressed it, and the mirror popped open.

"Oh, my God. There's another room back here."

Not much of a room. Nothing like the spacious, opulent chambers of the suite outside. This was more of a deep, hidden alcove.

Peering into the darkness, she saw a simple desk containing a computer workstation with a large monitor. If Neville Fielding had secrets, this was obviously where they'd find them.

"I'm going in." She stepped over the threshold.

"Carys, for fuck's sake, just be caref—"

"Gideon?" she whispered as she crept farther inside. "Gideon, are you there?"

Shit. Only silence answered. Their signal must have cut off, she guessed, taking in the soundproofed walls and ceiling that surrounded her.

She padded over to the desk. The computer on it was powered down, but still warm. Beside it was some kind of communications system.

What the hell was Fielding using this for? Who did he talk to on this secret workstation, hidden behind a concealed door in a house that only a man with ten times his wealth could possibly afford?

There was only one answer, of course. One explanation.

Opus Nostrum.

Dammit. She had to go back out and try to retrieve

one of the bugs she'd placed elsewhere. This was the room the Order needed to monitor.

She spun around and started hurrying back toward the hidden door.

"Gideon," she whispered. "Can you hear me?"

The transmitter in her ear was still utterly silent.

And in the quiet that engulfed her, she felt a queer prickling of her senses.

She wasn't alone.

Someone was there with her now.

She started to gather the shadows around her, but it was already too late. No sooner had she realized the danger, she came face-to-face with the big body and threatening stance of a Breed male now blocking the portal to the exercise room.

Oh, God. It was *him*.

The leader of Riordan's thugs who'd shown up at La Notte.

Now, he wore a tailored suit and a glossy silk tie, looking every bit the gentleman . . . except for the threatening twist of his mouth and the lethal coldness of his stare.

"Well, isn't this a surprise," he muttered. "The Breedmate bitch from Boston."

Carys swallowed hard, even as the blood drained from her face. She had to will her Breed instincts to heel under the freezing blast of the deadly male's glare.

"What are you doing here?" she asked, the only thing she could think to say.

"I think the better question is, what are you doing here? Snooping around in places you don't belong." He reached out and snatched the transmitter from her ear, moving so swiftly even her Breed senses could hardly track him. The tiny device disappeared into his clenched fist. "You're involved in a dangerous business, my dear. A careless girl could get killed if she crosses the wrong people."

Carys was smart enough to be afraid, but she couldn't worry about herself in that moment. Not when this bastard had taken the man she loved. She hiked up her chin. "Where's Rune? What have you and Fineas Riordan done with him?"

He grinned, fangs flashing in the semidarkness. "If you want to see him alive again—if you want to leave this house with your pretty throat intact—you'll come with me now."

CHAPTER 33

B rynne smiled and nodded, not even half-listening as
one of her human JUSTIS colleagues regaled her
and a few other party attendees with a long-winded
account of his recent golf holiday in Scotland. Holding
her warm, untouched glass of champagne, Brynne
scanned the gathering for any sign of Carys.

It had been more than an hour since she's last seen
her.

Brynne had watched her slip away from Simon
Fielding to escape outside alone. When Carys hadn't
returned to the ballroom, Brynne had assumed she'd
begun her reconnaissance mission in the councilman's
chambers upstairs.

But even if she had disappeared into the shadows at
that time, Carys was taking much too long to finish. The
absence was making Brynne more than a little nervous
now.

And with each minute that passed, she couldn't
shake the feeling that something was wrong.

"Will you excuse me, please?" she murmured to her group of colleagues. "I just remembered I have to make a quick call."

She ditched her glass on a passing server's tray and already had her comm unit in hand to contact the Order's headquarters when the phone buzzed with an incoming call. Gideon's deep voice came on as soon as she picked up.

"Brynne, is Carys with you?"

"No." And the fact that he had to ask made her pulse tick even faster. She stepped into a quiet corner and spoke just above a whisper. "I haven't seen her for a while now. Aren't you in contact with her through the transmitter?"

"I lost the connection about an hour ago, when she was inside Fielding's chambers. The GPS signal is still reporting from the building, but I haven't been able to reestablish audio yet."

"Are you sure she's here? I've been watching for her all this time, and she hasn't come back to the ballroom or any of the other reception areas."

"That's why I called," Gideon said. "I don't have a good feeling, either. I was hoping you'd do a quick search for her, just to confirm we have visual on her."

"Of course." Brynne was already walking.

"I have your comm's GPS signal in front of me now," he told her. "Carys's signal is due south of yours, moving at a good clip."

Brynne picked up her pace, trying to walk casually, yet swiftly. She weaved through the crowd of party guests, heading in the direction Gideon sent her.

"I think the kitchens are back this way," she told him, nearly to the tall, open doors at the back of the main reception room. She'd seen dozens of tuxedoed servers pass through those doors most of the night with food and beverage trays.

As she hurried along, someone called her name and waved to her from within the throng. The Breedmate of her supervisor, smiling and trying to get her attention. Brynne shot the woman an apologetic look and pointed to her phone as if she was on a call that couldn't be interrupted. Which was certainly the truth.

"Carys just turned a corner now," Gideon advised. "She's moving away from you, Brynne."

"Shit." She ducked through the tall doors behind one of the exiting servers. She followed the curving corridor, which dumped her into the clatter of the busy kitchens. Catering people and servers were all over the place, hustling here and there with their trays. "Am I getting closer?"

"Yeah, you're practically on top of her now. She should be right in front of you, not even two yards away. She's stopped moving now."

Brynne frowned, pivoting where she stood. There was no one near her except cooks and kitchen staff.

"Gideon, you must be mistaken. She can't be in here. I don't . . ."

The words dried up on Brynne's tongue as her gaze landed on a serving tray that had apparently been recently returned to the kitchen. Used glasses and soiled linens lay heaped on the tray. And there was something else there too . . .

"Oh, my God." Brynne's stomach plummeted.

Peeking out from within the folds of one of the white napkins was a small wire and earbud.

"Gideon, she's been found out. Carys is gone.

Someone's taken her."

~ ~ ~

Fineas Riordan's Darkhaven was an ancient, craggy stone castle that looked exactly like the kind of place that would house a monster.

Carys didn't know what she'd been expecting after her captor—Riordan's brother—took her out of London in a piloted private jet, then dumped her into the backseat of a chauffeured car that drove them several miles outside of Dublin. But as they drew nearer to the forbidding fortress, her heart bled for the boy who'd been raised in this place under the violent conditions Rune had described.

She ached even more sharply for the man she loved, and she could only pray that Riordan's brother hadn't been lying when he'd implied Rune was still alive. That there was still hope he might be able to leave this place unharmed and return home to Boston, where he belonged.

It was that thin hope that had convinced Carys to play her captor's game by pretending she was, in fact, merely a Breedmate. Everything Breed in her vibrated with aggression and seething hatred. It had been nearly impossible to walk along docilely out the back of Fielding's house, and to resist the powerful urge to leap on Riordan's brother and tear out his throat.

She had to admit, the holstered semiautomatic pistol he carried on his hip helped keep her in check too.

He held the gun on her as they exited the vehicle and he took her by the arm. The nose of the pistol jabbed against her ribs was a steady reminder to maintain her composure as she was led across the gravel drive and into the castle's main entrance.

Carys was taken down a flight of stone stairs that descended from the heart of the fortress to at least a full story below ground. Far enough down that the heavy sounds of mortal combat and bone-chilling, animalistic roars coming from somewhere in the bowels of the keep hadn't been audible until she neared the bottom step.

Now, the awful sounds filled her ears. Dread made every step seem endless as she walked through the corridor with her captor. Up ahead, two other Breed males waited on a catwalk suspended above an open chamber below. One of them, a hulking guard holding a nasty-looking assault rifle, stood at sober attention. The other leaned forward as though he didn't have a care in the world, his elbows resting casually on the railing of the catwalk.

She didn't have to guess who the second male was.

Fineas Riordan shared the same sharp features and dark hair as his brother. The same cold eyes and thin, cruel mouth. He leered at her as she approached, his tongue sliding out to slowly, deliberately, wet his lips.

"Come," he beckoned. "Ennis, bring her over before she misses the best part."

A sick feeling gnawed at her insides as she stepped onto the wide catwalk. Just as she didn't have to guess who Fineas Riordan was when she saw him, there was no need to guess at what lay below, where the sounds of brutal, hand-to-hand fighting emanated.

Carys glanced over the railing . . . just in time to see Rune lunging for his opponent in the pit below. The pit where his father had forced him to fight as a boy.

Death matches, like the one taking place before her

eyes right now. The broken, bloodied bodies of two other Breed males lay on the floor as Rune dealt with his current threat.

Oh, God, Rune.

"He's got remarkable stamina," Riordan said casually. "I've lost track of how many hours he's been going down there. He always was a tireless bastard."

Rune was fully transformed, with fangs flashing and eyes ablaze with amber fire. He wore only the pants he'd had on the night before in Boston, but now they were filthy and torn. His *dermaglyphs* were livid with the dark colors of rage and aggression, seething on the sweat-soaked, bruised and shredded flesh of his back and chest.

Yet as dangerous as Rune looked, his opponent appeared even more so. The big male was wild-eyed, savage. Insane with violence. His fangs dripped saliva, and his *glyphs* were so saturated with furious color, they looked oily and black.

Rune now had his snarling, crazed opponent in a head lock. One big palm gripped the flailing vampire's skull, while Rune held the male's neck in the muscled V of his bent arm. His massive biceps flexed at the same time he wrenched the other male's head back.

Bone and tendons crunched, severing instantly. Rune dropped the corpse and wheeled back on his bare feet.

Oh, God . . . he looked so battered and weary. His breath heaved out of him, fatigue in every powerful muscle.

He lifted his head to look up at the catwalk and his blazing amber gaze lit on her.

The roar he let out when he saw her shook the stone walls and the rafters high above.

Carys's hand flew to her mouth, tears stinging her eyes. "Rune!"

"Carys? No!" His outraged eyes went to his father. "How did you get her? Goddamn it, let her go!"

Ennis Riordan chuckled as he sent a sidelong glance at Rune's father. "I told you the bitch we saw in Boston was more than just a fuck to our boy, Aedan."

"Obviously something more than he wanted us to believe. But what was she doing in Fielding's house tonight?"

"She hasn't told me anything so far. Said she wanted to see him first." He smirked at her. "I think we can persuade her to talk now."

"Let her go," Rune growled from in the pit. He ground out a low curse. "Don't hurt her. You sick fuck!"

His father's brows rose. "You haven't seen sick yet. When we're done with you, boyo? Oh, what fun we're gonna have with her."

And then, it all happened so fast.

Riordan glanced at his guard. In response, the male reached over to pull a lever mounted on the stone wall at the end of the catwalk. Down below, one of the iron-grated portals built into the wall of the fighting pit began to open.

Another feral Breed male sprang out like a lion set loose in a gladiator's arena. Bigger than the last one, his massive body was unmarked and fresh for combat. And, like the other, he seemed too unhinged to be fully sane. Bloodthirsty and vicious, he circled Rune, prepared to lunge.

"Now, let's make it more interesting." Riordan nodded to his brother.

In a flash of motion, the other male drew his pistol

and shot Rune in the shoulder.

Carys screamed.

The sound started out high-pitched and anguished, but quickly changed to something powerful and otherworldly. Her transformation from woman to Breed female was sudden, and unstoppable.

Her fangs punched out of her gums in an instant. Her vision burned red as her Breed nature took over and her pupils narrowed to vertical slits within her amber irises. She leapt at Riordan's brother, seizing hold of him. Her body slammed against his, lifting him off his feet.

Her immense forward momentum sent them both airborne.

"Holy shit!" Rune's father jumped back against his guard on a curse.

His brother shrieked in abject terror in Carys's grasp, his eyes wide.

It took less than a second for Carys to understand why. As they sailed over the railing of the catwalk, into open air, sparks exploded as if they'd crashed into something.

The blast of light was blinding, filling her vision like the blast of a thousand suns.

Then her nostrils filled with the smoky stench of burning skin and hair.

What the hell?

The Breed male she'd held fast in her fists was gone. Disintegrated in her fingers.

Suddenly, she wasn't holding anything anymore. The ashes of Ennis Riordan's body rained down around her like snowflakes as she plummeted to the floor of the fighting pit.

CHAPTER 34

Nova's sketches of Riordan's castle lay spread out on a work table in the rear of the Order's private jet. Chase and the other warriors had been gathered around the diagrams for the past hour or so, reviewing entry points and running through possible infiltration plans.

He drummed his fingers on the table as he considered the confined chambers and limited exits on the drawings. "How many guards are we looking at once we get inside?"

"Could be a couple dozen," Lucan said. "We can only guess, based on the security camera images that Gideon's been collecting on the place."

Dante smirked. "Well, shit. We've taken out nests of Rogues in bigger numbers than that."

Chase and the Order's other longtime members chuckled at the reminder. Two decades ago, missions like this one were commonplace, when they'd all worked together from the original compound in Boston. It wasn't often they came together on a joint patrol now, but it was always easy to settle back into the old rhythm of the tight brotherhood they still shared.

Rio glanced over at Mathias, a smile stretching the scars that marred his left cheek. "What kind of party favors are we bringing these assholes tonight?"

"My team will have extra arms and ammunition waiting for us in Dublin. They're also bringing explosives, should we need to blast our way in—or out."

Kade gave a wolfish grin. "Show of hands. Who besides me wants to play with the fireworks?"

With the exception of Nathan, the team from Boston all thrust their hands up, along with Aric. Then Dante and Brock joined them too.

As the jokes and chuckles traveled the table, Lucan's comm unit buzzed with an incoming call. He left to take it while the discussion continued.

"It's going to be close to sunrise when we land," Hunter said. "Even if Riordan anticipates that we're on to him, I doubt he'll be prepared for a full-scale attack in broad daylight."

Chase nodded. "And we'll be covered on that front. Mathias's vehicles are equipped with light-blocking windows, and we'll be storming Riordan's gates wearing full UV tactical gear."

"What about females or young children?" Tegan asked. Once the coldest member of the Order, having a mate and an adult son of his own had added a new, protective dimension to the lethal male. "We gonna have to sweep for civilians once we get inside?"

Mathias shook his head. "Not a concern. Riordan hasn't been mated for years. Unfortunately, his Breedmates seem to have an unhealthy habit of dying under mysterious circumstances. He does have a brother, Ennis, whose reputation is almost as repulsive." Mathias cleared his throat. "Then, of course, there is the matter of Riordan's son."

Chase grunted at the reminder. He wasn't about to forget the delicate matter of potentially going into combat against the male Carys loved. Tavia had stressed to him that she and their daughter both expected him to reserve judgment, to do what he could to spare Riordan's son if at all possible.

He'd given his word. But he couldn't guarantee the male wouldn't be caught in the crossfire if things went south inside the stronghold.

With those grim thoughts riding him, he nearly didn't notice that Lucan had gone markedly quiet, still on his phone call at the other side of the jet's cabin. But everyone else had stopped talking now too.

Lucan's sober expression and silence drew more attention than if he'd been roaring vicious curses at the top of his lungs.

He ended the call and walked over, his grave eyes locked on Chase.

"What's going on, Lucan?"

"It's Carys." Two words, spoken so seriously, it seemed to suck all the air out of the room. "She's gone missing from the party in London."

"Gone missing?"

Chase felt his veins freeze over. At the table with him, Aric exploded with a shout of disbelief and worry.

"What do you mean, gone missing?" Chase murmured. "For how long? Where would she go? For fuck's sake, tell me we're turning that house upside down looking for her right now."

"Brynne searched the house. Gideon had Carys's

GPS signal on site and active, but when they located her earpiece . . ." Lucan shook his head. "It appears she's been gone for more than an hour."

"Someone took her?" Chase knew the answer without asking it. He knew who, as well, and the ice that had settled in his blood turned arctic. "Riordan."

Lucan's stark gaze confirmed it. "Gideon's tap on the security cameras showed her arriving there with Ennis Riordan. She hasn't been there long."

"One second in that place is too goddamn long," Chase muttered. "And we're how far from touching down in Dublin?"

"A couple of hours. I've already told the pilot to push this bird as hard as he can."

Chase thought about his mate, who'd stayed behind at headquarters with the other women. "Has Tavia been told?"

"Gideon thought you'd want to be the one to break the news to her."

"Yeah. He's right." And Chase should have known Tavia hadn't yet been informed. He would have felt her anguish through their blood bond. The way she was most certainly feeling his now. "It'll be best if she hears it from me."

As he got up from the table to make the dreaded call, he put his hand on his son's strong shoulder. He couldn't imagine what Carys's twin must be feeling. The siblings had been so close as children. There had been strains in their bond recently, but it was on the mend now and their love had never dimmed.

Aric looked at him with eyes the same green shade as Tavia's. His gaze was stark, unblinking. When he spoke, his deep voice was firm with resolve. "We're gonna bring her back. She's going to be all right. And those fucks who took her are going to pay in blood."

The other warriors murmured their support, but the assurances did little to numb the dread clawing at Chase. He'd never felt so helpless, realizing that he was hundreds of miles and too many damn hours away from reaching her.

He knew Carys was strong. God knew she was stubborn. His daughter had never backed down from any fight, but she'd never been tested by something like this.

She had never faced the kind of evil that Fineas Riordan was reputed to deal in, and the thought of his little girl being taken—being touched by filth like Riordan—was almost too much for him to bear.

As the jet's engines roared and the agonizing wait until landing began, Chase found himself pinning his hopes on an unlikely ally.

With him and the Order too far away to help, her best chance of survival could be Riordan's own son. The same Breed male Chase had been reluctant to accept and all too quick to condemn.

Now, he never prayed so hard to be proven wrong.

~ ~ ~

"Carys!"

Rune's panic flooded him like electricity in his veins.

Even though his mind knew she couldn't be harmed by UV light, his heart had seized with horror when the invisible web overhead had exploded like a supernova.

His relief came just as swiftly as he watched Carys drop to the floor of the pit behind him, wholly intact.

She landed on her feet with all the grace of a cat—and came out of her slight crouch with all the ferocity and power of a Breed female.

Her fangs glinted behind her parted lips. Her bright blue irises were devoured by crackling amber heat. She glanced past his shoulder in alarm.

"Rune—look out!"

His second of inattention cost him. The drugged vampire Riordan had released into the pit saw his chance to strike. He charged at Rune, taking him down to the floor on his back.

Carys roared. She grabbed at Rune's opponent and tore the big male off as if he weighed nothing. Then she sent the snarling savage against the stone wall and pulled Rune to his feet.

Above them on the catwalk, Riordan gaped in shock. "What the fuck? She's a goddamn daywalker!" He pointed into the pit and swung a furious look at his guard. "Shoot the bitch! Kill her!"

Bullets started hailing down in a rapid barrage.

Rune felt a round hit his side as he threw himself around Carys. The shot bit into him, but he leaned on his ability to absorb the pain and kept moving. He grabbed her hand, dragging her behind him so he could be her shield.

"Under the catwalk," he shouted, racing for the scant cover with her.

The gunfire couldn't reach them directly below Riordan and his guard, but they couldn't hope to stay under the shelter forever.

Riordan bellowed in outrage. "Get her, you idiot!"

The bullets slowed as the guard ran from one side of the catwalk to the other, trying to get Carys in his sights.

Rune held her close, adjusting their position as the gunman fired off a handful of wasted shots. Damn, he wanted so badly to embrace her, kiss her. He wanted to hold her and never let her go. She needed to know how sorry he was that he failed to keep his father's evil from touching her. Most of all, she needed to know how deeply he loved her.

But there was no time for any of that now. The gunfire kept coming, and Carys's survival was his sole focus.

Rune knew the moment she scented his fresh injury. Her face lifted to his, alarm sparking in her transformed eyes. "Oh, shit. Rune, you've been shot?"

"I'll live. Don't worry about me."

And he intended for her to live too, which meant he had to find a way to get her out of there.

But now, across the pit from them, Rune saw the vampire shaking off his daze. The big male got up from his sprawl where Carys had flung him. His feral eyes looked past the other dead in the pit, seeking out his prey.

Rune stepped in front of Carys, shielding her. The snarling Breed male prowled forward, fearless of the gunfire, his fangs dripping pink-tinted saliva from the powerful narcotic Riordan had fed him.

He couldn't let the beast get close to her. On a snarl, Rune charged forward. He plowed into the center of the big vampire, driving him down onto the floor of the pit. They rolled and thrashed, Rune trying to avoid the snapping jaws and razor-sharp fangs.

"Over here!" Riordan's shout to his guard alerted Rune that Carys was on the move again. "Don't let her get away this time!"

As Rune struggled and fought with his out-of-control assailant, he caught a flash of movement in his peripheral vision.

A blur of shadows as Carys crossed the open floor of the pit at full Breed speed, then dashed back under the catwalk before his father's gunman could lock on to her.

Rune and his opponent came up from the floor, both pounding each other. One of Rune's blows connected under the vampire's chin. The male staggered back a couple of paces.

Then all at once, he convulsed violently as a sudden, lethal barrage of bullets tore into his broad chest.

Rune swung his head in the direction the shots had come from.

Holy hell.

There stood Carys beneath the catwalk, holding Ennis Riordan's smoking pistol in her hands.

CHAPTER 35

Carys didn't let go of her breath until Rune was standing with her under the meager cover of the catwalk.

Once he was there, she sagged against his warmth and strength, her arms hanging limply at her sides. Emotion overwhelmed her. Most of all, she felt a profound relief to feel his arms wrapped around her and his voice murmuring tender words against her ear.

He lifted her chin on the tips of his battered, bloodstained fingers.

"Carys," he whispered, his deep voice urgent and raw. Emotion stormed in his blazing eyes. "You're the last person I ever wanted to see here, in this place. I wanted to handle this for myself . . . for us."

"I know." She gazed up at him, seeing the torment in every line and hard angle of his face. "I know that's why you left with them. I never doubted you. Not for a second."

A strangled moan leaked out of him. Then he kissed

her, deeply and fiercely, as if they weren't standing in the midst of death and carnage, with the threat of still more perched on the platform over their heads.

But the threat was real.

And Riordan wasn't finished with them yet.

"Fuck the sentimental reunion," he snarled from above them. "Release the last fighter."

The heavy gate on one of the pit's perimeter access portals lifted, freeing yet another feral Breed male.

"Oh, hell, no," Carys muttered. She broke out of Rune's loose hold. "Not this time."

She aimed her pistol at the snarling vampire as it loped into the arena. She squeezed the trigger several times and . . . nothing happened. Just a hollow *click-click-click*.

No bullets left.

"Stay back," Rune said as she tossed the empty weapon down. He swept her behind him and prepared to face this new opponent. "I need you to stay safe, Carys. Promise me."

No, she couldn't give him that vow. Everything Breed in her wanted to fight this battle with him. Everything female in her was determined to stand by her man—to her last breath, if it came down to that.

Up on the catwalk, Riordan chuckled sadistically. "As soon as either of them comes out from under here, shoot them dead," he told his guard. "Both of them!"

Carys growled at the command. As scared as she was, her rage was stronger. She knew Rune would meet this new threat the same way he'd confronted all of the ones that had come before, but damn it, enough was enough.

Shots rang out the instant Rune and the other Breed

male clashed with the start of their combat. In the tumble and roll with his opponent, Rune somehow managed to evade the sudden spurt of gunfire. But Carys knew it was only a matter of moments before his father's guard hit his mark.

She wasn't about to let them get that chance.

Carys's body was in motion even before she had decided what she would do. She slipped her shoes off and inched backward on her bare feet, out from underneath the catwalk.

With Riordan and his shooter preoccupied with trying to hit Rune off the front of the spectator platform, neither of them realized she had leapt up from the pit until she was already on top of them.

Carys didn't waste a second. She shoved the guard over the railing, gun and all. He barely had time to scream before the UV barrier consumed him.

She wheeled on Riordan, lips peeled back off her teeth and fangs in a hiss. His eyes rounded with surprise. Then, coward that he was, the bastard bolted away from her.

In a flash, he had vanished from the catwalk, disappearing into the gloom of the castle corridor.

Dammit!

Carys longed to go after him, but down in the pit, Rune was still locked in a dangerous fight.

And to her horror, she saw that he was injured even worse than before. Fresh bullet wounds peppered his back. Yet he kept fighting. Nothing short of death would slow him down.

No way in hell was she leaving him. Not even in the hopes of killing the bastard who'd raised him.

Carys perched on the railing and waited for her

chance to spring. When the struggle down below brought Rune and his opponent within range, she leapt off. Sailing down, she dropped right onto the other male's back just as he was about to lunge for Rune.

The impact drove him to one knee beneath her, but he was immense. As hard as she hit him, her lighter weight didn't collapse him. He reared back, trying to toss her off him. His big arms grappled for her while she clutched his mane of greasy hair and wrenched his head back.

Rune was right there, not even a second after she landed. With the vampire thrashing wildly, hissing and snarling in rage, Rune pulled his fist back and sent it driving home like a battering ram—straight through the other male's sternum.

The vampire went rigid, his scream of shock cut short as he convulsed in a violent shudder. Then the body slumped in a heap on the floor of the pit, blood pooling from the gaping hole in the vampire's chest.

Carys jumped away from the carnage and flung herself into Rune's arms. "Thank God, it's over."

Rune held her, but tension vibrated in every hard muscle of his body. His voice was gravel, raw and deadly. "Where's my father?"

She twisted to gesture to the empty catwalk. "He ran down that corridor when I pushed his guard over the railing."

Rune drew her away from him, a bleakness in his eyes. "This won't be over until the son of a bitch is dead. Come on. We have to get out of here before he sends reinforcements down to find us."

CHAPTER 36

With Carys running beside him, Rune snatched the dead guard's assault rifle from the floor of the pit and headed for one of the portals. The iron-banded grate was sealed closed, but a blast of gunfire at its center splintered the thick wood.

Rune rammed it with his shoulder—*once, twice, three times*—smashing a gap big enough for them to slip through. He took her hand, then he and Carys ducked into the dark, vacant cell on the other side used for holding the pit's less-than-cooperative fighters.

Another iron-banded door waited across the bare room, and together he and Carys shot and crashed through that one too. The cell opened onto a narrow tunnel, one of many that snaked through the underground bowels of the fortress.

Thin yellow light from flickering, bare bulbs mounted in the ceiling illuminated their path. The stench of urine and old blood offended his nostrils, but the cramped corridor was empty. Nothing but the echoing sounds of his and Carys's footsteps as they hurried along in the dank gloom.

Rune had been staving off his pain during the combat in the pit, but each step was making it harder keep a hold on his ability. Agony seared him in more places than he could count, but it wasn't the pain slowing him down now. His injuries were taking a toll.

Added to the gunshot wound in his side were the three bullets he'd taken in his back during the last fight. His breath sawed out of his lungs in a wet, wheezing rasp. Each inhalation was a knife-sharp jab of fire in his chest. Blood ran into his eye from a laceration on his forehead. Still more cuts and bruises covered his hands and arms and torso.

The way he felt, it was a damn miracle he was still on his feet at all.

No, not a miracle.

It was Carys. Her daring move back there on the catwalk had, without a doubt, saved his life.

And it was Rune's love for her that spurred him forward now, when every shredded muscle and broken bone in his body threatened to drop him on his ass in the middle of the passageway.

In spite of his determination, though, his feet were getting sluggish. Carys had slowed beside him to match his pace. She studied him in the scant light of the tunnel.

Her fangs had retracted now, and her eyes had returned to their arresting shade of blue.

She looked at his glowing irises and fully extended fangs. Her gaze drifted to his *glyphs*, which were still furious with color, betraying the trauma he was hoping to hide from her.

Her beautiful face pinched with concern as she took

in his condition. There was no mistaking her grave expression. She knew he was in bad shape and worsening by the moment.

"Let's stop for a while, Rune." Her fingers tightened around his hand as her footsteps dropped to nearly a halt. "Please, stop. We don't know what's waiting at the end of this tunnel and you need to rest."

"No." He tossed his head, impatient. "We have to keep pushing forward. I need to get you out of here."

He tugged her hand, but she wasn't budging. "Listen to me. The Order is on the way. They know your father is part of Opus Nostrum. They're coming for him tonight. Lucan Thorne, my father, most of the other warrior commanders . . . they could be here in as little as an hour."

Rune paused, considering. He felt no sympathy for anything that might happen to Fineas Riordan, but if the Order was going to be of any help to Carys and him, they needed to be kicking down the castle doors right now.

"We have to keep moving," he insisted.

She shook her head, refusing to let him start off again. "You can't go on like this. You can't fight like this." She reached up to touch his battered face. "All we have to do is stay safe until the warriors get here. I can't cover both of us in shadow if we're in motion, but I can do it if we find someplace to hide and wait for the Order to get here."

"It's too risky. My father and his men aren't going to stand around wondering where we are. They'll hunt us down. Hell, I have no doubt they already are. They're going to shine a light in every crevice and corner of this damn place, and unless we get out of here first, they're going to find us, Carys."

He didn't even want to consider what Riordan and his thugs would do to her if they got their hands on her again.

"There are a couple of back ways out of the castle," he said, resting the rifle on the floor of the tunnel. He was already planning their best chance of escape while he used their pause to catch his breath and try to find his reserves of stamina. He may have one foot in the grave right now, but his primary goal was her safety. He'd worry about his own ass later. "We'll have to get through the main floor, but once we do, we can steal a vehicle out of the carriage house behind the kitchens."

Once she was secured somewhere far away from his father's house, he'd go back in alone and finish the bastard. He'd be damned if he was going to wait around for the Order to do that for him, either.

He could tell by the look in Carys's eyes that she understood his intentions. "You're going to try to kill him. Alone?" She shook her head. "You're not going to leave me again. We belong together."

He cursed under his breath. "Yes, we do, love. But don't you see? I can't move forward now without knowing I've put my past in the grave. For good this time."

"Then I'm going to stand with you. You're not going to keep me outside your walls anymore. Not for my protection. Not because you're afraid I won't understand. From now on, we fight together." Her soft voice broke with emotion. "I love you. I have loved you from the very beginning, Rune."

"Rune," he said, then slowly shook his head. He reached out, tenderly cupping her beautiful face in his hands. "I wasn't honest with you. Not even about my name. I owed you so much more than that. I still do, Carys. Hell, I can't pretend I'll ever be the man you deserve."

She brought his battered fingers to her lips and kissed them with unbearable sweetness. "I fell in love with a man who is kind and good and loyal. A strong, fearless man who owns every room he walks into, whether it's the arena or the bedroom or the fancy lobby of the MFA."

Her kiss moved to the centers of his grit-covered, lacerated palms. "I fell in love with a man who makes his living delivering pain, yet who touches me with so much tenderness, it makes my heart ache."

Devotion smoldered in her eyes as she held his tormented stare. "That man's name is Rune," she said. "I know everything about him that I need to know, and there's no other man I will ever want."

"Christ, you humble me. And I love you, Carys. So damn much." The words were a raw whisper on his lips as he lifted her chin and claimed her mouth in a deep kiss filled with longing.

There was regret in it too, because, even though she absolved him of his lies and didn't hate him for the situation they were in together now, she didn't know his whole truth yet. She didn't know the full depth of his shame.

He broke their kiss on a sharp sigh. "I can't forgive myself until he's dead and this place is destroyed forever. He's done terrible things. I don't mean everything he did to me. None of that matters to me now. It's the other people he's hurt. My mother. The Breedmate who came after her. And to the little girl, Kitty. What he did to her is unspeakable."

Carys soberly nodded her head. "I know. But she's strong, Rune. And she's coping as best—" Her eyes widened when she saw his confused frown. "Oh, my God . . . you don't know. Of course, you don't know. Your sister, Catriona—Kitty. She lives in London now. She's mated to an Order warrior, Mathias Rowan. For the past few days, they've been in Boston, staying at my family's Darkhaven."

He couldn't believe what he was hearing. "She's alive? She's okay?"

"Yes. And she's happy, Rune. She's in love. And there's more. She's expecting a baby with Mathias."

"Holy shit." The shock of it, combined with his injuries, made him rock back on his heels. He leaned his ass against the wall of the corridor as his brain worked to process the details. "So often, I've wondered what happened to her. I've worried that she was dead."

Carys nodded gently. "She's been worried about you too."

"You've talked to her about me?"

"We've become friends. Even before we knew we had a love for you in common."

Rune swallowed. He dreaded asking, but he had to know. "Does she blame me for leaving her here? Does she think I knew what was happening to her?"

"No, she doesn't blame you." Carys leaned her shoulder against the wall beside him, standing close, caressing the worry from his face. "She didn't allow you to know any of her pain. Just as you hid yours from her."

He lowered his head. "Jesus Christ. My little sister is alive. I never thought I'd see her again."

"Then let's get out of here so you'll have that chance. We both want to see you come home where you belong."

Home. He hadn't known the meaning of that word for a long time. If he ever really had. But now it burned in front of him like a beacon in the dark, lighting the way.

And as he looked at Carys, he knew that path would always lead to her. She was the only home he would ever need.

He pressed a kiss to her forehead, then threaded his fingers through hers. "Let's go, love."

He stepped away from the support of the stone wall and her sharp intake of breath made him pause. She was looking down at their feet. At the dark pool of blood that had collected beneath him where he'd stood.

"Oh, my God. Rune . . ."

"I'm okay," he told her. But she saw through his lie. He knew that for the rest of their time together, whether it was measured in minutes or centuries, Carys would always see through him to the truth. And he didn't want to hide anymore. "I'll be all right once we're out of here. I can heal when I'm home."

"No, Rune. You can't. You won't heal, not from wounds like this. Not unless you get blood right now." Her Breed instincts were already responding to the fresh red cells on the ground. Amber light sparked in the blue of her eyes. The tips of her fangs now glinted behind her parted lips. "You need to feed, Rune. The only thing that can heal this is the bond. My blood."

Even as he growled in denial, everything Breed in him ached for what she offered.

In his heart, in his soul, Carys already was his mate. In all ways except this one. And he wanted it with her more than anything. But not now. Not like this.

He shook his head, scowling furiously. "I've never

wanted to bond with anyone. Not until you, Carys. I sure as hell never wanted it to happen in this hellish place. With you offering your vein out of worry for me, or, fuck . . . out of pity."

"Is that what you think I'm doing?" Anger gave her voice a sharp edge. "I love you, Rune. And if drinking from me now, in this place—under these fucked up circumstances—saves your life, then I can't think of any better time or place to do it."

He blew out a low chuckle in spite of his pain and doubts. "You are a stubborn female."

"Goddamn right I am. You said you love me."

"Christ, yes. More than anything in this world."

"Then drink, Rune." She didn't give him another second to refuse.

Bringing her wrist up to her own mouth, she sank her fangs into the flesh. Blood pumped from the twin punctures, red and sweet and powerful.

The fragrance hit his senses more intensely than any drug his father or Opus Nostrum could ever hope to concoct.

He took her hand and forearm in his grasp and lowered his head over her wrist. The instant her blood hit his tongue, the rush of power was so swift and immense, he staggered back as if he'd been punched.

Holy hell.

He'd had no idea what to expect. Nothing could have prepared him for the astonishing roar of liquid energy that coursed down his throat with each hard draw of his mouth. Carys's strength poured into him, feeding his injured cells and tissues. Nourishing him the way no human's blood had even come close to doing.

His veins lit up as his bond to her took root.

She had been his from the moment they'd first met. Now, she was his forever.

He only had to prove to her—and to himself—that he could be worthy of her gift.

CHAPTER 37

C

Carys sucked in her breath in amazement as Rune's mouth settled over her wrist and he took the first few pulls from her veins. Seeing him feed from her was more intimate than she could have imagined, more profoundly sensual than anything she'd ever experienced.

It felt so right, her blood nourishing him, bonding him to her.

And, oh, God, it was erotic too.

The suction of his mouth, every tug of his lips and tongue, stoked a powerful heat in her core. It bloomed outward, into her veins and arteries, into each crackling nerve ending.

Her eyes were burning with desire, even as contentment poured through her while she stroked Rune's dark head and watched him drink his fill.

She moaned when he finally stopped sucking and sealed her wounds closed with a swipe of his tongue.

He was panting as he drew away and met her gaze,

his own eyes blazing like hot coals too.

"Jesus Christ," he hissed thickly. His fangs were deadly sharp, glinting as bright as diamonds in the dim light of the tunnel. "Carys, holy fuck. That was . . ."

He didn't seem capable of describing it. Nor did he seem to have the patience to try. With a possessive growl, he wrapped his palm around the back of her neck and pulled her to him for a fierce, hard kiss.

Love and desire swept through her like wildfire, and it was all she could do not to bury her fangs in his neck and complete their bond.

"I want that too," he murmured against her mouth. He lifted his head and stared at her, his hot gaze filled with awe. "I can feel you inside me, love. I can feel you in my veins, in all of my senses. God, Carys . . . you're a presence in me now that's as bright and strong as lightning."

He licked his lips, his amber eyes drifting to her throat. His grin was purely male and so primal it made her sex clench with yearning. "I can't wait to do this again when I have you in bed with me."

"Neither can I," she said. "So let's get the fuck out of here."

He nodded. "Yeah. The sooner, the better."

He was still bleeding from his many bullet wounds. They would need tending as soon as possible, but his color was better already thanks to her blood. As they resumed their flight through the tunnel, she couldn't have been more relieved to see him moving with renewed strength and stamina.

He was alive and her blood would keep him that way. At least, long enough for him to get help once they were out of this place. They had their whole future ahead of them now, and it waited just on the other side of this hell.

We will make it out of here together.

We have to.

It was her mantra as she ran with him, deeper into the darkness.

"There's an old tower stairwell up here that'll take us to the main floor," Rune told her, glancing over his shoulder at her as they hurried along. "With any luck, we can make the climb before the guards think to block it. Promise me you won't let me slow you down."

"No," she replied, refusing to even consider the thought. "We do this together. No matter what."

She knew what he was telling her. Normally, with their Breed genetics, it would take no more than a few seconds to speed from one location to another, but Rune's injuries would not permit that now. He was too depleted, and she wasn't about to do it without him.

They reached the entry to the tower stairs. "This way, Carys."

Rune went in ahead of her, holding his gun vertical in the confines of the narrow stairwell. The worn stone steps spiraled upward, around and around and around, one blind turn after another.

Low voices sounded from somewhere above now— urgent shouts coupled with the heavy pound of boots across the floors.

"Be ready," Rune cautioned her. "We're coming to the main floor now."

"Okay. Let's do this."

No sooner had they reached the archway that opened out from the stairwell than they saw a pair of guards heading their way.

"There they are!" the men shouted, opening fire the instant they saw Rune and Carys.

"Get back!" Rune pulled her behind him as gunshots chewed into the stone beside their heads.

Flying shrapnel exploded, biting Carys's cheek. She felt blood run in a warm trail down her face, just below her left eye.

Rune saw it too. Now, through his blood-bond to her, he would also feel her pain. Rage ignited in his eyes. On a bellowed roar, he returned a spray of gunfire.

"You have to run," he growled at her. "Flash past the guards. I'll cover you from here. Use the shadows, Carys. You have to make it through the great hall to get to the kitchens and the carriage house outside."

She swiped at the streak of blood that dripped off her chin, peering around him as he continued to volley shots with the advancing guards. "I'm not leaving without you."

"We only have one gun, Carys. Both of us can't hope to make it past these two men. More will be coming any second. You have to try to get away, damn it!"

She didn't answer him. He wouldn't want to hear it anyway. No matter how bad their odds, she had no intention of leaving him behind to save her own life.

But maybe there was something she could do to help them both.

With Rune and the two guards alternating bursts of gunfire, Carys looked to the shadows around her and in the gloom of the tower. She gathered them close, concealing herself.

Then she slipped out from behind Rune and charged their assailants.

CHAPTER 38

She was gone even before he realized what she was
doing.

"Carys!" Rune felt her whisk past him like a cool gust
of air. He saw the formless drift of shadows move
swiftly, stealthily, avoiding the gunfire. She was difficult
to track, but Rune kept the gunmen busy dodging his
bullets and drawing theirs to him instead of her.

Not even an instant later, one of the two guards was
thrown across the room by invisible hands. His startled
comrade pivoted around with his assault rifle to find the
attacker.

Rune seized the opportunity. His bullet flew, nailing
the guard in the back of the skull.

The gunmen dropped, lifeless.

Rune redirected his aim and shot the other one too.

Carys materialized that same moment. She quickly
retrieved the fallen weapons, giving Rune a fangy smile
as he ran over to meet her.

He couldn't decide whether to kiss her or chew her

a new one for the stunt she'd just pulled. While she was cool as could be, his heart was banging in his chest like a fucking jackhammer.

"Now we have two more guns," she said, handing one of them to him.

He slung the backup rifle's strap over his shoulder. "We're gonna talk about this later," he snarled, but he could hardly hold on to his anger when the fact was they made a damn good team.

But they still weren't home free.

Not even close.

The commotion had drawn a lot of unwanted attention. Now, more guards started pouring in from other parts of the fortress. Amid the thunder of rushing boots and the jangle of weaponry, he heard his father's furious voice, shouting kill orders to his men.

"This way. Hurry!" Rune grabbed Carys's hand and led her through another antechamber that would skirt the main corridor and take them into the great hall. They barely made into the huge room before Riordan and half his garrison were on their heels.

Rune pulled Carys with him behind a stone alcove. They ducked as far as they could into the meager shelter as a fresh hail of bullets ripped through the air all around them.

Rune shot back, but only squeezed off a handful of rounds before his magazine emptied. He threw the rifle down and swung the backup into his hands to continue shooting at the dozen men now advancing into the great hall with his father.

"Give it up, boyo. You're rats in a trap." Riordan's voice boomed over the staccato spurts of gunfire. "What's it gonna be? You want us to shoot you like vermin, or take you alive and then lay waste to your woman while you watch?"

Rune glanced at Carys, neither of them acknowledging the threat. Their gazes locked in determination. They had their plan of escape. They had each other. All the rest was simply noise and obstacles to overcome.

"Flush them out of there," Riordan commanded his men. "We can have just as much fun if we take them captive in pieces."

The guards opened fire again, moving into new positions around the great hall.

"They're going to corner us," Rune whispered. "We need to get across the room if we can. The exit to the kitchens is that door to the left of the fireplace."

Carys glanced that way, then gave him a nod. Rune knew she wouldn't do it without him, even though her speed could take her there twice as fast than if she waited for him. So, he had no choice but to lay down heavy gunfire and try to take out as many guards as possible if they were both going to make it across.

Carys held her weapon at the ready too. No fear in her eyes, only a steely determination that galvanized his own.

There was a lull in the barrage. Rune gave her a signal. "Go."

They ducked out from behind the wall. Both of them spraying rounds, they hustled across the wide room as swiftly as they could. A number of guards cried out as they were hit, several going down for good.

The return fire came at them hard now. Rune felt a bullet rip into his thigh. He stumbled, nearly brought down by the crippling impact.

He refused to let it slow them down—not when Carys's life was on the line.

With rounds still zinging at them, they made it into the mouth of the room's central hearth. The ancient fireplace, with its heavy walls made of massive stones, was tall enough for them to stand upright in it and deep enough to hold a dozen men. But there was less cover here than where they just been. Though now they were just steps away from where they needed to be.

Carys looked down at his fresh wound in horror. "Oh, shit, Rune."

The hole in his thigh was gushing blood. Not good. On top of all of his other injuries, it was catastrophic. Her blood was still a vibrant force inside him, but it wouldn't stop him from bleeding out.

And as the feeling started to fade from his leg, he knew he wouldn't be able to run now. Hell, at this rate, he'd be lucky if he managed a slow hobble.

Damn it, no!

"I can smell your blood, Aedan." His father's gleeful voice rang out over the straggling shots. "You may not know it yet, but you're dead, son. Gonna be a shame you won't live long enough to see me and all of my men rape your Breed bitch until she's begging for us to kill her too."

Rune gently lifted her chin and held her gaze. "That's not going to happen," he told her firmly. "I'm not going to let them touch you. Not ever. We're going to get out of this."

"I know." She nodded, but he could see the flicker of fear in her eyes now.

Her doubt nearly killed him. Far more than any bullet could.

Even he had to acknowledge that things didn't look good for them. More guards poured into the great hall now. His father's personal army was closing in, diminishing their chances of escape with each second that ticked by.

"We have to make a break for it," he told her.

She shook her head. "You'll never make it."

"But you might." When she parted her lips to protest, he cut her off with a kiss. "Please, Carys. I love you. Do this for me."

Misery swam in her gaze. "No. No, I won't! Rune, we're staying togeth—"

Her words cut off as a sudden explosion rocked the fortress.

Dust fell from the heavy rafters of the hall. Outside the room, a sudden, frantic commotion kicked up.

Fineas Riordan shouted to his men, "What the fuck was that?"

A panicked voice answered. "The main gate, sir. Holy shit, they've taken it out!"

Carys swung a wide-eyed glance at Rune. "The Order. Rune, they're here!"

In the middle of the great hall, Riordan was barking commands to his guards. "Get out there and push them back! All of you, look alive—hold this keep! Whoever's at our gates, blow them away! And kill these two right fucking now!"

Chaos and gunfire erupted.

But apparently, his father had no intention of sticking around to lend his own blood and sweat to the battle. Rune saw him grab a weapon from one of his men, then he flashed across the great hall to an archway leading to the east tower of the castle.

Carys saw it too. "He's getting away!"

When her body tensed with purpose, Rune felt her fury emanate through his bond to her. She was pissed as hell and ready to kill.

"Don't even think it, love." Rune grabbed her arms and ground out a curse. "Forget about him."

But his woman was Breed, and her power coursed through her as ferociously as it did him. As it did in any other of their kind. Her blue eyes burned bright amber in an instant. She tossed her head in defiance, fangs bared. "I can't forget about him until I know he's dead."

She pulled out of his hold. Then she vanished into shadow and was gone.

Rune bellowed her name as he pushed to his feet behind the shelter and opened fire on his father's guards.

CHAPTER 39

Carys flashed up the tower stairs only seconds behind Riordan.

There was a small chamber at the top, and a door that appeared to open out onto the battlements. Riordan had his hand on the latch as Carys caught up to him. He yanked it open—then shrank back on a cry as the early morning sun's rays reached for him.

He slammed the heavy wood panel on a curse and wheeled around.

Carys stood there, her assault rifle aimed on him. "Like a rat in a trap," she said, throwing his own words back at him.

But Riordan had a gun too. He raised it on her. "You think you're man enough to take me on?"

He fired.

She dodged the shot with ease. Her Breed speed took her to the left side of the small room. Riordan pivoted and fired on her again. Another dodge, and this time instead of letting him see where she ended up, she gathered the shadows and taunted him into wasting more rounds. She zipped and zagged, taking far too much satisfaction in his wild, ineffective aim.

His panicked shots ricocheted off the stone walls.

Then his rifle jammed.

Carys felt a cold smile spread over her face as she let the shadows fall away. She stood directly in front of him now. "I'm not man enough to kill you. But I am woman enough."

She fired on him twice—a bullet in each shoulder. He jerked back with the impact, his arms hanging limply at his sides. He dropped his useless weapon, howling with pain.

Carys's vision burned red with contempt for him and all the evil he had done. "That's for Rune's mother and the other Breedmate you killed."

As he hissed and coughed, she lowered her aim and blew out both of his knees. He dropped to the floor it utter misery, writhing and convulsing in a tight ball at her feet. "That's for Rune and his sister, Kitty."

Carys stood over him, her gun's barrel leveled at the spot between his furious amber eyes.

Riordan snarled, thick spittle dripping from his open mouth and fangs. He stared at her in seething outrage. But Carys saw fear in his gaze now too. He was beaten and he knew there would be no coming back from it now.

"Just do it, you bitch! Kill me, you fucking daywalker freak!"

"No." She shook her head. "A bullet would be too merciful. And I'm fresh out of mercy where you're concerned."

"Huh?" His confusion was short-lived.

Carys slung her weapon over her shoulder and reached down to grab Riordan by his collar. As soon as she started dragging him across the floor, he began screaming. He wailed and thrashed, begging her to let him go. All in vain.

She opened the door to the roof.

She hauled Rune's tormentor outside, into the clear heat of the morning sun. She didn't flinch, didn't blink, merely watched in pitiless silence as the lethal rays devoured him.

~ ~ ~

Chase was at the head of the Order's charge as the warriors poured through the exploded main gate in full UV gear. Debris and smoke plumed in front of his face shield. Bullets zipped past him as he and his comrades stormed the courtyard, returning fire on Riordan's guards who shot at them from windows and arrow slits inside the fortress.

Lucan's voice came over the shared audio link that fed into the warriors' earpieces. "Units, fan out as discussed. First team, secure all entry and exit points. Second team, sweep every corner of this goddamn place until you locate Carys. We take out anyone who stands in our way, except Riordan. I want that bastard taken alive."

So did Chase, because he wanted to be the one to kill him.

With the assigned units splitting off to carry out their missions, Chase, Lucan and Dante advanced on the castle's main entrance along with Nathan, Aric and the team from Boston.

Half a dozen of Riordan's guards confronted them as soon as they crashed through the door. A heavy gunfire exchange lit up the central corridor before the warriors mowed down their assailants.

More shots rang out deeper inside the fortress. Lucan motioned for Chase and the others to follow him toward the commotion. They took out a couple more gunmen in the corridor as they came up on the great hall. Nearing the arched entryway, Chase wasn't quite sure what he was looking at.

The bodies of several gunmen lay scattered and bloodied across the wide expanse of the room. Three more guards crouched in various positions in the room, exchanging fire with another Breed male who was hunkered behind the massive stone shelter of the ancient fireplace.

The warriors picked off the trio of Riordan's men one by one.

In the sudden quiet, the other shooter held up his weapon in surrender and slowly limped out from behind his cover. The immense, dark-haired male was gravely injured. He had a makeshift tourniquet tied around his blood-soaked thigh and was bleeding from too many other places to count. His face was bruised and lacerated, his eyes bleak, but hot with amber fire.

"Jesus Christ," Aric gasped. "It's him. Carys's fighter."

And from the look of him, he'd been busy taking on his father's thugs alone until the Order arrived.

Chase lifted his face shield. "Where's Carys?"

"She went after him." He pointed to a stairwell entrance in the corner of the great hall. "She wouldn't let me stop her."

Dread and disbelief swamped Chase. "She's gone after Riordan? Alone?"

No. Please . . . fuck, no.

"The stairs go up to the tower roof," the fighter said, already moving in that direction despite his serious injuries.

Chase didn't wait another second. Summoning every ounce of strength his Breed genetics had given him, he flashed into the stairwell with his heart in his throat.

Intense light poured out from the small chamber at the top of the stairs. He stepped into the room and immediately closed his visor, his arm raised to cover his eyes, even though they were shielded from the UV rays by his protective gear. It took a moment for his vision to adjust.

It took even longer for his mind to process what he was seeing.

The access door to the roof was wide open.

Carys stood outside in full sunlight.

She held something in her hand—a tattered shirt. Swirling around her in the morning breeze was a cloud of dark ashes. They scattered away into nothingness as Chase stared, dumbstruck.

Carys turned then. She looked over her shoulder at him, fangs bared, eyes ablaze with molten amber.

Chase could hardly breathe as he looked at her now. He'd been terrified that he would reach the top of the tower and find his beloved little girl destroyed by the evil that lived here. Instead, he found a vengeful Valkyrie, with the wind stirring her hair like a tempest, and the tattered remains of her enemy clutched in her unforgiving grasp.

Her eyes softened on him now. She let go of

Riordan's empty shirt and it fluttered away, forgotten.

"Daddy!" she cried, and rushed into his waiting arms.

Chase shut the door on the sun and lifted his face shield as he held her close. "I'm so glad you're okay," he murmured into her hair. "Your mother and I have been out of our minds these past several hours. When we heard you'd been taken, we thought . . ."

He let the worry go without finishing the sentence. She was safe. She was back in her family's arms. Soon, she would be back home with Tavia and Aric and him.

But his little girl *was* gone, he realized as he held Carys now.

She'd been gone for a while, but he'd been too stubborn to see it.

He saw her clearly now. He saw a strong, courageous, impressive woman.

She was magnificent. Formidable.

And her father had never been more awed by her, nor more proud.

CHAPTER 40

"Holy shit," someone murmured from behind Carys and her father.

She realized only then that they weren't alone. Aric, Nathan and his team from Boston, even Lucan and Dante, stood just inside the room.

On a curse, her brother broke away from the group and moved in to hug her too. Carys wrapped her arms around him and her father, so grateful to be reunited with them.

The danger was over. Riordan was no more.

Relief and joy flooded her, but she couldn't rest yet. Her heart still had somewhere else it needed to be.

She raised her head, peering past the thick knot of warriors to the top of the tower stairs.

And there he was.

"Rune." Tears choked her when she saw him.

He was alive.

And he was looking at her with so much love, it stole her breath away.

She flew to him on a strangled cry. They kissed desperately, hugging each other close and murmuring private, tender words. She didn't care that they had an audience. She didn't care about anything except the fact that Rune was there with her, telling her that he loved her. Kissing her as if he never wanted to let her go.

But the scent of his blood was a potent reminder that he wasn't out of danger yet. She drew away from him and glanced at the warriors.

"Rune needs help for his injuries. I gave him my blood a while ago, but it's not enough."

She saw her father's chin lift in understanding. There was no disapproval in his eyes at the acknowledgment that Rune was bound to her now. Only concern as his gaze took in the extent of Rune's wounds.

"Rafe," he said, motioning to Dante's son and a member of the Boston team. The blond warrior had inherited his mother's gift for healing with a touch. He'd mended worse injuries than Rune's before. He and Tess had even worked together to bring another of the Order's family back from death not so long ago.

"I believe our introduction is overdue," Chase said, stepping forward to extend his hand to Rune. "This isn't the way I'd envisioned us meeting, but I can honestly say it's an honor."

Carys held on to Rune, resting her head against his bare chest and smiling as he took her father's hand and shook it firmly. "An honor for me too, sir."

"Call me Chase. Or Sterling."

"Just don't call him Harvard," Dante drawled, grinning.

Chase chuckled. "Feel free to ignore anything that one tells you. It's always worked for me."

Rune's laugh vibrated warmly against Carys's ear. "All right. Chase it is." He glanced down at Carys then, his gaze intense and meaningful. "My name is Rune."

Chase nodded solemnly. "Thank you for protecting my daughter, Rune. Thank you for keeping her safe and alive."

"Not at all, sir," Rune said. "She's the reason I'm alive. She is my reason for everything."

He caressed her cheek and her heart was so full, she couldn't resist lifting up to kiss him again.

When their lips parted, Aric stood before them. He shook Rune's hand too. "I guess this is going to make us brothers now."

"Aye," Rune said. "Maybe in time we'll even be friends."

Aric smirked. "Got a feeling my sister won't have it any other way."

Now Lucan strode over and introduced himself. "I don't know whether to thank you or offer condolences that things had to go this way."

Rune shook his head. "This was the only way it could go with my father. I have no regrets, other than the fact that I didn't end him a long time ago. Before he had the chance to hurt so many other people."

Lucan grunted, his cool gray eyes thoughtful. "You and I have more in common than you know, Rune." He turned that contemplative gaze on Carys. "And you deserve more credit than anyone has been willing to give you, myself included."

"Thank you," she murmured, both humbled and proud.

Rafe came over and began working on the worst of Rune's injuries as the other Boston team members came forward too. They all greeted Rune and Carys with praise and genuine interest, falling into an easy camaraderie with both of them.

It felt good, being accepted by all of them. Oddly, it felt right. She didn't know exactly what her future was going to look like after she got home to Boston, but she couldn't help thinking that as much as it would include Rune, it was going to include the Order as well.

She had a feeling no one in the room with her now was going to tell her no again.

CHAPTER 41

A couple of hours after Rafe worked his magic, Rune was cleaned up and seated in the great hall with Carys, feeling as if his multiple gunshot wounds and broken bones had been nothing more than bee stings.

His body was healed and he was breathing a hell of a lot easier knowing Carys was safe and sound. She was nestled against him now, speaking on the phone to her mother who was waiting not so patiently for her family to return to the Order's headquarters in D.C.

As Carys ended the call, she glanced up at Rune. "Yes, of course. I'll tell him for her. We'll see you soon. I love you." She murmured a tender goodbye, then put the comm unit away.

"You'll tell me what?"

"Nova wants you to know that she'll be waiting to greet us as soon as we arrive, no matter what time it is. She's very excited to see you."

"Nova," he said, testing out the name his sister had been using since she fled this place to begin her new life in London years ago.

Carys had explained what she knew of Nova's journey from Dublin to London, and the circumstances that had brought her into Mathias Rowan's orbit.

It seemed both Rune and his sister had wanted to deny where they had come from—to hide from the monster who'd terrorized their past. They had both learned the hard way that some monsters couldn't be outrun. They had to be confronted and destroyed in order to truly break free of their hold.

"Are you nervous about seeing her?" Carys asked, softly caressing his bare chest.

Rune nodded. "I'm not sure how she'll react to seeing me after all this time. I'm different now. I'm not the brother she remembers."

Carys smiled. "I think you'll find Nova to be something of a surprise too. A good one, though. Just as you'll be a welcome surprise to her."

Mathias Rowan had been a welcome surprise as well. Rune and the London commander for the Order had been introduced when the group came down from the tower. He seemed to be a good man. A Breed male who loved Rune's sister with the same depth of feeling that Rune felt for Carys.

He wanted that for Nova. God knew, she deserved some kindness and decency after the hell she had endured in this place.

He glanced at the bloodstained floors and bullet-pocked walls of the room. The battle was over at last. The monster was dead. The bodies of the fallen had been cleared away to the courtyard where the sun would claim them. Now all that was left to do was take stock of whatever intel Fineas Riordan might have left behind.

Rune told the Order where to find the storage chamber of UV weaponry and narcotics his father had showed him. The warriors were busy assessing that cache and combing through all the other chambers for further evidence of his Opus Nostrum ties.

"Are you okay with all of this, Rune?"

He glanced down at her, idly stroking her arm as he held her. "I am. I feel freer than I ever have, knowing my father is gone. His evil can't touch me or anyone else I care about. Now, we need to make the same thing true of Opus Nostrum."

He considered all of the terror the organization had caused. All of the misery they could still deliver if they had arms and chemicals like the ones his father was stockpiling. He considered the war his father had boasted about, yearned to make happen.

"I'm ready to fight that battle," Rune murmured. "Whether it's as a part of the Order, or in any other way they can use me. All my life, I've been fighting inside a cage. Fighting for survival, then fighting for nothing because it was the only thing I knew how to do. I can still fight. Now, I just want it to mean something."

Carys's gaze was soft on him, but lit with a shared fire. He felt her flare of agreement through his bond to her. It sparked bright, then burned hot and unwavering. "I want that too, Rune. I can't walk away from this fight now either."

God, he loved her. He was proud to have her at his side and in his arms. In his corner, fearless and ready to stand with him against anything or anyone.

He bent his head to hers and claimed her mouth in a hungry kiss. His body stirred on contact, his arousal impossible to hide. She sat up, taking in the sudden churning of his *dermaglyphs*, and in the crackling heat that warmed his irises.

When she glanced down to his rather obvious erection, her eyebrows rose and her cheeks flamed a sexy shade of pink.

He chuckled, unashamed. "I'm feeling stronger now."

"So I noticed." She shook her head and leaned in close, her lips teasing, barely brushing his. "I should thank Rafe for your speedy recovery. It's amazing what he was able to do with his ability."

"Yes, it is, but I can't give the warrior all the credit." Rune grabbed the back of her neck and ended her teasing. He kissed her again, then rested his forehead against hers and gazed into her eyes. "Your blood kept me alive. Your love kept me fighting, Carys. Now that I'm healed, I can't wait to get you alone again and complete our bond. I want to lock you in forever, before you change your mind."

"Never. I'm yours. I have been from the start."

Their mouths met in a deeper joining, both of them relishing the closeness, the passion that ignited so swiftly and burned so strongly between them.

Things might have gotten embarrassing fast if not for the sound of approaching footsteps across the floor of the great hall.

Aric cleared his throat. "It's going to take me a while to adjust to seeing this without feeling like I need to step in and defend my sister's virtue."

Smiling, Carys gave him an arch look. "My virtue is none of your business. And we'd rather not have you watching us, so we're all learning to cope here."

Her brother laughed. "Fair enough. We should be

ready to roll out soon. The other warriors are wrapping up the sweep of the place now." Frowning, Aric glanced to Rune. "I saw the fighting pit. We also located a medieval torture chamber that looks like it's seen recent use. Some fucked up shit here, man. If Carys hadn't ashed Riordan, I would've gladly done it myself."

As he spoke, Chase, Lucan and Mathias entered the room.

"We took a look at the crates of UV weaponry and narcotics," Chase said. "We're collecting samples of everything to analyze and will try to trace them back to their manufacturers."

Lucan glanced at Carys. "We can't interrogate Riordan about Opus's activities, but recovering this cache could be even more important. Lots of Breed lives will be saved by keeping this shit off the streets."

Mathias nodded. "Unfortunately, there's too much of it to haul away."

"And we can't leave it behind either," Chase added. "The risk of any of this shit leaking out to the public is too big to chance."

"What will you do?" Carys asked.

"Destroy it," Lucan said. "We'll take our samples, but I want the rest of it neutralized before we leave here. The UV cylinders, the drugs, all of it."

"We also located a hidden room in back of the storage chamber," Chase said. "Riordan's got a workstation and a secured communications system in there. Gideon's been unable to hack into it so far, so we're packing it all up and taking it back to D.C. with us."

Carys sat at full attention. "Fielding has one of those rooms too. I found it just before Ennis Riordan grabbed me."

"Gideon doesn't know about it?" Lucan asked.

She shook her head. "My connection to him broke off as soon as I entered the room. It had the same kind of equipment in it, and the room was hidden, just like Riordan's."

The three Order commanders exchanged a grave look.

"What is it?" Carys asked. "What's wrong?"

Chase exhaled a sigh. "Fielding is dead. We got the word from Brynne as we were touching down in Dublin. He killed himself, just like Hayden Ivers, that human lawyer you led us to."

Nathan and Rafe strode into the great hall at that same moment.

"We're loading up the vehicles now," Nathan announced. "Tegan and Hunter want you to know we can be ready to roll out within the hour."

"Good," Lucan said. He turned a glance on Rune. "Like we said, the cache downstairs is too dangerous to be left behind. We need to destroy it before we go. This was your home at one point, so if there's anything you want to take away from here—"

Rune gave a firm shake of his head. "This was never a home, not to anyone. And I already have the only thing I need to take with me," he said, drawing Carys further under his arm. "When I left Boston two nights ago, I promised myself I wouldn't come back until my father was dead and this place was razed to the ground."

Lucan held his gaze solemnly, then nodded. "Okay. That's all I needed to know."

~ ~ ~

Less than an hour later, Rune sat in the back of a UV-shielded vehicle with Carys. Chase occupied the seat facing them in the big SUV. Up front, Aric was behind the wheel with Nathan riding shotgun.

Theirs was the last car in the line of idling vehicles parked in the castle's sunlit courtyard. The other warriors in their UV gear had just finished packing up what they needed to take back with them to headquarters and were preparing to depart for the Dublin airport.

Chase touched his earpiece and listened for moment. "All right, Lucan," he murmured into his mic. "We're rolling out."

Rune drew Carys close as the fleet started moving. She glanced back, looking out the rear window as they left the courtyard and the castle. He felt her faint shudder. Through his blood bond to her, he felt her overwhelming relief as the place they'd narrowly survived fell farther and farther in their wake.

They'd come through fire together in that place.

They'd emerged stronger, inseparable. Invincible, as long as they had each other.

Rune had no need to look back. There was nothing to see there anymore.

His life lay ahead of him now. With Carys at his side.

As his mate.

A formality he intended to complete as soon as they arrived back in the States.

She pivoted back around and settled against him with a sigh. Rune stroked her cheek, then couldn't resist lowering his head to kiss her. He didn't even care that her father was sitting across from them.

When he glanced up, Chase's blue eyes were locked

on him. He held something in his hand. "Whenever you're ready, son."

Rune took the small remote detonator. As he stared at it, Carys looked up at him, her gaze filled with love and tenderness.

He held his future in his arms.

His past would never touch him again.

So, hell yeah. He was more than ready.

Rune pushed the button, then tossed the remote aside. As the percussion sounded in the distance behind them, he cupped Carys's beautiful face in his palms and kissed her with all the love—and hope—he felt in his heart.

CHAPTER 42

When they arrived at the D.C. headquarters later that night, everyone was waiting to see them.

"Oh, my girl!" Tavia rushed to fold Carys into her tight embrace as soon as she entered the mansion.

When Carys turned to introduce Rune to her mother, Tavia ignored his extended hand and wrapped him in a warm hug too. Carys grinned as she watched her big, tough fighter get swamped by her mother's boundless affection. He stood stiff and awkward at first, but eventually his strong arms relaxed and a smile curved his mouth.

There were a lot of relieved, happy tears from most of the Order's women. A lot of worry and concern about everything Carys had endured. And a lot of questions about how she and Rune had managed to not only survive their ordeal in Riordan's hands, but to triumph over him and his men virtually on their own.

All of the questions and buzzing conversation slowed to a pause the moment Nova quietly came around to the front of the noisy reunion. Her blue eyes were shy under the angular sweep of her blue-and-black hair. Her smile was uncertain as her tattooed hands fidgeted with the hem of her black shirt.

Rune stared. She glanced up at him and nodded mutely. That was all it took.

He stepped forward and scooped Nova into his arms with a shout of joy. When he set her down again, he held her face between his palms, drinking her in.

"You're all grown up. You look amazing," he said, his deep voice thick with emotion. "You look . . . happy."

"I am," she replied. "I'm happier now that you're back in my life too, Aed—"

"Rune," he said. "If that's okay with you."

She nodded. "Nova."

The siblings hugged again. Rune reached out to snag Carys by the arm, pulling her into their happy family. Then Mathias drifted over to join his Breedmate. With one arm around Nova, he reached out and clasped Rune's shoulder.

Soon, the fancy drawing room of the mansion was filled with the entire Order and all of their mates. Rune was introduced to all of the women, and Carys enjoyed the numerous, approving looks she got from the other warriors' mates as they all greeted her man.

She held his hand, feeling so proud to belong to him. She couldn't wait to begin their future, away from all of the commotion and the reality of all the dangerous missions that still lay ahead for the Order. Maybe even for Rune and her too.

As warm as their welcome was—and as grateful as she was for the love they were receiving from everyone there tonight—now that she was home with Rune, Carys couldn't wait to be alone with him.

Gabrielle seemed to understand how she was feeling. Lucan's mate came over to Carys and leaned in close to her ear. "There's an empty guest room on the third floor at the end of the hall. If you and Rune would like to use it to freshen up or rest for a while, consider it yours."

Carys murmured her thanks and gently squeezed Rune's hand. They slipped away at the first opportunity, heading immediately for the stairs.

They ducked inside the guest room and Rune kicked the door closed behind them. Carys had her arms and legs wrapped around him, held aloft in his strong arms. They kissed like mad, eyes blazing with desire, fangs tangling in their frenzy for each other.

Rune carried her to the king-size bed and laid her down. His big hands trembled as he stripped off her ruined clothes.

"We should clean up first," Carys murmured.

He shook his head. "Later. Right now, I just need you."

She needed him too. It had always been like this for them, but now, the desire was even more intense. Carys watched him, enthralled, knowing that the passion they shared would always be this fierce and undeniable.

Rune was naked now as well. He crawled over her on the bed, his immense body radiating heat and power and so much love it stole her breath. His wounds were healed over. The faint red welts left on his skin would be gone by morning.

He looked so strong and formidable. So incredibly sexy.

And he was hers.

Tonight more than ever, they belonged to each other.

She needed him, right now. On a throaty growl, she pressed her hands against his chest and tossed him onto his back. She straddled his hips, her wet cleft sliding along his length as she leaned down and met his mouth with a deep, demanding kiss.

A shift of her hips positioned him at her core. She wanted to prolong the delicious feeling of their bodies moving together in a teasing tempo, not yet joined. But her hunger for him was too intense.

She lifted her pelvis, seating herself on the upward jut of his cock. He hissed as she sank all the way down. When she started riding him, he held on to her and groaned in pleasure, his neck tendons straining as taut as cables.

"Damn, you feel good," he rasped. She kicked up her pace and he sucked in a sharp breath. "Ah, fuck. Slow it down, baby. Let's make this last a while."

She tossed her head and grinned down at him. "We've got all night to slow it down. You said yourself you're feeling healed and strong again."

"Oh, yeah," he ground out, bucking hard beneath her as if to show her just how revived he truly was.

"That's good," she purred. "So there's no need for me to go easy on you, then."

His eyes ignited with amber fire. "Holy hell, you are a force to be reckoned with. And, Christ . . . you're ruthless too."

He grabbed her hips as she rocked on him and undulated in deep circles. She slid in an unhurried, but purposeful rhythm up and down his length, delighting in his pleasure.

She felt his muscles tense. His hips thrust feverishly, meeting her strokes, hungry for more. She showed him no mercy as his climax swiftly built to a frenzy. His big body shook, and a jagged shout tore loose from him as he exploded inside her.

Carys kept moving on him, relishing the way his body responded to her.

He gazed up at her from under heated eyes. "I can see we're gonna have to lay down some ground rules about who's in charge."

She smirked. "You know how I feel about rules."

He reached up to caress her cheek. "How do you feel about forever with me, love?"

Elation sent her heart soaring. She licked her lips. "I thought you'd never ask."

With her eyes fixed on his throbbing carotid, she leaned down and sank her fangs into his neck. Rune let out a sharp moan as her bite took hold. Then his arms wrapped around her protectively, possessively while she began to drink from him.

And as his blood roared down her throat and into her body's cells—into her soul—Rune rolled her beneath him and began to make love to her slowly, showing her just how passionate and perfect their forever was going to be.

~ * ~

ABOUT THE AUTHOR

LARA ADRIAN is a *New York Times* and #1 international best-selling author, with nearly 4 million books in print and digital worldwide and translations licensed to more than 20 countries. Her books regularly appear in the top spots of all the major bestseller lists including the *New York Times*, USA Today, Publishers Weekly, Amazon.com, Barnes & Noble, etc. Reviewers have called Lara's books "addictively readable" (Chicago Tribune), "extraordinary" (Fresh Fiction), and "one of the consistently best paranormal series out there" (Romance Novel News).

Writing as **TINA ST. JOHN**, her historical romances have won numerous awards including the National Readers Choice; Romantic Times Magazine Reviewer's Choice; Booksellers Best; and many others. She was twice named a Finalist in Romance Writers of America's RITA Awards, for Best Historical Romance (White Lion's Lady) and Best Paranormal Romance (Heart of the Hunter). More recently, the German translation of Heart of the Hunter debuted on Der Spiegel bestseller list.

With an ancestry stretching back to the Mayflower and the court of King Henry VIII, the author lives with her husband in New England.

Visit the author's website and sign up for new release announcements at **www.LaraAdrian.com**.

Find Lara on Facebook at
www.facebook.com/LaraAdrianBooks

Look for the next story in the
Midnight Breed vampire romance series

Stroke of Midnight

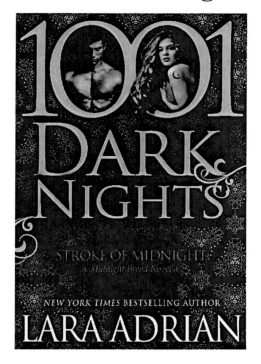

Available October 13, 2015

Available in ebook and trade paperback

For more information on the series and
upcoming releases, visit:

www.LaraAdrian.com

Thirsty for more Midnight Breed?

Read the complete series!

A Touch of Midnight (prequel novella)
Kiss of Midnight
Kiss of Crimson
Midnight Awakening
Midnight Rising
Veil of Midnight
Ashes of Midnight
Shades of Midnight
Taken by Midnight
Deeper Than Midnight
A Taste of Midnight (ebook novella)
Darker After Midnight
The Midnight Breed Series Companion
Edge of Dawn
Marked by Midnight (novella)
Crave the Night
Tempted by Midnight (novella)
Bound to Darkness
Stroke of Midnight (novella, October 2015)

. . . and more to come!

More romance and adventure from Lara Adrian!

Phoenix Code Series
(Paranormal Romantic Suspense)

"A fast-paced thrill ride." –Fresh Fiction

Masters of Seduction Series
(Paranormal Romance)

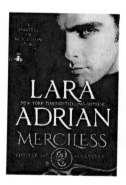 

"Thrilling, action-packed and super sexy." –Literal Addiction

Connect with Lara online at:

www.LaraAdrian.com

www.facebook.com/LaraAdrianBooks

www.goodreads.com/lara_adrian

www.twitter.com/lara_adrian

www.instagram.com/laraadrianbooks

www.pinterest.com/LaraAdrian

www.wattpad.com/user/LaraAdrian

CPSIA information can be obtained
at www.ICGtesting.com
Printed in the USA
LVOW08s1541240317
528385LV00003B/511/P